Spirit Wind

Fire Ant Books

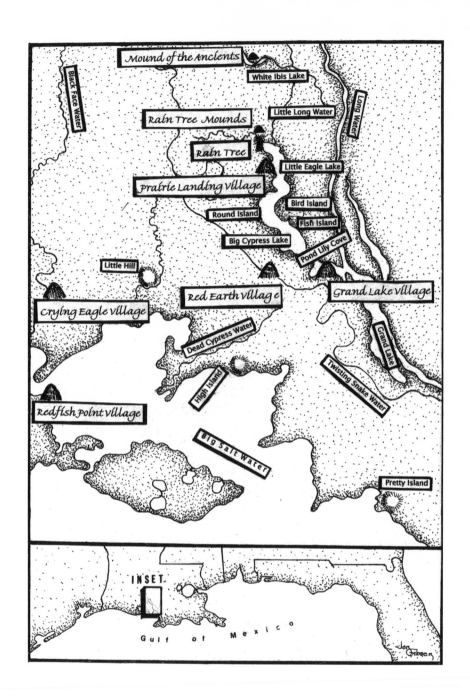

SPIRIT WIND

Jon L. Gibson

The University of Alabama Press, *Tuscaloosa*

Copyright © 2009
The University of Alabama Press
Tuscaloosa, Alabama 35487-0380
All rights reserved
Manufactured in the United States of America

Typeface: Bembo

∞

The paper on which this book is printed meets the minimum requirements of American National Standard for Information Sciences-Permanence of Paper for Printed Library Materials, ANSI Z39.48-1984.

Library of Congress Cataloging-in-Publication Data

Gibson, Jon L.
  Spirit wind / Jon L. Gibson.
        p.   cm.
  "Fire Ant books."
  Includes bibliographical references.
  ISBN 978-0-8173-5572-2 (pbk. : alk. paper) — ISBN 978-0-8173-8248-3 (electronic) 1. Chitimacha Indians—Fiction. 2. Indians of North America—Fiction. 3. Atchafalaya River Valley (La.)—Fiction. I. Title.
  PS3607.I269S65 2009
  813'.6—dc22
                                                                    2009020599

Cover illustration: "Seeking the Swamp Medicine" (oil pastel by Jon Gibson).

For
Mary Beth

Contents

Preface

There are many ways to tell a story. This book is one, an anthropological story told in fiction. It is a story about the prehistoric Chitimacha Indians of the Atchafalaya swamp in South Louisiana. Cultural details are as accurate as documentary accounts permit—largely John Swanton's, J. O. Dyer's, Albert Gatschet's, and Faye Stouff's, as well as my own ethnographic and archaeological investigations. The only liberties taken with cultural details have been to fill in minor gaps with information and interpretations based on nearby Lower Mississippi tribes and histories. Depictions of the Atchafalaya swamp and the coastal marsh are based on personal familiarity, and while place-to-place details may have changed, land-shaping processes have not—at least, not for the past few thousand years. Even the people and events fictionalized here had real counterparts. This book is fiction only because we do not know real names, personal histories, or the specific details of their everyday lives.

Names for people, places, and things have been fabricated in order to be faithful to the aboriginal and prehistoric setting, but they are as congruent with the contemporary landscape as today's science, ethnology, and archaeology can make them. For readers who wish to follow Storm Rider's journey through his watery world, I correlate ancient and modern place-names in the glossary. Serious students of Chitimacha and Attakapa life also can find identifications of various native terms in the glossary.

For thousands of years, the Chitimacha people and their ancestors lived on Bayou Teche and in the vast Atchafalaya swamp on the western edge of the Lower Mississippi Valley near the Gulf of Mexico. They still do.

This story takes place around a thousand years ago, long before French explorers and Acadian refugees came into the area. It is a time that archaeologists call the Late Woodland, or late Coles Creek, period. People of the time lived in villages along bayou banks and lakeshores. They ate fish, clams,

roots, acorns, and game but did not grow maize or grew it only when water conditions favored farming. They built earthen mounds—flat-topped
platforms to support their fire temples and conical mounds to entomb their
honored dead. They wove beautiful cane basketry with tri-dyed rectilinear
and curvilinear designs. They made durable grog-tempered pottery bearing decorations that mimicked their fancy baskets—paddle-stamping resembled weaving, and straight-line and curvilinear patterns, often painted,
depicted traditional basket designs. Their everyday equipment and facili-
ties came from natural materials—dugouts hewn from cypress, lodges constructed from palmetto and mud, portable tools made from cane and bone,
and occasionally stone arrowpoints, especially those known as Friley points,
were obtained via trade with peoples living along the Red River in central
Louisiana.

This is an anthropologically accurate fictional story of a totally native way
of life shaped by its watery domain and its social and political histories—
including the war clubs of the neighboring Attakapa.

Today, the Chitimacha people live where they have always lived, but their
reservation of 283 acres is only a tiny parcel of the enormous territory they
once called home. The reservation has about 300 residents, and the tribal
roll lists over 600 people—a small fraction of their once sizeable aboriginal
population.

Writing this book retraces a personal journey for me. For more than 30
years, I lived and worked on the edge of the Atchafalaya basin. Bonds of
friendship with the Chitimacha people were forged and the magical spell of
the magnificent swamp cast. I fished many of the honey holes mentioned in
the text and examined archaeological sites from Krotz Springs to Pointe au
Fer and Charenton Beach to Bayou Sorrel—sites which correlate with villages mentioned herein. I hunted ducks and geese in the marsh, shrimped in
Vermilion Bay, and picked up prehistoric pottery on the cheniers. The stamp
of these enduring people and the majesty of the great swamp and marsh are
indelibly imprinted in my psyche. This book is my way of recounting that
journey.

Acknowledgments

The inspiration for a book about the Chitimacha people was born in 1969, when I first set foot among the moss-draped live oaks on the Chitimacha reservation near Charenton, Louisiana. For time eternal, the Chitimacha made their homes here along Bayou Teche and in the Atchafalaya wilderness. For years, Emile Stouff and Faye Stouff, traditional chief and his wife, Leroy Burgess, former tribal chairman, and Roger Stouff, grandson of Faye and Emile, shared their stories with me. The tribal council endorsed this project, and Kim Walden of the tribal Cultural Department has been an unwavering advocate since the beginning.

The storyline was developed during the course of back porch discussions with my wife, Mary Beth, who taught fifth-grade youngsters in another lifetime. The plot largely is hers; the details of culture and place are mine. Mary Beth also served as sounding board, chief critic, and on-call copy reviewer. Erin Faherty, my daughter and former creative writing instructor, gave the book its first critical read. Reviewer Julian Granberry, Native American Language Services, helped smooth out ethnographic scuff marks with linguistic buffing. Reviewers Charles Hudson, University of Georgia, and Bob Neuman, retired, Louisiana State University's Natural History Museum, scrutinized content for its fidelity and policed its tone, a tone that reminded Charles of "Harry Potter in a breechclout."

I thank the staff of The University of Alabama Press and Judy Goffman for leading me through the valley of the shadow of red-ink queries, style sheets, typesetter codes, and troublesome hyphens.

Spirit Wind

I

Spirit Child

The red-winged snake fluttered in the bushes overhanging the flooded bank. Cloud Bringer and his paternal nephews, both Esteemed warriors, heard a tiny cry, followed by a scraping sound like tree limbs rubbing together.

"There," said Cloud Bringer, his black eyes peering at the movement in the leaves, "next to the dead cypress tree. See, there it is again."

The warriors paddled harder, sending the dugout knifing through the storm-swollen water toward the red figure bobbing up and down in the thick bushes.

Uprooted cypress and tupelo gum trees littered the shores of Grand Lake, and broken limbs floated everywhere, buoyed by still-green leaves. Dead fish caught in the current streamed through the big lake until their silver sides merged with the silver surface of distant waters. The mighty alligator floated by motionless, its hurricane-stilled eyes attracting swarms of green flies.

"Uncle, look, a dugout is caught in the bushes."

Waves slapped against the snared dugout, and the red emblem painted on its prow rolled and pitched with the motion. It was a strange figure—a winged rattlesnake biting its tail, the snake Cloud Bringer saw in the bushes. The image was unknown to the Many Waters People, as they called themselves. Friends and foes throughout the rest of the great swamp, the tall grass, and the waving grass called them the People of the Lakes.

Frantically pulling away the branches, the searchers freed the dugout but drew back instantly for lying in the boat were two canebrake rattlers, tails buzzing, slit eyes fixed on the men. They guarded a large split cane basket.

"Let us leave this place," exclaimed one of the warriors, "Spirit snakes protect the basket. Their bite will steal our shadows and send us to the Wasteland."

A small cry came from inside the basket, and, as if a cue, the rattlers slithered over the sides of the canoe and dropped into the choppy water.

Pulling the basket closer with his paddle, Cloud Bringer craned to see inside. His eyes widened as he saw the tiny sun-lit face and arms reaching for him. Still, he did not pick up the golden-faced baby until the sun completely illuminated the interior of the basket. He did not fear snakebite—he knew the medicines and healing words—but he did not know what other power, good or bad, might be lurking in the basket with the baby.

When he was convinced there was nothing else in the basket, Cloud Bringer gently untied the soft leather strap holding the baby in his makeshift cradle. He saw the snake design on the baby's deerskin tunic, the same design as on the dugout. Strange clothes, but the clothes were not what filled the men with concern. A streak as white as feathers of the Great White Heron ran through the baby's hair, and there was more, the baby's eyes—one was brown, but the other was as blue as the waters of Grand Lake on a cloudless day. The Many Waters People's babies always had black hair and black eyes.

And those bicolored eyes looked straight into Cloud Bringer's. The baby, who looked to be about a year old, held up its small arms wanting to be picked up. Cloud Bringer lifted the baby to his shoulder.

The men looked at each other in amazement. The baby had uttered two syllables, soft but absolutely clear and unmistakable.

"Eenjee."

The Ancients' word for father!

Cloud Bringer's heart touched the clouds. The baby called him father in the old language. From that moment on, the old man and baby were tied together with a bond stronger than life itself.

"Nephews," said Cloud Bringer, "Sun Woman sends us to search for her and Great Sun's lost baby daughter, who was carried away by the Mighty Wind and instead we find a spirit child."

"What should we do with him, uncle?"

"We need to ask *Old Traveler*," he said.

Cloud Bringer laid the baby on the bottom of the dugout and raised his thin arms toward the sky.

"Hear this man, *Old Traveler*, Great Spirit, Knower of All Things, who is this child? Where does he come from? Why do you send him to us now in the aftermath of the Mighty Wind?"

The men waited, intently listening, watching, waiting. The dugout pitched in the waves. A solitary tree duck preened its feathers in a distant cypress tree. High feathery clouds slowly drifted by, but *Old Traveler* did not answer.

Finally, Cloud Bringer spoke: "Nephews, let us take the spirit child to Bent Woman. She will know why the baby was sent to us and why he speaks the ancient language. She will see the future and tell us what we must do with the child."

The men paddled through the debris-filled lake. A lookout at the landing saw the child on Cloud Bringer's shoulder and summoned the villagers, who jubilantly rushed to the lake bank thinking the baby was the Sun family's lost daughter. Great Sun and Sun Woman, his wife, waded out into the lake awaiting the dugout. As it neared the shore, unbridled joy turned into abysmal shock. The child in Cloud Bringer's arms was not their daughter. The Sun family suffered the stabbing pain of losing a child for a second time. They collapsed in the shallow water, smearing their faces and hair with handfuls of mud from the lake bottom.

A loud wail went up from the assembled throng. Always Frowning and Fire Watcher, Great Sun's younger brothers, waded into the lake and led the Sun family to the shore.

Bareheaded and mud-caked, Great Sun looked like an ordinary man, a father trying to endure the heart-wrenching agony of losing his child twice on consecutive days. But he was not ordinary. In the people's tradition, he was divine. His line was descended directly from *Old Traveler,* the creator, through his spiritual mother, *Noon-Day-Sun,* who lights the day.

Fighting to regain his composure, Great Sun asked Cloud Bringer: "Whose child is this?"

"I do not know, Great Sun" answered Cloud Bringer, "We found the baby near Fish Island."

"Where are the parents?" asked Great Sun.

"The child was alone in a dugout. It was adrift but had gotten trapped in some bushes."

The baby stirred on Cloud Bringer's shoulder, and Great Sun held out his arms to take the child.

Cloud Bringer handed the infant to Great Sun, who recoiled in shock when he saw the baby's eyes and white-streaked hair. Holding the baby at arm's length, he asked Sun Woman to remove the baby's tunic. He raised the boy child above his head, inspecting him for other abnormalities.

"Healer, what manner of child have you brought us?" said Great Sun.

"A spirit child!"

Uneasiness ran through the villagers, and speculation raged.

"He is a water spirit from the submerged village in the middle of the lake," said Three Fingers, the village's best alligator hunter.

"No, he comes from the Upper World. See how a shooting star scorched his hair and blinded one of his eyes," explained a narrow-faced woman.

"I am afraid of him," said a young mother, gathering her children around her legs. "He looks like a witch."

"People, he is a lost, helpless baby, delivered to us on the Mighty Wind," said Cloud Bringer's sister.

"Ah-e," replied Cloud Bringer. "Do not fear him. He is one of us. Rattle-snakes protected him, which makes him a Snake, one of our most honored clans."

"Snakes protected him?" inquired a tribal councilman, one of the Beloved Men. "Then surely, he is special. We must hold council to talk about this spirit child."

"The child is everyone's concern," said Great Sun. "All who wish to speak should be permitted. People, reassemble in the plaza when *Noon-Day-Sun's* shadow reaches the village pole."

Always Frowning, Great Sun's middle brother and the Village Keeper, rushed to the plaza along with his assistant and two Red Stick slaves and began removing broken limbs, downed lodge posts, and scattered piles of thatch and other debris, clearing an area for the people to gather. He scrounged mats from the ruins of the temple so Great Sun and Sun Woman would not have to sit on the wet ground.

"The Beloved Men will either have to find mats for themselves or get their rear ends wet," he thought, smiling. "I am glad that Great Sun did not tell me to prepare his litter because it was stored in the temple anteroom, which is now scattered among the crowns of the live oaks on the edge of the plaza. Thank goodness, the old sun's bones had already been moved from the temple or his shadows would have never found each other, forever doomed to wander the land crying for his bones."

Always Frowning knew Great Sun did not want to hold a formal council meeting without the sanctioning power of the sacred fire, which had been doused when the temple blew away. Great Sun had already sent runners to the villages at Prairie Landing and Red Earth to secure renewing coals from their fires. Everyone knew that without the sacred fire, the village was vulnerable to all manner of malady, especially of the supernatural kind.

"The grounds are as clean as I can make them on such short notice," he said, trying to convince himself. "I hope Great Sun approves."

People began drifting into the plaza, followed by a palatable cloud of anxiety. There was muted talk, even fear of the child, whom many felt was a bad omen, coming as he had during the Mighty Wind that knocked down their village and stole Great Sun's daughter. Great Sun and Sun Woman entered the plaza, forsaking litters and warriors' shoulders. Neither wore their public garments or headdresses. They took seats on the mats that Always Frowning placed next to the village pole, which had survived the Mighty Wind, unscathed. The divine couple came as sad parents who had lost a child, and the people felt their pain.

Great Sun opened the meeting, speaking slowly in the formal deep-throated speech he used in public gatherings.

"People of Grand Lake village, we have suffered the loss of our homes and possessions, the fish are all dead, and the animals scattered. A sharp cane knife stabs at your Sun's heart. His precious daughter no longer warms his arms and makes him laugh."

He fought the lump rising in his throat.

"The ways of *Old Traveler* sometimes are hard to understand, even for his earthly son. One day after the Mighty Wind takes away my child, he sends us another marked by his own hand.

"I wish to know what the Many Waters People think about this infant. We must decide whether to adopt him into the tribe or return him to the lake. I ask our honored Snakebite healer, Cloud Bringer, to speak with us now."

Great Sun returned to his mat, and Cloud Bringer approached the village pole and struck it three times with his feathered cane.

"Hai, hear this man," he said. "I stand before you with a heavy heart. I grieve for my cousin's missing daughter. Though I do not have a true child, I have doctored so many of your sons and daughters that I feel like they are mine. I suffer each time *Old Traveler* decides to take one of our little ones before they have completed their life's journey. So, I too have lost many of my children, and my heart bears the sorrow for them all.

"The Mighty Wind brings us a spirit child, one who carries the words of the Ancients on his lips. I think the Ancients speak to us through him.

"My nephews and I found him strapped in a basket guarded by two rattlesnakes, but when the snakes saw that we meant no harm, they left him in our care. When I gathered him in my arms, he called me father in the old language. I believe this is a sign that *Old Traveler* intends for me to raise this child as my own. In my old age, the creator gives me the son I always wanted.

"Hai, I have spoken."

Great Sun then asked Bent Woman, the fearsome village prophet, to address the people. She took the strange baby from the wet nurse and hobbled to the village pole. She pursed her lips, spitting a thick, brown stream of tobacco juice on the sacred pole. Silence gripped the crowd. From bravest warrior to shyest toddler, all stood in awe, partly of the powerful prophet and partly of the spirit baby with the white-streaked hair and eyes of different colors.

The spirit baby did not cry, not even when Bent Woman held him high for the people to see.

"Hear my words, people of Grand Lake village," Bent Woman began.

"*Old Traveler* gave First People their civil laws and religious commandments, but, soon, believing themselves just as wise as he, they created their own laws patterned after their selfish hearts. When *Old Traveler* saw their folly, he grew sad, but his sadness turned to anger as First People continued to turn from him and his teachings. He decided to send a great flood to rid the world of these bad-hearted people."

Bent Woman paused and stared at the strange infant cradled in her arms. For a long while, the only sounds were the crackling fire and a dog barking at the landing.

"Is she asleep?" asked a big-eyed child pulling on his mother's hand.

"Suhhh."

"No! She's old. She forgot the rest of the story," answered his bored adolescent sister.

"Be quiet, both of you," whispered their mother. "She will finish the story when she gets ready."

Bent Woman's eyes fluttered, her head shook, and she bared her yellowed teeth in a silent grimace before she resumed her story.

"Among these law-breakers were two good people, a man and a woman. They watched the water rise in Grand Lake, and the woman begged *Old Traveler* to tell them how to save themselves. Knowing they were the only two law-abiding people left, *Old Traveler* came to the woman in a dream and told her to fashion a large clay pot. He instructed her and her husband to climb into the pot, which was beginning to float on the flood waters pouring into the village. Rising water covered the lodges. Soon even the tops of the tallest cypress trees disappeared, and the good woman and good man found themselves floating alone on a great lake without shores. No other people survived. Their dugouts were all eaten by flying white ants.

"Hear me, people of Grand Lake village, *Old Traveler* speaks to us through the lesson of the great flood.

"Swimming alongside the clay pot were two rattlesnakes. *Old Traveler* sent snakes to guide and protect the good man and good woman, just as he sent snakes to guide and protect the baby.

"The baby is not a spirit. He is not evil. Rattlesnakes protect him, just as they protect our most powerful clan, the Snake People. If they had not been guardians, the baby's inner shadow would be wandering the Wastelands now instead of being here with us.

"The white streak in his hair is the mark of *Lightning-Spirit-Bird,* powerful sister of *Thunderer* and *Noon-Day-Sun.* It is meant to remind us that he came to us during the Mighty Wind when *Lightning-Spirit-Bird* filled the night with her jagged light spears and wind from her great wings. His brown eye is for seeing during the day, his blue eye carries the color of the daytime sky, so he can see in the dark. *Old Traveler* himself marked the baby so the people can see how special he is—he is destined to be all-seeing, a great prophet of the Many Waters People.

"*Old Traveler* takes away Great Sun's infant daughter. He extinguishes the sacred fire on her shoulder—the red birthmark showing her divinity—just as he extinguished the sacred fire in the temple. Then he feels sorry for us and gives us another baby, one marked by his own hand, too. I asked the spirits if this was a fair exchange, could any living child really replace the Sun child. They are silent. I am sure they will give us our answer in time. I have spoken."

Finished, Bent Woman joined Cloud Bringer at Great Sun's side. The baby she carried in her arms clearly was awake but made no sound. She handed him to Cloud Bringer and shuffled through the plaza, mumbling incoherently. The throng parted ahead of her and watched nervously while she disappeared into the live oak shadows.

Great Sun called on Tattooed-All-Around to speak for the Beloved Men.

The old man struck the village pole, and the people respectfully fell quiet.

"Hai, hear this man," he crackled. "The council has talked about this infant. We have listened to our noble leaders. We have personally examined his strange markings and accept Bent Woman's explanation. We believe sky spirits sent him to us and protected him until they led Cloud Bringer to him. They have placed him in our care, and we should respect their gift. If we give him back to the lake, we risk offending the spirits and suffering greater calamities. People of Grand Lake village, we think he should be taken into the tribe as one of our own.

"These are the words of Tattooed-All-Around, spoken on behalf of the Beloved Men."

Great Sun thanked the Beloved Man.

"People of Grand Lake village, I would like to know what you think about the baby," asked Great Sun.

A murmur ran through the assembly.

"Great Sun," replied a frail old man, leaning heavily on his warrior son's arm as he approached and struck the village pole with his hand, carefully avoiding the wet brown stain.

"Hear this man. The last time the people were gifted with a special infant, it was a child with a crooked body who grew up to become Bent Woman, the greatest prophet our people have ever known. Many of us remember our mothers telling us that the people debated whether she should live or die. The snake-protected child should live. And that is what I have to say."

A hum of assent ran through the people.

Great Sun raised his arms quieting the crowd, and he motioned for Cloud Bringer to bring the baby and stand by his side.

"Hear my words, people of Grand Lake Village. Cloud Bringer wants to adopt the foundling and teach him the healing way, the Snakebite medicine. Great Sun favors adoption. Bent Woman favors adoption, The Beloved Men favor adoption. Do the Many Waters People favor adoption?"

Their voices rang out as one, "Ah-e, Ah-e! Yes, Yes!"

"Cloud Bringer, you have become a new father," said Great Sun.

From the ring of onlookers, a bright-eyed girl of five winters tugged on her mother's hand and whispered, "Mother, I heard the spirit baby talk. What does *Eenjee* mean?"

Cloud Bringer rejoiced. His son, his apprentice, had been sent by *Old Traveler* himself.

2

The Healing Way

Weeks after the mighty gulf storm, thirty new lodges rose from the clamshell-strewn shore of Grand Lake, their thick palmetto thatch browning in the steamy sea breeze. Bright yellow dugouts lined the water's edge, smelling of freshly hewn cypress and smoke. Village life returned to normal, except for fishing.

"I only catch grunters and garfish in my nets," complained a fisherman, throwing two hand-sized drum fish in a clam basket.

"I am not going to set out my nets again until the water clears up," said his friend, dumping a basketful of clams into the coals, raising a hissing white smoke.

"I know several places where the water has cleared up, but nothing lives in it—it smells too bad, worse than Black Face dung."

"Fishing has never been this bad before," said their squint-eyed companion, who was busy spreading bear oil on the bottom of his overturned dugout. "If it does not get better soon, the mother of my children is going to starve. She refuses to eat even one more clam."

"Ah-e, my wife says our children's skin is becoming milky. She is afraid they are going to turn into clams."

"Fish will come back after the weather turns cooler," predicted the old leathery-skinned man, grinding a bone fishhook out of a deer toe bone. "Cooler weather brings rain from the north and freshens the water. Now, the lake is poisoned with water from the Big Salt Water. Only clams and grunters thrive. Grunters eat clams like we do. So, where you catch grunters, there are always lots of clams in the mud."

The men nodded at leathery-skinned man's assessment.

"Well, I am ready for the north wind," said the man raking his steamed clams from the ashes. "I barely remember what whisker mouth tastes like."

"We should go thumping for alligators," said the squint-eyed man. "I had rather eat grilled alligator tail than grunters and clams, and I know where the father of alligators makes his den."

The fishermen agreed.

"Do you think we ought to ask Three Fingers to go?" asked the leathery-skinned man. "He knows more about thumping than all of us."

"No, he is too old and feeble," replied the clam baker. "He would probably fall in the lake and become alligator bait."

"Let us meet here in the morning then," said squint-eyes, "I will bring my thumping pole."

The men caught the giant alligator, and no one howled louder than Three Fingers, who in his youth had been the village's best alligator hunter. What meat was not eaten was rolled up in the hide and packed in sun-dried salt from the springs on Pretty Island. The hunters gave the head to Three Fingers, who placed it on the ant mound behind his lodge. In several moons, the ants would strip all the soft tissue, and he would pry loose the teeth, drill holes in them, and string them into a necklace for his grandson.

Months after the north winds carried away the rotten-egg smell in the water, fish gradually returned to Grand Lake. Wind-stripped trees sent out new leaves, and pokeweed, ragweed, and blackberry vines invaded the new sun-lit openings in the woods. Ferns and large black ants overran the decaying skeletons of uprooted trees. Time slowly healed the hurricane-scarred land.

Long after the mourning was over—the time of blackened faces—Great Sun and Sun Woman, his wife, continued to grieve for their daughter, who was lost during the hurricane. The people watched sadly as Great Sun and his wife paddled into the lake when bright stars danced on the water. They always carried an article of clothing or toy that belonged to their missing daughter. They always returned empty-handed.

Cloud Bringer felt sorry for the Sun family, but he knew they were still young enough to have other children. He, on the other hand, was old and without a wife but had become a proud new father—*Old Traveler* had blessed him with a child, a special child, a child destined to become a famous prophet of the people. He named the boy Stormy.

"I should have brought Stormy with me today," he thought, as he headed toward Howling Wolf's lodge. "He knows how to make the medicine, but he needs to see how it is administered and listen to the song that makes it work. Next time, I will let him come."

Cloud Bringer was passing the brush arbor when a group of women called to him and motioned for him to talk with them.

"Great Healer," said the corpulent one, "We sometimes hear strange noises coming from the lake in the wake of Great Sun's dugout. We wondered if you have ever heard anything?"

"Only bullfrogs and alligators," he said.

"I once heard a sound like a panther wailing," spouted one of the gossips.

"Sounded to me like doves cooing," exclaimed another busybody.

"Land creatures do not live in the middle of the lake," a third meddler reminded them. "Unless they are spirits. Cloud Bringer, do you think they could be evil spirits, maybe the *Long Black Being?*"

"Huh!" growled a wrinkled-faced woman with disheveled hair, "The only thing I hear on the night wind is somebody playing a flute."

"Women, stop worrying," Cloud Bringer said, "The noises you hear are happy sounds of a reunited family. Great Sun and his wife are visiting their baby daughter, who has now become a water spirit living in the underwater village in the middle of the lake. She only comes out of her lodge at night when the flickering fires of the Upper World shine on the water."

Satisfied with Cloud Bringer's explanation, the women returned to pounding lotus-root flour and fussing about Always Frowning's insatiable demand for new baskets and mats.

The year *Noon-Day-Sun* hid her face and darkened the land, Cloud Bringer passed his seventieth winter, his sixteenth since the great gulf storm. He cherished his adopted son and avid pupil. Every day, the old man was amazed how quickly Stormy learned the healing ways, how reverently he handled the medicine plants, and how well he sang the curing songs. It was like he already knew them. The old healer often wondered who was really teaching whom.

Cloud Bringer taught Stormy how to recognize the plants and when and where to look for them. He showed Stormy what part of the plant he needed to make the medicine—the leaves, seeds, berries, roots, or bark.

"Do not kill the plant," instructed Cloud Bringer. "Only take as little as you need to render the medicine. If you take the plant's life, its healing power will be lost or weakened because its own gift of life is gone."

Sitting around the fire each night, the men would go over and over the day's collection of plants until Cloud Bringer was sure Stormy recognized them all and knew what medicines they rendered.

"What is this?" asked Cloud Bringer, holding up a long, narrow red bean.

"Red Seed, make a tea with the leaves and use to treat coughing sickness," recited Stormy. "Also place crushed seeds and leaves in an open weave basket and put in sheltered water to stun fish."

"Okay, now this one?"

"Black Drink Bush, brew a tea and serve hot, treats sickness of stomach and bowels and, when boiled down to a thick paste and chewed, sends patients to the dream world."

One after another, Cloud Bringer held up the plants. Stormy identified them without hesitation, all of them.

"Swamp Bush, make tea for fever and a poultice for eye sores.

"Yellow Wood, make a tea of boiled leaves and inner bark to speed up slow heartbeat.

"Big Leaf Tree, a tea made from the leaves helps old people with aching joints and shuffling disease."

"Brother, enough for tonight," his sister insisted. "Stormy needs his rest, and so do you."

"Your aunt is right, Stormy. We will not be awake to greet *Noon-Day-Sun* if we do not get some sleep."

"Where are we going tomorrow," asked Stormy.

"Wherever the wind takes us, my son."

"I hope you pay attention, old man, so you can find your way home," said Stormy's aunt, settling onto her sleeping mat.

Her rhythmical breathing told Cloud Bringer she was asleep, and Stormy soon fell still. Cloud Bringer watched the lodge ceiling in the flickering light from the dying lodge fire. No matter how many times he stared at the ceiling, it was never the same, always alive with dancing shadows, changing faces, and vivid memories. There, by the hanging bundle of dried lizard tail roots, was the face of young Broken Plaits, his only true love, and next to the door was a Black Face warrior trying to enter. He rolled onto his side and looked at his son, watching the firelight play across his handsome face.

"Son, you have learned the healing ways well," he thought. "You remind me so much of myself at your age, so serious, so eager, so single-minded, but you need to find your true love and have children of your own or your life will not be whole. Do not wait for *Old Traveler* to send them to you. He might wait too long, and old age comes quickly."

Father and son spent the day searching in vain for lizard tail to treat wounds, sores, and teething babies' gums.

"Lizard tail does not grow in the swamp," said Cloud Bringer. "I have never seen it far from the waving grass. We will have to plan an overnight journey to Pretty Island before the green wings return."

Frogs and crickets began their nightly song, as lengthening cypress shadows reached into the lake.

"It is getting dark. We must paddle hard, or Pale Sun will be high above the trees by the time we get home. Your aunt will be afraid that we have been taken by *Long Black Being*."

The tired men dragged the dugout onto the shore just as the large orange orb was peeking through the trees.

"Father, I am going to see Speaks Twice, if he is not out running his fish lines," said Stormy. "I'll be home later."

Cloud Bringer entered the lodge, where his sister was waiting.

"My brother," she said, "You fill Stormy's days with lessons and more lessons. He needs to be with young people his own age. He should be hunting with the other young men and learning how to make blowguns and bows. He should to be playing hoop ball, chunky, running races, and wrestling. He should be noticing girls. Why, he is so shy, he does not even look up when girls walk by him, giggling."

"I gave him my blowgun," Cloud Bringer, "and he restrung my old black thorn-wood bow with string he plaited from the plant with hairy roots. He already can shoot better than most warriors," Cloud Bringer weakly protested.

"Brother!"

"But he already runs like a deer and has never been interested in wrestling or playing chunky or hoop ball."

"How do you know?" asked his sister. "Have you encouraged him?"

"No, but. . . ."

"Cloud Bringer, he is grown. He needs to be making his own decisions now."

"You are right, sister. I will ask him what he wants to do," Cloud Bringer said dejectedly.

"No, brother, you must tell him his apprenticeship is complete. Tell him you have taught him all you can."

Cloud Bringer pretended to be asleep when Stormy crept into the lodge.

"What can I say to him?" the old man thought. "Do I tell him that he no longer needs his father? Do I tell him that he must make his own way? Do I tell him that he needs to start his own family now?"

Cloud Bringer spent a restless night.

"Your father was so tired yesterday. He sleeps late today," said Stormy's aunt. "Why not go see if Speaks Twice needs help with his traps?"

After Stormy left, Cloud Bringer put on the cape he wore to healings and, with his heart on the ground, went to see Great Sun. The men were cousins. Great Sun was the oldest son of Cloud Bringer's father's brother.

"Why do you wish to see me, my cousin?" asked Great Sun, inviting Cloud Bringer to sit on the checkered mat beside his.

"Stormy's training is finished. I can teach him no more," said the old Snakebite healer sadly.

"So soon? Are you sure?" asked Great Sun. "He is only sixteen winters old. If we make him Snakebite healer now, he would be the youngest the people have ever recognized."

"Seventeen winters," corrected Cloud Bringer. "True, he is young, but he already knows the medicines, the songs, and the ceremonies. The lessons he must learn now can only come from the people," replied Cloud Bringer. "He must grow wise so he can best use his knowledge."

Heaviness settled on the old healer like a warm night's mist on cold water. His shoulders slumped, and he stared at the flickering fire.

Great Sun eyed his cousin closely. He knew how much the healer loved being with his son and teaching him the healing way. Over the years, he had watched a sad old man smile again and rediscover the spring in his step. A fresh strength replaced the tired old-man voice at council meetings, and he heard that many of Cloud Bringer's patients recovered sooner and more completely when doctored by father and son together. Cloud Bringer had even told him that his shadow could fly to the Upper World without remorse because the sacred Snakebite medicine was safe for another generation.

But as he continued to watch Cloud Bringer, he only saw a tired old man.

The old Snakebite healer rose from the mat. Head bowed, he politely backed toward the door. Great Sun felt Cloud Bringer's sadness. He knew the feeling well. It was never far from his own heart.

"I will call a public meeting for two sleeps hence. I would like for you to announce the completion of Stormy's training. I will tell Always Frowning and Fire Watcher to make arrangements."

Cloud Bringer nodded. There were no more words to be said.

3

Snakebite Healer

Stormy stood beside his father on the mound platform, flanked by other healers and village officials. Doing his best to imitate their stern look, he thrust out his chin and narrowed his eyes as though looking into the great mysteries outside the circle of firelight.

Excited children ran through the square grounds shouting, "He comes, Great Sun comes." A little girl tugged on her mother's skirt begging to be picked up so she could see. An excited murmur ran through the crowd and then quieted. All eyes turned toward the porch of the temple where Great Sun would speak.

Stormy quickly forgot about trying to look priestly and became a wide-eyed seventeen-year-old. His knee twitched, and he shifted from foot to foot.

Cloud Bringer noticed and frowned at him to be still.

The twitching stopped, but the pounding in his temples did not.

"I am about to become the youngest Snakebite healer the people have ever recognized," Stormy thought.

He took pride in the honor but worried that the naming celebration might be too much for him to bear.

"What if I collapse when Great Sun touches me with the sacred pipe?" he worried to himself. "Or choke on its magic smoke? What if I trip in my new palmetto sandals and fall down the temple steps? What if I forget the words of thanksgiving my father had me memorize? I cannot remember even one of them now.

"Guardian spirit, help me remember the words," he pleaded silently. "Do not let me dishonor Great Sun, Bent Woman, or the priests. Do not let me embarrass myself, my clan family, my friends, and, above all, the man who raised me, my adoptive father."

Stormy was still fidgeting when he watched Great Sun enter the plaza riding on the shoulders of two strong warriors. The men kneeled at the time-worn bench in front of the temple, and Great Sun dismounted. Stormy had never seen anyone look so important. Great Sun's shiny turkey-feather cloak flashed in the firelight, and he was sure he saw a golden glow envelop the chief.

Sun Woman took her place beside Great Sun.

What a magnificent pair they were, Stormy thought—Great Sun, tall and dignified; his wife, strikingly pretty with kind eyes. The people respected Great Sun because he was fair and kind, but nobody dared approach him or talk to him without being spoken to first. He was not an ordinary man. He was the brother of *Noon-Day-Sun*. His power was absolute and fearful. Like him, Sun Woman was of noble blood, but her wisdom and advice were sought by everyone from fussing neighbors to new mothers, and it did not matter whether they were nobles or commoners.

The stern temple priest, Turkey-Buzzard-Man, emerged from the temple carrying a beaver-skin bundle. Stormy wondered how the frail priest kept from entangling his long curving fingernails as he unwrapped the bundle containing the sacred pipe stem. The stem was covered with symbols of the Upper and Lower Worlds—Stormy could make out frogs and snakes, as well as panthers and strange pointy-eared figures. Attached feathers of the cardinal, snowy egret, and red-winged blackbird fluttered in the breeze and seemed to make the pipe stem fly. The bamboo tube showed the polish of many hands, the varnish of great age.

Stormy watched intently as the priest took a white clay pipe bowl from a lidded cane basket. His father had told him about the pipe bowl. Still, he was amazed when he saw it up close. It was shaped like mighty *Thunderer*, brother of *Lightning-Spirit-Bird*. It looked so real that Stormy imagined the mighty spirit bird was about to fly off with its prey. But its prey was what really caught Stormy's attention—*Thunderer* held a man in his talons and was eating him.

"The sacred pipe was given by *Old Traveler* to First People and has been passed down since the great flood," his father had told him. "Long ago, the people were at war with all their neighbors, even with bands of their own tribe living on the eastern side of the great swamp. The sacred pipe has seen much blood.

"Since the battle at Red Earth village on the Twisting Snake Water, only the man-eating Black Faces and skinned-headed Red Sticks have remained our mortal enemies. Should we and our enemies ever smoke the calumet officially marking an end to hostilities between our peoples, the pipe bowl is meant to send a clear message that violators will suffer the fate of the man being torn apart by the razor-sharp beak of *Thunderer*.

"The people smoke at village ceremonies and intertribal meetings to honor *Old Traveler,* the Giver of Life," Cloud Bringer explained. "We will send smoke at your naming ceremony, but we use the sacred *Thunderer* pipe bowl, not to frighten or intimidate, but to remind everyone that we are able to observe our village rites only because we remain strong and committed to defending our way of life. Bent Woman says that our village ceremonies are possible only because we know war and that, without war, we would not know peace. She says if there were no war or peace, there would be no reason for the Many Waters People to celebrate our traditions—friends and foes would all be one people without differences."

Stormy was jolted back to the present by Turkey-Buzzard-Man's deep voice, singing the Joining Song. Stormy knew the pipe bowl was the spirit of war and the stem the spirit of peace, and although they were brothers, the song kept them from fighting each other while they were united.

Turkey-Buzzard-Man pushed the long decorated stem into the back of the heavy pipe and packed the mixture of tobacco and sumac into the bowl. He handed the calumet to Great Sun, careful to avoid scratching him with his long fingernails. Fire Watcher, another temple priest, lit the mixture with a burning stick taken from the fire on the temple apron.

Great Sun inhaled and, turning slowly clockwise, blew smoke in the four directions. Then, raising his lips, he sent the gift of smoke up toward the dark sky. The last puff was directed toward the ground at his feet. He then passed the calumet around the circle of Beloved Men and village officials who each smoked in turn.

When the calumet was handed back to Great Sun, he motioned for Stormy and Cloud Bringer to come forward. He blew smoke over them, purifying their bodies and preparing their inner spirits for their exposure to the great mysteries.

A dog on the water's edge barked at a raccoon. The fire popped, sending a shower of sparks into the night, but not a word was heard among the spectators. Many children had never seen a naming and honoring ceremony held at the same time and did not quite know what to expect, but wide eyes revealed their fright. Even adults who had attended naming or honoring rites before were nervous about the upcoming brush with the spirits.

Great Sun broke the silence with his booming voice.

"Hai, Hear this man, Many Waters People. We are gathered tonight to name our newest healer. He is the youngest person to ever complete training in the Snakebite medicine. I ask Cloud Bringer to come forward and introduce our new healer."

Great Sun moved aside relinquishing the front of the apron to Cloud Bringer.

"Hai, listen to my words," said Cloud Bringer. *"Old Traveler* brought this person to us during the Mighty Wind. Two rattlesnakes watched over him until a feathered serpent biting his own tail led this man to him. The people accepted him as one of us and consented to his adoption by this Snakebite healer. The Snakes are his adoptive clansmen. Now, this person has completed his training and mastery of the Snakebite medicine. He can cure the bite of the white-mouthed snake and the other vipers. The people can be assured that snake bite will not condemn them to the Wasteland where their shadows can never be together. This person now has reached the first step in fulfilling his destiny that Bent Woman foresaw many winters ago."

Cloud Bringer's words left no doubt about who the new healer would be. Everyone now knew it was Stormy. The story of how he had been found after the Mighty Wind had been told around campfires for many winters. Nonetheless, the crowd remained respectfully quiet until Cloud Bringer finished.

Stormy heard Great Sun call his name and saw his father's face beaming with pride, but the moment he started toward the mound edge, the calm was shattered by a commotion at the corner of the temple mound.

A low figure darted through the crowd and scurried up the mound steps. Startled, Stormy drew back. The creature jumped through the fire scattering sparks. Babies cried, and frightened toddlers hugged their mothers' legs. Even adults who had seen honoring ceremonies before were stunned by the suddenness of the intrusion and the grotesqueness of the figure.

The creature was covered with curly black hair, which resembled moss stripped of its gray sheathing. The constant leaping and waving of its limbs hid its shaggy coat in the dim firelight. It had a head but no eyes, ears, nose, or mouth. It seemed to have three legs and an arm or maybe two legs and an arm used like a leg. Its unearthly screams brought fear to normally brave people and had more than one warrior reaching for his knife.

"I am not afraid, I am not afraid," Stormy kept thinking over and over, but his pounding heart and shaking knees did not agree. "Father warned me to expect the unusual, but he could not have foreseen something like this."

The creature darted in and out among the seated council elders and temple priests, sometimes coming within inches of their faces with a scratcher made from a garfish jaw. Stormy was astounded. None of them had raised their cane knives. They seemed to be amused by the monster, that is, all but Fire Watcher, who was nowhere to be seen. Sun Woman stared straight ahead, her face expressionless. Stormy was dismayed to see smile wrinkles in the corners of his father's eyes, and why was Great Sun watching him instead of rising up against the creature?

With a quick motion, Great Sun grabbed the hairy being with both hands. Immediately, the jumping and screaming stopped, and the figure assumed the posture of a man.

"It is time," said Great Sun.

The shaggy being approached and without a word started scratching Stormy's bare shoulder with the garfish jaw.

Stormy wanted to run, wanted to hide under Cloud Bringer's mantle like he used to when he was small. The scratching hurt worse than brushing up against a greenbriar vine, but he did not cry out or flinch. The last thing his father had told him was to be brave and show no fear no matter what happened.

Blood oozed from the scratches, only to be quickly wiped away on a hairy arm. From beneath its shaggy coat, the creature produced a bamboo tube, sprinkled charcoal on the scratches, and rubbed hard.

Then, the creature spoke using the formal speech of the nobility.

"Hai, Cloud Bringer's son has earned the healer's mark," said the monster in a gravelly voice, which sounded a great deal like Fire Watcher's. "From this moment on, he is a Snakebite healer of the people."

Then, as quickly as it appeared, the shaggy being dropped to three legs and scampered wildly through the crowd, disappearing into the darkness behind the temple. For a few steps, it could be heard running through the palmetto. A dog growled, and then there was a silence, heavy with unseen forces and spirits.

The people's attention flew back to Stormy as Great Sun approached him. Stormy stood as straight as a cane and as tall as he could stretch without tiptoeing. Great Sun touched his bleeding shoulder with the stem of the calumet and then rubbed the pipe over all over his body.

"Hear this man, people of Grand Lake village," said Great Sun. "The boy named Stormy, adopted son of Cloud Bringer, no longer exists among the people. The man now standing before you shall be called Storm Rider. As is our custom, his father, Cloud Bringer, now walks away from his old name and shall hereafter be known as Father-of-Storm-Rider.

"People, I say to you. *Old Traveler* smiles, Great Sun smiles, the Beloved Men smile, and the temple priests smile. Great Sun welcomes Storm Rider into the rank of healers. There have only been three other Snakebite healers in the history of our people, and we are fortunate to have two with us now. Storm Rider is the youngest Snakebite healer the people have ever honored."

The people stomped their feet on the ground and howled their approval.

Great Sun raised his arms, quieting the people, and called Storm Rider to the front.

"Do you have words for the people, Storm Rider, formerly called Stormy, adopted son of Cloud Bringer, member of the Snake clan, and now Snake-bite healer?" he asked.

Storm Rider stood there stiffly, groping for words, his acceptance speech completely forgotten.

"I am honored and will try my best to keep the people healthy. Oh, and I like my man-name, too," he finally blurted out.

The people laughed and howled.

Red-faced but buoyed by his new status and name, Storm Rider scanned the crowd, looking for Speaks Twice and Spotted Fawn. He heard the blue jay whistle, the greeting among the three friends and, following the sound to its source, found their broad smiles and waving arms in the crowd. Their joy released his happiness. His grin reached across his face, and his spirit soared like an eagle floating on a thermal.

"*Old Traveler,*" he promised silently. "I accept the responsibility that has been given me. I shall protect the sacred knowledge of the ancestors and use it only for the good of the people. Guardian, thank you for not letting me choke on the smoke or fall down the steps."

His eyes watered but not from tears, and his face felt like he was standing too close to the lodge fire. He did not feel the pain of the tattoo. That would come tomorrow, but now, as he moved toward his friends, he heard Spotted Fawn trilling, and then his aunt's voice rang out, "Storm Rider, Storm Rider." Others joined in, and soon his man-name carried over the waters of Pond Lily Cove and reached into the swamp beyond. Hoot owls repeated the chant, as did wolves hunting at Fish Island.

And in the old cypress tree beneath which a special infant had been discovered seventeen winters ago, the Great Horned Owl turned its big yellow eyes toward the distant glow on the southern horizon and raised its voice in praise.

4

Lessons in Healing

Nearly everyone at Storm Rider's initiation was happy for him, but a few people were jealous. One family of the Panther clan whose son was training to be a healer resented naming an orphan as a powerful Snakebite healer.

"He was not born of the people or of nobility," complained the matriarch. "How can he be a healer? There is no way he would have been named Snakebite healer if his adoptive father had not been Great Sun's cousin. Uummh, family patronage!"

Another young trainee of the Bear clan was upset that Storm Rider's apprenticeship was so short.

"That person could not have possibly learned all the plants and the healing songs," he was overheard complaining to his teacher. "It has taken me twice as long, and still there are cures I have not mastered. Do people think he is special, just because his father says he is? His father is old and forgetful."

And then there were Buzzard and his four Panther clan brothers, the village ruffians. They enjoyed scaring youngsters and ganging up on their peers who would not stand up to them.

Buzzard disliked Storm Rider, which was nothing unusual for he liked few people, but his disdain for the newly recognized Snakebite healer was especially intense. He even refused to call Storm Rider by his man-name. His dislike had been festering for many winters. It started when they were boys, and Storm Rider refused to join him and his bully gang making fun of Speaks Twice, who stuttered, and Spotted Fawn, who was covered with freckles. That they were Storm Rider's best friends did not matter to Buzzard. To be in Buzzard's inner circle, you had to do exactly what he wanted, when he wanted, to whomever he chose. And the problem was that Buzzard was big and strong and quite capable of carrying out his mean-hearted capriciousness. People were afraid of him and tried to avoid him and his gang.

Even curs slunk away when he came near, usually followed by a barrage of clamshells.

But his real clash with Storm Rider came the day Storm Rider and his father passed through the plaza going to a healing. Buzzard was picking his team for a hoop ball game.

"Hey, you," Buzzard yelled at Storm Rider, "Come play on the winning side. We are going to beat these sissies so badly they will go back to playing dolls with their baby sisters."

Storm Rider shook his head and kept on walking with his father. Buzzard's face turned as red as a sunrise before rain, and he threw the ball as far as he could into the surrounding woods.

"How dare you refuse to play on my team?" he screamed after the healers. "You'll be sorry."

Nobody had ever refused to play on his team before. They were afraid he would bash their heads with his fist or insult them unmercifully.

The young healer obviously was not afraid of him, and that infuriated Buzzard, who thrived on the fear he created.

"The son of Strikes Blows has a real problem," said Father-of-Storm-Rider. "He is lost and needs to find his way."

"Ah-e. I try to stay away from him."

"We need to find a calming medicine for him."

"Huh! Maybe a mad bear might teach him a lesson," said Storm Rider.

Fists clenched and chest heaving, Buzzard watched the healers until they disappeared down the trail leading to Bead Basket's lodge. "One day soon, I will teach that pretender a lesson he will not forget," he fumed under his breath before stomping off toward the landing, his bully gang following a safe distance behind.

As long as Storm Rider was under his father's protective arm, Buzzard dared not do anything amiss that might get back to the old Snakebite healer. Like everyone else in Grand Lake village, except maybe Great Sun and Bent Woman, the ruffians were afraid of Father-of-Storm-Rider's magic.

One of Buzzard's clan brothers reminded him that he had heard a village elder say that Father-of-Storm-Rider could turn grown men's arms into fins and their legs into tails and make them spend the rest of their lives flopping like catfish in the bottom of a dugout.

"If he can do that to grown men," the brother said, "just think what he can do to us young men."

The miscreants did not wish to be turned into catfish or worse, so they avoided picking on Storm Rider in public and offending his father.

But since his initiation, Storm Rider no longer spent his days with his father. He went to the swamp by himself. Buzzard boiled with anger whenever he saw the courtesy people paid the young healer when he walked through the village.

"Tell me what the mongrel with the white-streaked hair and the cur-dog eyes has done to earn such respect?" Buzzard asked his brothers, not expecting an answer.

"Bead Basket's snakebite he supposedly cured when he was a boy was only a story started by Father-of-Storm-Rider, who was by his side the whole time. Now, who do you think really did the curing?" Buzzard asked smugly.

"Bead Basket said Storm Rider drew out the poison without even leaving a swelling or a bruise," one of the gang members reminded Buzzard.

"Do you really think so? How would she know? She was out of her head."

"What about Howling Wolf's stomach sickness he cured? Do you remember how much blood he threw up for days? Everybody thought he was dying."

"Cured? All that cheat did was take credit for the cure. Howling Wolf just ate too much bloodweed. He did not know it had been boiled only once.

"Brothers! You are making me angry. Quit defending this imposter. He is not born of the Many Waters People. His veins do not carry a single drop of noble blood. He is nothing but a poor cast-off, raised by a feeble old man and his sister. He would be eating scraps with the dogs if Father-of-Storm-Rider had not taken him in."

Buzzard's lips grew thinner, his eyes narrowed. He glared at his companions. They did not say another word. They knew better.

For days after his initiation, Storm Rider held his chin high as he walked through the paths between lodges on his way to the swamp to gather medicines. People smiled and congratulated him. They even left small gifts at his lodge door. Even old Snapping Dog gave him an arrow point he had gotten from the Stone-Arrow-Point People up on the Water-Runs-Red. Storm Rider was surprised. Snapping Dog was the village grouch, always complaining, never having a nice word for anyone. His aunt said the point probably was the first gift he had ever given anybody.

The attention was nice but embarrassing. He wished it would stop. Always before, the attention he received was because he looked different. Little children gawked at his white streak or begged him to look at them so they could see his eyes of different colors. Stories about snakes protecting him had been told in all the lodges. Now, he was accepted by the tribe. He was finally one of the Many Waters People, and the feeling swelled his chest.

Still, the young healer sensed there were dark days ahead.

Despite the apparent ease he had shown in mastering the medicinal arts, he had worked hard. Sometimes, he fell asleep humming the words and vocables of the healing songs. He had learned to recognize medicine plants by the shapes of their leaves, and often, while busy with other matters, he caught himself imagining what this leaf or that leaf looked like. His father also taught him to recognize plants by their bark and by the kinds of insects and fungus that lived on them.

"Sickness and injury have no season," his father said one wet morning during the Season of Falling Leaves, as they searched for roots of the Five-Leaf vine to treat Spotted Fawn's aunt's recurring fever.

"You must be able to find roots when the vine is dead and recognize shrubs after the leaves have fallen. Every patient must have fresh medicine. Old medicines lose their power."

Storm Rider watched as his father pulled at the root until he exposed six rootlets. These he cut off with his cane knife. Then he had reburied the root. He remembered how gently his father handled the plant, how respectfully.

"It will continue to grow and provide us with new roots whenever we need them again. Our medicine will be stronger because the plant lives.

"People trust you to make them feel better," his father continued. "If you cannot find the right plants during all seasons, you will not be able to treat people properly. With fresh medicine, you can be confident in your ability to help them, and, my son, if you have confidence in yourself, people will have confidence in you. Faith is the best medicine of all. I have seen people recover from bad wounds and life-threatening sicknesses because they believed I could heal them. These are the cases when *Old Traveler* intercedes, so you must always ask for his help and guidance during a curing ceremony."

Storm Rider remembered the strange look that clouded his father's eyes one day while telling the story of his grandfather, his father's clan father. The old Snakebite healer stared into the distance as he recalled the story.

"If people lose faith in you, they will think you are a witch like they did my clan father. They carried him away, bound from head to foot. I did not know where they took him, and many sleeps passed before circling vultures led me to his remains on Bird Island. The birds and the turtles had nearly finished with him. His eyes and mouth were open holes, and his bare bones were visible between his bindings.

"The elders would not let me take his body to the bone house. They did not want his bones buried in Rain Tree mound. They said that witch's bones should not be covered with Mother Earth's fertile robe. They said it would make new witches grow."

Father-of-Storm-Rider paused.

"After many moons, I went back to Bird Island. His bones were scattered, and I found only a few of them. They were bleached as white as the clam shells on the shore. Wolves and wood rats and big black ants had also found them. I did not see the fox or owl forms that the outside shadow assumes when it lingers near the bones, and I did not hear their unearthly barks or hoots. I prayed that *Old Traveler* would let his two shadows be reunited. He did not deserve to have his spirits wander the Wasteland. His punishment was unjust.

"That was the last time I set foot on Bird Island. I will not go there again."

The lesson of Father-of-Storm-Rider's disgraced clan-father and teacher was not lost on Storm Rider. He thought of it whenever he went to a sick person's lodge and sometimes on rainy days in the quiet of his lodge. He promised never to lose a patient because he administered the wrong medicine or sang the wrong song. He knew he would never intentionally harm anyone with his medicines. His self-confidence grew daily, an inner strength drawn from his father's thoroughness and his trust in the healing power of nature.

"You will not be able to heal every patient," his father told him, "but remember those you cannot cure go to a better place in the Upper World where game is plentiful and nobody gets sick. Make sure the patient's family understands this first, and then perform the healing."

Storm Rider worked hard to please his father. He loved to see approval in his father's eyes. Now that he was Storm Rider, Snakebite healer of the Many Waters People, he still cherished his father's approval above all else.

"I hear your heart singing," he often heard his aunt say when she and his father spoke of him after they thought he was asleep. He swelled with love and pride for his father.

Storm Rider remembered the last days of his training when his father showed him the slight-of-hand tricks that made healing ceremonies magical.

"Do not think of the quickness of your hands and the pocket hidden in your sleeve as foolery or deceit," his father said. "Our tradition tells us that by pretending to remove the harmful object from the patient and making it disappear in a clay pot filled with water, you really are removing the poison from the body. The real poison sees itself spat into the water and is fooled into thinking it has drowned. It leaves the patient and enters the water, where it really does drown. When the patient and his family see that you have removed the stone or feather or thorn that was causing the sickness, recovery will be quick, that is, if *Old Traveler* wishes."

Although medicinal training dominated their days, his father taught him many other things—life lessons. Storm Rider learned how to speak with birds and animals. He learned to listen for the cackle of the ivory-billed woodpecker, which warned of intruders in the swamp—bears, panthers, Black Faces! He learned to watch the wren, who told him with its changing call and perked tail when he was about to have visitors and from which direction they would arrive, when and where danger lurked, when good luck was about to happen, and when rain was on its way. He learned to pay attention to the tree frogs' promise of oncoming rain. A bright red sky in the morning meant it would be raining in the afternoon. The scream of the screech owl during the daylight told of a serious illness or death in the village. The howl of the west wind told him that bad luck or death would soon follow. The playful gray squirrels, which ate live oak acorns out of his hand and sat on his shoulder, told him when visitors were approaching by their jittering flight to the nearest tree. They taught him when hair grew thick on their bellies and they cached acorns instead of eating them that the winter would be long and hard. The locusts told him by their shrill singing that frost would cover the ground three moons later.

His father taught him that people's eyes told their true feelings better than their words. Illness can hide in their words, not in their eyes.

"If someone has to tell you something with words, the true meaning may already be lost," Father-of-Storm-Rider once told him. "Words are deceptive. Use them sparingly and with great care. Do not make idle talk. Look into the person's eyes, and try to feel what the person is trying to say. Feel the patient's pain in your mind and then with your fingertips."

Storm Rider delighted in his new status, but praise and smiles quickly proved to be no substitute for trips into the swamp with his father. Their days had been long and tiring, but they were special because man and boy enjoyed each other's company beyond all else.

Storm Rider still lived in his aunt's lodge and spent each evening with her and his father talking about the day's events, but it was not the same. Storm Rider sorely missed the days spent with his father. The old man missed them even more. He grew frailer and started taking long afternoon naps. People began asking Storm Rider to tend to minor illnesses and injuries instead of bothering his father. Still, when the death wind was near, the people wanted the Father-of-Storm-Rider to care for their loved ones.

"My father's inside shadow will soon journey to the Upper World," Storm Rider said to Speaks Twice. "The people will cry. They know there will never be another Snakebite healer like him."

"Except his son," thought Speaks Twice.

5

The Red Bead

The eastern sky was beginning to lighten as Speaks Twice crossed the village plaza headed for Storm Rider's lodge. He listened to the distant growls and yelps of a wolf pack fighting over scraps left from the night's kill. A woodcock burst out of the palmetto, sending the lanky youngster's heart pounding as he fumbled for the door catch on the lodge.

"Storm Rider asked me to wake him before daybreak," mumbled Speaks Twice under his breath, "but he didn't warn me I was going to be attacked by an angry woodcock. Maybe it is a sign."

Speaks Twice ducked under the palmetto flap covering the door and tiptoed around the lodge fire pit. A single ember winked at him like the blinking eye of the great owl.

"Come in, Speaks Twice," said the old man softly, "A woodcock told me you were coming."

"I didn't mean to w-w-wake you, Father-of-Storm-Rider."

"You didn't. The dark before *Noon-Day-Sun* begins her journey is the time when I talk to my dream shadows. Storm Rider has already left. He's waiting for you at the landing."

Leaving, Speaks Twice tripped over the blowgun leaning against the lodge pole but managed to find the door covering and emerged into the gray and pink streaked morning.

"Sorry," he whispered back at the old man, who was now standing in the doorway.

"Hummm," he thought, "I didn't see Father-of-Storm-Rider rise from his sleeping mat."

"Young fisherman, watch out for the giant alligator that killed two Prairie Landing children while they were playing in their father's dugout."

"W-w-we will sleep with our eyes open, great healer."

Speaks Twice ran easily along the well-worn path toward the landing. Storm Rider was sitting in the dugout, paddle lying across his knees.

"What took you so long, my friend?" kidded Storm Rider.

"I w-w-went to wake you like you asked. D-d-did you forget, or did a dream shadow scare you awake?" grumbled Speaks Twice, perturbed.

"I could not sleep. My father told me to get in the dugout and imagine our trip, every step of the way, there and back. He said that going through a hard journey in your mind takes away half the anxiety because you have already been there before."

"Yes," fretted Speaks Twice, "And I could have slept while you were t-t-thinking."

Speaks Twice threw his gear into the dugout next to Storm Rider's. They traveled lightly, sleeping mats rolled and tied around a shoulder sling, but Speaks Twice had packed a fishing line and Storm Rider a double-weave waterproof basket containing a small fire drill and tobacco. Neither carried food, they would eat off the land.

They pushed away from the landing and snaked their way through the tall moss-draped cypress trees before paddling northward across the open waters of Grand Lake. A stiff sea breeze helped push the craft along, but the choppy water made for a rough ride.

"I s-s-smell rain coming," said Speaks Twice, thrusting his chin toward the ominous black clouds building in the south.

"Fisherman, we should get to the shore before *Thunderer* turns angry."

The muscles in their bronzed backs rippled as they paddled harder, their pointed paddles reaching deeply into the dark water. They beached the dugout, overturning it as a shelter against the rain. They were pushing their gear under the dugout as the cloud burst drenching them with hard stinging rain.

"Ouch, feels like t-t-tattoo needles," laughed Speaks Twice, his long warrior lock plastered to his face and chill bumps rising on his arms and legs.

"Are you afraid of getting tattooed?" kidded Storm Rider.

"No, b-b-brave healer, but I see that your t-t-tattoo did not waterproof your skin either. You're as p-p-puckered as a p-p-plucked duck."

The storm passed quickly, but thunder kept up its steady rumbling as the wind and rain spread up the lake toward Prairie Landing village. Every now and then the loudest claps jarred the dugout. Mist steamed off the rain-cooled water like tiny fingers of smoke reaching for the sky, and the damp air was heavy with the smell of ozone and rotting leaves.

"*Thunderer* heads for White Ibis Lake," said Storm Rider.

They righted the dugout and stowed their gear.

"P-p-pull, harder, Storm Rider, or we'll be p-p-paddling in mud."

The boys dragged the heavy dugout off the lake bank, agilely jumped in without tipping the unsteady craft, and resumed their strong, graceful paddling. They stayed close to the shoreline. Grand Lake was still agitated from the storm.

Speaks Twice began to sing—singing always calmed his stuttering: "Fish, you are lucky, lucky indeed. I cannot catch you when I am on my knees. Saved by a paddle, a paddle indeed. I cannot catch you when I am on my knees. My net is empty, empty indeed. I cannot catch you...."

As Speaks Twice's song went on and on, Storm Rider sank into his inner thoughts. "I wonder if my mental journey made *Thunderer* and *Lightning-Spirit-Bird* follow our path? No, has to be coincidence. If *Thunderer* is really tracking my mind's journey, I would feel it here, in my heart."

He glanced back at Speaks Twice who stopped singing and was watching a brace of wood ducks winging toward their nesting cavity in a dead cypress tree ahead. A startled Great Blue Heron jumped into flight from a nearby privet bush, showering both boys with rain drops and scolding them with loud, raucous calls.

"H-h-heron does not like anyone t-t-trespassing on his hunting grounds," said Speaks Twice.

"Nor do we," replied Storm Rider, noting that the big bird's flight followed the storm to the north, the direction of White Ibis Lake.

The sun came out, quickly drying their breechcloths and hair. With it came the heat and humidity. Perspiration ran down their backs and chests and stung their eyes.

Storm Rider stopped paddling and trailed his hand in the water, splashing his face. Speaks Twice leaned over the side, dipped a double handful of water, and drank thirstily.

"Ahhh, good. No w-w-water is sweeter than Grand Lake's. We leave our lake now, healer, and enter B-b-big Cypress Lake, the lake of our b-b-brothers, the people of P-p-prairie Landing village."

"We must stop at their landing. They will wonder why two Grand Lake clansmen have come to their lake. We must tell them where we are going."

The narrow connection between the lakes opened into a large expanse of open water, which was still white-capped from the passing thunderstorm. A flock of ibis trailed after the tempest, and a giant garfish rolled over, slapping the water with his tail and sending a spray of water into the boat. Soaked again! But neither boy noticed. They were watching four canoes rapidly approaching from a clearing in the wooded shoreline. Then they saw smoke rising from the distant weathered lodges and knew that warriors from Prairie Landing village had found them.

Storm Rider made a sweeping motion with his arm, palm down, the Many Waters People's greeting among friends and relatives.

"Brothers," said the powerful tattooed warrior standing in the prow of the largest canoe, "What brings you to our lake?"

Storm Rider noticed the other canoes had deftly encircled their dugout, and the occupants all had their hands on their bows. Ignoring the tenseness, Speaks Twice slowly rose to his feet smiling and making the familiar sweeping greeting.

"We are h-h-heading to the B-b-big Salt Water. Can you point us in the right d-d-direction?" Speaks Twice sat down with a beseeching expression on his face.

The Prairie Landing men looked at each other quizzically. Then the powerful one started laughing so hard he almost tumbled out of his dugout. Belly-laughter consumed the little flotilla dispelling the tension.

"I am Storm Rider, son of Cloud Bringer, who is now called Father-of-Storm-Rider, great healer of the Grand Lake village, and my friend here is Speaks Twice, son of Laughing Otter, famous fisherman of our village. Sometimes, he jokes, too."

"I am Red Club, member of the Wolf clan and war chief of the Prairie Landing village. My men are merely being vigilant. Our scouts have watched your progress since you put your boat in the lake after *Thunderer* passed."

"My father speaks fondly of you, Red Club, and Bent Woman sings your praises around winter fires. Your exploits and bravery are legendary in our village."

"So, you are the young prophet. Yes, I see now, the streaked hair, the eyes of different colors. Is your father well? He was born in Round Island village, one of our old villages, but moved to Grand Lake when it was abandoned. His reputation honors all our villages."

Turning to Speak Twice, Red Club continued: "I know your father too, lanky one. We were members of the war party that raided the Black Faces the year the lake froze."

Storm Rider rose to his full height.

"Great warrior, we have come to your lake because we are on a quest. We seek the Mound of the Ancients on White Ibis Lake," he said thrusting his chin toward the north. "My father told me of seeing strange apparitions there and finding objects that belonged to the Ancients. We hope to recover one of their objects and place it in our temple. Our priests believe it will help restore protection to our village, which was blown away by the Mighty Wind that took away our Great Sun's infant daughter."

"I know you are eager to continue your journey," said Red Club, nodding. "We will escort you as far as the Rain Tree. You are welcome in our village anytime. I hope you find what you are seeking. May you and your fathers live long and kill many Black Faces."

The dugouts paddled past Bird Island, where Father-of-Storm-Rider's clan father, the accused witch, was left to die. They skirted Eagle Point, where the majestic birds gathered to raise their young, and they knifed their way through the narrows of Little Eagle Lake and entered the live oak–shrouded Rain Tree Water, where the sacred Rain Tree and Rain Tree burial mounds hid on the shadowy banks.

"Be vigilant," warned Red Club. "We leave you here. The Black Hairs, rotten brothers of the Black Faces, live higher up on Twisting Snake Water. They often send raiding parties against our villagers at Red Earth and Cottonwood. If they catch you, they will eat you. And another thing, paddle slowly past the Rain Tree. If you splash one drop of water on it, the sky will open, and it will rain for days."

"We will be careful," said Storm Rider. There were warrior hand shakes, and then the Prairie Landing warriors were gone.

Speaks Twice looked at the Rain Tree, and then turned to Storm Rider and said, "D-d-don't look at me. I'm not g-g-going to make a splash."

The boys continued upstream. They stopped talking as they neared the burial mounds and quieted their splashing paddles by using them like sculls to propel the dugout through the ghost sickness zone. Two bends upstream, Storm Rider finally relaxed, expelling his breath loudly.

"Ghost sickness can't get in if you don't breathe," he explained.

Speaks Twice nodded.

"It's getting dark," said Storm Rider. "We shouldn't camp near the mounds. Do you think we're far enough away?"

"L-l-let's go one more bend."

The boys dragged the dugout from the bayou and covered it with moss, so it couldn't be seen by night raiders. They spread moss on the ground, covered it with sleeping mats, and, without building a fire, fell instantly asleep.

At dawn, Storm Rider was jolted awake by a cold shower of raindrops on his face.

"Looks like squirrel could have found another limb to jump on."

Speaks Twice grunted, "W-w-what? I can't see you, healer."

"It would help if you would open your eyes. We need to go."

They each ate a raw cat-tail root dug from the muddy bank and drank handfuls of bayou water.

"G-g-good for a dry throat," croaked Speaks Twice, "but not nearly as sweet as Grand Lake w-w-water."

They uncovered the dugout, scattered the moss about so that it looked like it had fallen naturally, and pushed the boat into the stream, brushing away their tracks with beaver-felled cat-tail stalks. A mother beaver attracted by the commotion in her food patch swam downstream to investigate. Startled by the oncoming dugout, she slapped the still water with her tail and, followed by her litter of four kits, dove into the underwater entrance of her den.

Half a bend ahead, the boys turned into a fast-flowing stream with high banks lining its unusually straight course. Cloud Bringer told them this would be the Little Long Water and that it would take them northeastward toward the Long Water, near their destination.

"The c-c-current carries lots of drift," said Speaks Twice, pushing away a floating log with his paddle.

"Look how muddy the water is, fisherman. It runs into the woods where the banks have caved in. We've got high water coming downstream."

"The w-w-whole bank must have c-c-collapsed nearby and let in the flood."

"Then, we better paddle faster," said Storm Rider, his flying paddle creating a continual fury of splashing water.

The boys knew that if they could reach Black Water Chute before the spreading backwater topped the banks, they would still be able to complete their journey. If they couldn't make it, well, they could always sleep in the dugout, though it would be a water-filled dugout. Thunder, lightning, and driving rain were back. A dead cypress tree crashed across the Little Long Water.

"We must hurry, my friend," yelled Storm Rider in the deluge, *"Thunderer* is flapping his mighty wings."

They ducked under the fallen tree, and then they saw the foaming black water pouring into the Little Long Water ahead. It was Black Water Chute.

Soaked but elated, they began the run up Black Water Chute. Just beyond the mouth of a drain pouring out of a small round lake, the source of the black water, they pulled their dugout out of the chute and laboriously dragged it a few steps across the palmetto-covered bank and into the cutoff lake.

"White Ibis Lake!" proclaimed Storm Rider, "Just where father said it would be."

They had made it. Rain dripped off the cypress trees into the dark water, which was encircled by a beaver dam, but both boys noticed muddy water spilling over the dam in several places, dyeing the black water brown.

"The f-f-flood is topping b-b-beaver's dam," exclaimed Speaks Twice.

"Let's pull over here," said Storm Rider, pointing to a recently repaired spot on the dam. "We've got to find the old mound quickly or we'll be going home like a pair of wet raccoons."

The rain slowed to a steady drizzle when they entered the narrow, muddy lake, and fog was rising, making it difficult to see into the woods on the bank.

"W-w-where is the mound?" asked Speaks Twice. "Y-y-your father said it would be on the left-hand b-b-bank near the l-l-little cove in the sharp bend in the lake. The rain and the fog hide everything. W-w-we can't see."

Storm Rider looked skyward, blinking in the drizzle. He heard his inner voice say, "A little farther, watch for the sacred flame."

"S-s-sacred flame," Speaks Twice puzzled, "W-w-we are nearly a day away from the c-c-closest fire temple at Prairie Landing village."

Suddenly, there was a bright flash and a loud crack. Lightning struck a tall water oak tree, setting the top on fire.

The tree was really no taller than others along the bank. It was merely higher because it stood atop the Mound of the Ancients.

"Paddle hard, Speaks Twice, the sacred flame lights the way."

They landed on the muddy bank. Storm Rider grabbed his gear, draped the carrying sling over his neck and shoulder, and began to slog toward the burning tree, Speaks Twice right behind using his paddle like a brace in the deepening mire. They had taken but a few steps when their sandals were lost, and a few more steps found them buried knee-deep in soft clinging muck. At first, they took turns using the paddle to pull each other along, but that was too slow. So, they started pulling themselves from bush to bush.

A mud snake half slithered, half swam between Storm Rider's bogged-down legs. He reached down about to grab the serpent when Speaks Twice raised his arm for him to stop.

"H-h-healer, healer," Speaks Twice whispered, "S-s-something's wrong. Look at the b-b-bushes. They're moving."

"Moving? There is no wind."

"S-s-snakes!" shouted Speaks Twice, "T-t-they're everywhere, every b-b-bush! The limbs are s-s-snakes. We're in a snake den. Aihee, I h-h-hate snakes!"

Speaks Twice recoiled as he realized that the limb he grabbed had begun to coil around his arm. Raising his paddle over his head with both hands, he flew toward the mound, his long wiry legs moving as fast as Spotted Fawn's pestle.

"C-c-come on, Storm Rider, hurry!"

"They will not harm you if you leave them alone."

"E-e-easy for you to say, snakes are your p-p-protectors, your totem. I am of the D-d-dog People."

They sat heavily on a rotten log at the foot of the mound, breathing hard but out of the deep mud, the drizzle streaking their muddy bodies and faces.

"Y-y-your war paint is r-r-running," joked Speaks Twice, jerky movements belying his calm. "N-n-never been in a snake's den before."

"We must not ascend the mound without purification," said Storm Rider. "Here, fisherman, hold my sleeping mat over my head while I make fire."

He extracted the small fire drill from the waterproof basket he carried in the rolled-up mat and a half dozen draws of the bow later had a wisp of smoke curling around his hand.

"Break off a piece of bark from the peeling-bark tree," he instructed Speaks Twice.

He placed a pinch of tobacco and sumac on the bark and dumped the smoldering cypress-bark shavings from the fire drill into the sacred mixture. The tobacco began to burn sending its aromatic plumes skyward. Storm Rider turned, offering smoke to the spirits of four directions before letting the smoke bathe his head and body and inner shadow.

"Put your hands in the smoke and waft it over yourself," he said. "The smoke is our prayer. It purifies our bodies and inner shadows. It prevents ghost sickness. It closes the snakes' mouths."

Purified and protected, the pair made their way up to the mound summit following the well-worn deer trail, made muddy and slick from the rain. Storm Rider went first, followed by Speaks Twice, carrying his paddle just in case a snake decided to ignore the smoke. They found the top of the mound completely bare, trampled by deer herds that had been bedding up here for years, safe even during the highest floods. They found no snakes.

Visibly relieved, Speaks Twice sat down in the mud but still held onto his paddle.

"N-n-now, what is it that we are s-s-supposed to see? I hope it is not s-s-snake s-s-spirits. There are enough real ones around. Where are the s-s-sacred objects? W-w-would you know it if you saw one, healer?"

Storm Rider did not have answers. He was wet and tired. He wanted a big bowl of his aunt's fish stew and kunti bread hot from the ashes.

"My father saw objects and apparitions on the mound," he reminded Speaks Twice, and himself. "The snakes must be protecting them, just as they do us."

"Y-y-you, Storm Rider, they p-p-protect you, not me."

The boys sat in silence. Speaks Twice mindlessly stirred the mud between his legs with his paddle.

"I am not going to sleep with the s-s-snakes," he said. "I am sleeping in the dugout in the m-m-middle of the lake."

He reached down, removing the mud caked on the end of his paddle. He felt something hard, a root maybe. No, too hard for a root. He cleared off some of the mud with his fingers, and a glimmer of red caught his eye.

"Storm Rider, l-l-look at this," he said, handing him the object. "It's rock."

Storm Rider dipped the rock into a water-filled hoof print and washed away the remaining mud. He dug out the dirt on the ends, revealing a small hole running completely through the finger-shaped rock. He held up the red stone to his eye, noticing that the hole was wider on the ends and narrower in the middle.

"Looks like Old Hair's beads," he exclaimed, "except that his are made out of shell from the Big Salt Water. Speaks Twice, you found a red rock bead that belonged to the Ancients. It's what we came for!"

"Is it s-s-sacred, Storm Rider? Some old woman p-p-probably wore it around her neck."

"It is sacred to us, my friend, even if it was not to the Ancients. My father says that the Ancients' spirit remains in everything they made or touched. Now, the spirit of the red bead will help protect our village. Before we leave this place, we must send thanks."

Storm Rider put the bead in the tobacco holder and stuck it inside his rolled-up sleeping mat. The boys slipped and slid down the mound and sloshed across the muddy, snake-infested privet thicket to the dugout, Speaks Twice fending off snakes with his paddle. They hurried to the dugout, dropped the sleeping roll and paddle inside, and waded noisily into the lake, washing off their muddy legs and arms.

Half a dozen large alligators noticed the splashing and came to investigate.

"Time to get in the dugout, Speaks Twice, unless you think you can charm the toothed ones with your smile."

They climbed in. Storm Rider unrolled his sleeping mat and removed the tobacco holder, preparing to send thanksgiving smoke.

"H-h-hand me the mat and I will hold it over your head while you start the fire."

Storm Rider sat transfixed, staring at the water dripping into his cupped palm.

"The tobacco," he lamented. "I did not put the cover on tightly enough. It is wet."

Before the boys could say another word, they were startled by a loud cracking. The top of the lightning-struck water oak split apart and crashed to the ground. Flames shot into the drizzle—toward the Upper World—losing themselves in a column of white smoke. One finger drifted north, one south, and others curled toward the remaining cosmic quarters.

The boys were awe-struck. They stared at the smoking tree.

Finally, Storm Rider found his voice.

"The Ancients send the prayer for us, not with sacred tobacco smoke, but with smoke just as powerful—a prayer sent from the sacred mound itself. We need to go, my friend, now, before the fire goes out."

They pushed off and swung the dugout toward the beaver dam. Speaks Twice looked over his shoulder and suddenly stopped paddling.

"L-l-look, Storm Rider, look at the s-s-smoking tree."

A smoke ring was rising into the darkening mist. It looked like a writhing snake biting its own tail.

6

Cloud Bringer,
Father-of-Storm-Rider

Heads lowered, Storm Rider and Speaks Twice ascended the temple steps and handed Great Sun the white doeskin bundle holding the red bead. Great Sun raised his feathered staff, quieting the murmur running through the crowd gathered at the foot of the mound.

"People of Grand Lake village," he began, "This is a special day for us. Storm Rider and Speaks Twice bring us a gift from the Ancients, a gift that we believe will shelter our homes from the Mighty Wind and protect us from the Black Faces and Red Sticks."

He unwrapped the red bead and held it up for the people to see.

"The Ancients," he explained, "sanctified this bead by their living and dying. They blessed its consignment to our temple by sending smoke themselves, a fire lighted by *Lightning-Spirit-Bird*. My people, this is a powerful relic. I will have Fire Watcher place it in the Fire Temple so that its power will mingle with sacred smoke from the eternal fire and keep the Many Waters People safe."

Great Sun paused and, placing his hands on the young men's shoulders, turned them around to face the crowd.

"People of Grand Lake village," he resumed his harangue, "These young men entered a snake's den and braved rising waters and unsettled spirits to bring this relic to us. We owe them our gratitude, and we thank their families for teaching them respect for the old ways and for raising them to be responsible young men, dedicated to the service of our village."

The people shouted their approval.

While the boys fidgeted under the attention, Father-of-Storm-Rider's chest swelled with pride, and moisture collected in the corners of his heavy, wrinkled eyes. He wiped it away. He found Laughing Otter and his wife in the crowd, their faces aglow with happiness. He nodded to Laughing Otter, and Laughing Otter reciprocated with a huge grin. His eyes returned to his son. Storm Rider was looking at him, brows peaked and lips pressed tight, as though saying, "Father, come get me. Tell them we must go gather medicine."

Father-of-Storm-Rider understood. He vividly remembered how he felt at his first honoring ceremony when he was ordained as a Snakebite healer, the first in the tribe in generations. It happened long ago, back when he was still named Cloud Bringer, before he became known as Father-of-Storm-Rider. He too wanted to run away and hide in the swamp.

The memory loosed a flood of other memories. He closed his eyes and relived the emotional ups and downs that his life as a Snakebite healer had taken. He recalled how his family and friends shared his joy, especially his clan father who was a healer and his teacher. Cloud Bringer remembered how the people looked up to him, but also how they started standing a little farther away from him and only speaking when spoken to. Women diverted their eyes when he passed, even the demure young woman he hoped to marry. Only the men seemed unaffected. He was a dignitary, but he was feared as well.

He understood. Snakebite healers were the tribe's most powerful shamans. They could cure the bite of the white-mouth snake, but they also became the most fearsome witches if they used their power for sinister purposes. He knew he would never become a witch.

Still, Father-of-Storm-Rider knew how transparent the line was between healer and witch. His own clan father was suspected of being a witch, and it weighed heavily on his heart because he knew the rumors were unfounded, started by Pretty-Man-Smiling's distraught mother and his sisters.

"Father, they say you killed Pretty-Man-Smiling with your magic. They say he should not have died from hornet stings. They say you gave him medicine to make him swell up and then stole his breath while he was in a trance. They say you wanted his pretty wife. Two of Pretty-Man-Smiling's sisters bathing at Pond Lily Cove said they saw you and her swimming together. Father, you must confront these liars," pleaded Cloud Bringer.

His clan father would not talk with him about the accusations. "Everyone knows they are not true," he would say. Yet, the vicious rumors took on a life of their own, even infecting some of the temple priests and village elders. The people lost their faith in his clan father, leaving him to suffer the fate of distrusted healers.

Cloud Bringer's clan father was publicly accused of witchcraft and sentenced to be bound and carried far from the village where he would be left to his fate. None of the six clan elders spoke on his behalf. Even Great Sun, his first cousin, would not defend him, knowing he would lose the trust of the people if he did. Pretty-Man-Smiling's wife's hair was shorn, her nose cut off, and she was given to Big Round Belly, who kept her busy sweeping the dance ground during the day and warming his sleeping mat during the night.

Cloud Bringer was not touched by the public outrage that consumed his clan father. He often wondered why. He was, after all, the accused witch's nephew and trainee. His sister offered the best explanation.

"They believe in you, Cloud Bringer, and they know you have sworn not to lie with any woman ever since Broken Plaits, your chosen, married Pretty-Man-Smiling's youngest brother."

Witches were not accorded the traditional public mourning. Even private weeping and sadness were viewed with suspicion and fear. So, Cloud Bringer busied himself in the healing ways, hiding his feelings until he was alone deep in the swamp. He used these medicine-gathering trips to search for his clan father, and nobody questioned his absences. One day, spiraling vultures led him to what was left of his clan father's remains. He offered the Two-Shadows-Joining prayer, hoping to right the injustice that condemned his father's outside shadow to wander the swamp. Then, he left, vowing to return in a year.

"When *Noon-Day-Sun* twice passes this place, I will return to see if your outside shadow has left to join your inside shadow in the Upper World. You will always live in my heart, clan father."

Cloud Bringer's reputation grew at home and even spread to nearby villages. His successes at curing snakebite were becoming legendary. Children told their mothers they wanted to be Snakebite healers when they grew up, and he overheard one scarred warrior grumble that soon there would be no warriors left to protect the people from the Black Faces when all the children became healers.

On the day he passed his twenty-fourth winter, he was finishing a healing song for a woman who had just given birth. The child was stillborn, and the woman was bleeding and fevered. He finished packing his medicine basket and started toward the lodge door when he heard shouting and screaming outside and then the war whoop.

"Black Faces! Cover the woman with the bear skin and get behind the storage baskets," he ordered her wide-eyed mother and sisters. "Do you have a bow and arrows?"

"No, our brother is hunting. We only have his war club."

"Give it me, quickly and then hide."

Cloud Bringer opened a crack in the door flap, just as a wild-eyed Black Face was about to enter, bow drawn. Cloud Bringer flew at him, catching him with a lowered shoulder and knocking him to the ground. Before he could rise, Cloud Bringer caved in his face with the heavy club, drenching himself with spurting blood.

Another Black Face raider saw his comrade die and raced toward Cloud Bringer, pausing only to release his arrow. The arrow impaled itself in the lodge post, and Cloud Bringer swung his club with deadly accuracy. The Black Face dropped like a stone.

Cloud Bringer stepped from the doorway, screaming at the remaining Black Face warriors. They looked at the wild man running toward them and turned and fled toward the lake where their dugouts were hidden.

The women emerged from the hut, frightened but armed with cane knives and smoldering sticks of firewood. Even the sick woman, weak and wan, stumbled outside, waving a wooden ladle and feebly mouthing insults. The women ran to Cloud Bringer, who was bending over the fallen Black Faces, making sure they would not rise again.

"Healer, healer, you saved us and our village," they exclaimed, wiping the blood from his arms and face with their skirts.

"I do not think the Black Faces will be back for a while," he said, and then strode quickly away from the crowd gathering to look at the dead Black Faces and the brave warrior who had foiled their surprise attack.

"Where are the warriors who did this?" one of the village elders asked.

"Beloved Man, this is not the work of warriors. It was the healer. It was Cloud Bringer," answered the sick woman's mother in a loud voice.

"Where is he?"

"He left, following the fleeing Black Faces," the woman explained. "He makes sure they are gone, but he carries only a war club. The Black Faces have bows and arrows!"

"Has anybody seen old Limp Leg? He sleeps under the big oak tree where the trail meets the lake," a concerned voice asked.

Warriors raced down the trail after Cloud Bringer and disappeared in the woods. A moment later, they reappeared, Cloud Bringer in the midst, anger raging on their faces.

"Limp Leg is dead," cried one of the warriors. "They took his head and cut off his hands and private parts."

"And they left one of their painted sticks in a gaping hole in his stomach, so we would know who killed him. It was clearly Black Face, but it was not Shark Killer's emblem."

"Limp Leg was a crippled old man, who wouldn't hurt a dog," cried a clan sister.

"Makes no difference to Black Faces," ranted another warrior.

The villagers cried for Limp Leg but knew they had been spared from a worse fate by the fierce Snakebite healer, who, with two swift blows from a borrowed war club, became an Esteemed warrior, one who had killed an enemy in battle. The people loved him.

The day following the attack, Great Sun summoned Cloud Bringer to his lodge.

"Cloud Bringer, my cousin, your bravery is on every lip. Esteemed warriors are saying you have a warrior's heart to go with the healer's heart. I want you to sit with the Esteemed warriors when they meet in council."

"Oh, Great Sun, I pledged to be a healer. My totem leads me in the healing ways, not the ways of war. I only killed the Black Faces to keep them from harming the people. I reacted. I did not go seek them in their homes in the waving grass. They are my hated enemies, and I will rise up against them next time they attack our village, but I am destined to heal our wounded and our sick. The way of war is for those born to it, for those trained in its arts."

"Nobody has ever refused my father's request before," said the old chief's son, eyeing the healer through narrowed eyes.

"I do not refuse," replied Cloud Bringer. "I ask Great Sun to consider this. Let me sit with the Esteemed warriors when they deliberate peace and let me sit with the healers when the council plans for war."

"So, part red, part white, half warrior, half man of peace. A fitting solution," beamed the Great Sun. "So it shall be."

"Maybe you should also join the village elders," said the great chief's son, the future Great Sun. "They could use somebody as skilled as you to find compromise in their word wars."

"Thank you, Great Sun. I am honored to join the warrior council."

Cloud Bringer backed toward the door but paused at the young Sun's words.

"Next time the Black Faces come, you might want to ask the warriors for help or carry your own war club. You are lucky there was a club in the lodge."

"Ah-e, I will carry a club," promised the healer, as he lifted the door flap.

As he entered the brightness, he thought: "Warriors would have been too late, young Sun. Black Faces would have our heads on their war poles by now."

Cloud Bringer walked briskly across the village to the admiring smiles of the women working under the arbor and through a mob of laughing children pulling on his breechcloth. Two grizzled warriors, veterans of past Black Face raids, acknowledged him with the friends' greeting, a circling motion of the arm, palm down. He surveyed the village, as much as he could see of it. Other neighborhoods were scattered among the live oaks, connected by trails. People were busy, working, talking, smiling. Life had re-

turned to normal in Grand Lake village just as quickly as it had been interrupted.

Suddenly, his knees felt weak and he had a splitting headache. He wanted
to be alone, drifting in his dugout, letting the wind and current take him
away, anywhere, far from people. He felt sorry for Limp Leg's family, but
death was an accepted part of life in the great swamp, an inevitable part of
life, whether from a Black Face arrow, illness, or old age. He had saved the
people from further harm, single-handedly, and he had done it with a war
club, not his medicines.

He would be leading a double life from now on, half Snakebite healer,
half Esteemed warrior. Yet, he did not worry about keeping the two sides in
harmony. He would always do what he believed was right. The people would
provide the checks and balances.

He reached in his medicine basket, extracted a piece of willow bark, and
chewed it. "Fly away, headache, fly away."

Cloud Bringer never married, though many maidens tried to get him to
forsake his vow. Clan widows joked with him unmercifully in the crass, sex-
dominated language that only they were allowed to use, and widows were
bolder than unmarried women, sometimes disrobing in front of him or sug-
gestively fondling their hickory rhythm sticks at social dances. He resisted all
advances but many times found himself calling for the help of his guardian
spirit.

"I will not suffer the fate of my clan father. I will not give some miscre-
ant an excuse to call me a witch."

Over the years, Cloud Bringer continued to administer to the sick and injured. He was the only healer in any of the western villages who knew how
to cure the bite of the white-mouth snake. That knowledge carried through
the villages like winds off the Big Salt Water, making him the most solicited
healer in the great swamp, but his kind heart and success at treating all kinds
of malaise of body and mind were what endeared him to the Many Waters
People.

Children loved him. They surrounded him every time he walked across
the plaza or along the trails between the neighborhoods. They wanted to
touch him, wanted him to pinch their little stomachs, pretending it was the
bite of the white-mouthed snake. They wanted him to pick them up when
they skinned their knees or bumped their heads.

The years flew by. The younger women and widows only smiled pleas-
antly at him now. But the children still flocked around him, and the heat of
the day often found him under the big oak at the landing telling stories to an
audience of quiet, wide-eyed youngsters. Other healers sought his advice on
this treatment or that, and his seat among the Esteemed warriors had steadily

moved around the council circle until he was at the right hand of the young Sun, who had ascended to the chieftainship when his father, the old Great Sun, had been killed by a Black Face arrow. Cloud Bringer no longer left the council debate when war was discussed—his advice was sought by both red and white factions, and it was his wisdom that often calmed the anger these sessions invariably provoked. He was also a village elder, his skill for ensuring common-sense decisions and settling disagreements so widely respected that he was often called to mediate stalled talks at the other lake villages.

So, it was that in the year he passed his sixtieth winter, Cloud Bringer came face to face with his mortality. He was heading toward his dugout when he felt a shooting pain in his upper arm and chest. He recognized the symptoms—he had seen them before in several of his patients whose shadows were now living in the Upper World. Overcoming his dizziness and nausea, he continued toward the landing. Not wishing to be seen, he turned onto an old disused path that led past several blown-down lodges and overgrown yards and arrived at the familiar lakeshore.

"Where are you bound today, healer?" asked the fisherman busy splitting catfish.

"To get fresh medicines. Never know when some fisherman might mistake his finger for a fish head."

"Ah-e, I am more careful now, healer."

Cloud Bringer pushed away from shore and paddled steadily across the lake. Reaching the far shore, he turned south and paddled until he was out of sight of the distant fisherman. Pulling aside the low-lying branches that hid the entrance to the secluded pool, he entered. There in the dark shadows, hidden from the eyes of the Many Waters People, Cloud Bringer lost his composure. In his despair, he, for the first time in his life, questioned his life's journey.

"I dedicated my life to healing the Many Waters People. Now that my earthly journey is nearly finished, I am filled with sadness. My love for Broken Plaits was unrequited, and now that I am old and her husband has died she teases me with the abandon of a young woman. I have no son to dig my bones, no daughter to plait my hair, no grandchildren to warm my lap. My only sister has no children. I gave my life to the people, forsaking my chance for an heir. The Snakebite medicine will not be passed on. It dies with this healer. I am worn out. I await my shadows journey."

Dusk gave way to dark. Stars created sparkling diamonds on the still waters, and jittery flying squirrels complained about the dugout afloat in their hidden world.

Noon-Day-Sun was flickering through the leaves when the nearby call of an ivory-billed woodpecker, the swamp's sentry, jolted the old man awake.

Cloud Bringer sat up. He could not remember when he had slept this late. He push-paddled his way out of the pool and into the wind-driven waves on the lake, every stroke of the paddle sending him deeper into sadness.

He was thinking about his lonely death, when he slowly became aware of someone tugging on his arm, jarring him out of the memories and into the present.

"Father, father," Storm Rider said, "Wake up, wake up. You were lost in the dream world. The ceremony is over. Turkey-Buzzard-Man takes the sacred bead to the temple."

"My son, you swell the heart of this man. I am proud of fisher boy too. You both carry on the old ways. I feared the snakebite healing way would be lost to the upcoming generation."

"Why do you worry, father? Medicine is my life."

"I know, Storm Rider, but I was remembering a time before you were sent to us."

"People are headed to the dance ground. Come, I hear the drum. Look, Speaks Twice is already out of sight."

"I am tired," said Father-of-Storm-Rider.

They saw Speaks Twice's head bobbing through the crowd toward them.

"C-c-come on, Storm Rider," he said with a big grin, "G-g-girls are waiting."

"Go, my son. Tell Spotted Fawn to come see me. I have missed our talks."

"I will, father."

"Storm Rider," said his father with a sad far-off look in his eyes, "Do not let her get away."

The old man left the boys and walked slowly toward his lodge, his heart singing: *"Old Traveler,* you gave me a son in my old age. By your own hand, you delivered him to me. The Snakebite medicine lives. This man knows great joy."

"W-w-what does your father mean?" inquired Speaks Twice. "W-w-where is Spotted Fawn g-g-going?"

7

"War"

Storm Rider was shorter than other boys of seventeen winters and was small boned, too. He always stood straight as an arrow in order to make others think he was taller than he was. Speaks Twice did not care how tall his friend was.

"D-d-don't worry yourself about the p-p-persimmons you can't reach from the ground," Speaks Twice said. "You can always c-c-climb the tree."

"I know how to gather persimmons, but I'm afraid Buzzard will beat me wrestling tomorrow. My father never showed me any wrestling holds, and I worry that if I lose the match, the people will say: 'There goes that loser. He can't even win a wrestling match, how can he heal people?'"

"N-n-no, they won't. They know the difference b-b-between a wrestling match and a cure for s-s-snake bite."

No matter how hard he tried, Speaks Twice could not get Storm Rider to stop worrying, even when he pretended to be a bossy wren, fluttering from stump to ground and back, flapping his arms like wings, and whistling loudly. Storm Rider tried to smile but only managed a tight-lipped sigh. He buried his head in his hands.

"I hate for people to lose faith in me because of a wrestling match. I worked hard to earn their confidence," he whined, refusing to be cheered up.

"T-t-then why did you accept Buzzard's c-c-challenge if you already knew you were going to lose the match and your r-r-reputation too," asked Speaks Twice, growing perturbed with his friend.

"If I had not accepted, I would have lost face for certain," reasoned Storm Rider.

"Then, stop f-f-fretting, healer. You are bound to lose either way. Even m-m-mangy curs know when to tuck their tails between their legs."

"I'm not afraid of him, only of losing."

"D-d-do you think a person who has already lost a w-w-wrestling match in his mind might be interested in a way to save his r-r-reputation?" Speaks Twice asked wryly.

"What are you talking about, Speaks Twice?"

"E-e-everybody can see how much b-b-bigger Buzzard is. They expect him to beat you w-w-wrestling. You need to c-c-challenge the big bully to a race before you wrestle him. N-n-nobody but Spotted Fawn and I know how fast you run. Y-y-you need be no t-t-taller than the mouse that lives in the s-s-seed basket to outrun a b-b-buzzard heavy with his own importance. H-h-he cannot keep up with the wind."

"Ah-e, a race! Maybe I can win," said Storm Rider, suddenly feeling the dark cloud lifting.

"W-w-wait until they announce the matches before you c-c-challenge him. Don't give him t-t-time to intimidate you or make excuses."

"That might stop his threats," said Storm Rider, "and make him an enemy for life."

"At least we m-m-might have a little quiet for a change, and I wouldn't w-w-worry about making an enemy. Last I heard, he was ranting about s-s-stuffing your head in a dark, narrow place. I hate to tell you, Storm Rider, but that is not f-f-friendly."

"You're right, but I keep hoping he will change."

"Humh, change! Y-y-you have a better chance of finding a friend among Black Faces. D-d-don't forget to bring your winged feet tomorrow."

"I'll come to your lodge in the morning," said Storm Rider.

That night, Storm Rider tossed and turned so much that he awakened his aunt.

"What's wrong?" she asked sleepily. "Are you worried about tomorrow?"

"I'm all right, go back to sleep."

When sleep finally came, sometime in the middle of the night, so did *Long Black Being,* who kept throwing him to the ground while the people laughed and scorned his healing. He woke just as *Long Black Being* was about to feed on his entrails.

"Buzzard, are you *Long Black Being?*"

He lay on his sleeping mat, going over the wrestling match in his mind, again and again. He could not see how he could throw Buzzard. Buzzard was too big and strong. Storm Rider decided that his only chance was to let Buzzard wear himself out and then trip him when he was off balance. He would have to keep away from Buzzard's powerful arms.

He did not rise until he heard the noisy mockingbird outside, fussing at the early risers gathering in the plaza. He donned the soft deerskin breech-cloth. On the waistband, his aunt had stitched the red snake emblem taken from his baby clothes. He did not put on his sandals. He knew he would be less likely to slip in bare feet, and besides he felt like he could run twice as fast barefooted.

"Remember, my nephew, your guardian spirit watches over you," said his aunt.

"You are too quick for him," said Father-of-Storm-Rider, propped on his elbow. "Do not let him goad you into a contest of strength."

"Okay, father," said Storm Rider, as he ducked under the lodge flap and jogged to Speaks Twice's lodge near the landing. Speaks Twice was sitting in his mother's flour-pounding mortar, whistling.

"F-f-finally! Did you lose your way in the dark? I was w-w-worried you had decided it was not a good day to s-s-skin your knees. People are already gathering in the plaza, and some are even b-b-betting on you."

"I've had skinned knees before, Speaks Twice. Had you rather wrestle Buzzard yourself?" Storm Rider asked, not in a mood for his friend's kidding.

"Huh! He would not dare w-w-wrestle me. Even thinking of me makes him s-s-shake in his sandals. He believes he will catch the s-s-stuttering disease if he touched me. So, you see, I have already b-b-beaten him."

They heard a blue jay whistle—the friends' signal to each other—and saw Spotted Fawn hurrying down the path to meet them.

"My father says you will win," Spotted Fawn said excitedly. "He says small and quick always beats big and slow."

"That might be so," admitted Storm Rider, "If only the small and quick contestant knew how to wrestle."

The three friends walked toward the plaza, listening to the noisy wagering.

"Buzzard's sure to win."

"I'll bet my best blowgun against your black thorn-wood bow."

"See, I told you his arms were bigger than my thighs."

"How about my bow and six fish arrows for your blowgun and dugout adze?"

"He's a head taller than young healer. Why would he want to challenge him?"

"I'll throw in a net spacer if he throws Buzzard."

"The healer is bound to get hurt."

The friends entered the plaza. Few people noticed, but Buzzard spotted them instantly.

"Ahh, look," he sneered. "Here comes a pair of ugly coots and their spotted girlfriend. Give them persimmon cakes just for showing up."

Buzzard's clan brothers laughed and patted him on the back. The one called Broken Tooth must have patted him the wrong way because Buzzard hit him on the shoulder so hard he winced in pain.

"That, my brothers, is only a sample of what I am going to do to that skunk head," he said, baring his teeth. "Next time, he will beg to play on my hoop-ball team, and I will tell him we don't play with mongrels with hair like a skunk and eyes like a cur dog."

Buzzard was so confident that he sauntered over to his father, Strikes Blows, who was standing with three other warriors and assured them a quick victory.

"Better make your bets now. The fake healer won't be standing long," promised Buzzard. "Look, he is so scared, he forgot his sandals."

"I see no fear in his eyes," said Strikes Blows. "And footing is better with bare feet."

"Until you get a thorn or cut your foot on a broken shell," replied Buzzard. "How is the wagering going?"

"So far, it is about two to one in your favor," said his father's companion.

"You mean people are betting on that loser?" Buzzard said in shock. "Has rabbit tricked them? They are going to lose their bets."

"My son, take care that you do not underestimate him. Three Fingers, here, tells me that he saw him drag a dugout across the neck of land between Long Lake and Little Long Lake. You know how far that is and how heavy heart-cypress dugouts are. He is stronger than you think."

"Who did you bet on, father?"

"You, Buzzard. I know you can throw him if you do not go crazy."

"Buzzard, Bear Tracks is calling for contestants to gather at the village pole," said one of the men. "You better win or I will lose my best blowgun."

Buzzard stalked back to his clan brothers. Broken Tooth held out a tiny clay pot containing a mixture of ochre and bear grease. Buzzard dipped two fingers in the pot and drew two red lines from the corners of his mouth to his earlobes.

Seeing the red paint, one of Strikes Blows' friends shouted, "Where are you going, Buzzard, to a wrestling match or to war?"

Only Broken Tooth was close enough to hear Buzzard's answer.

"War."

The contestants gathered around the village pole in the middle of the plaza, waving their bows and blowguns, whooping and yelling, and making their fiercest faces, trying to intimidate their opponents. Storm Rider said something to Bear Tracks, bringing a nod from the contest announcer.

Bear Tracks raised his arms, and the participants fell quiet. He began calling out the challenges.

"In wrestling, Broken Toe challenges Long Legs, and Buzzard challenges Storm Rider. In foot racing, Little Turtle challenges Sleepy, and Storm Rider challenges Buzzard. In swimming, . . ."

Bear Tracks continued announcing the contests, but Buzzard no longer heard him. His temples were pounding like a water drum, and his black eyes shot white-hot daggers at Storm Rider.

"That scrawny little wood rat dares challenge me to a foot race? Who does he think he is? He will not be able to walk, much less run, after I twist his legs around backward and tie his arms in knots."

His clan brothers drew back, and Broken Tooth darted behind the village pole. Buzzard was big and strong, but they all knew he was not fleet of foot.

Buzzard shook in anger, but for the first time, he worried. Nobody had ever dared challenge him before. How could this happen now? He wanted to beat the imposter so badly that people would stop singing Storm Rider's praises and put the name of Buzzard on every tongue. After all, he was a true son, not a foreigner. He was the son of Strikes Blows, an Esteemed warrior of the Many Waters People, not a foundling. He was the strongest young man in the village: no one else but his father could break a cane simply by bending it in his hands—certainly not the pretend healer.

And now, the pretend healer had the audacity to challenge him to a foot race. He was not blind. He suspected many young men could run faster, but none had ever dared race against him. He challenged only those he knew he could outrun legitimately or by intimidation. He had no idea how fast the orphan healer could run and not knowing gnawed at his stomach. If he lost, then his certain victory in wrestling would be for nothing. Losing would keep things as they were. People would still be praising Storm Rider and not giving him the attention he rightly deserved.

"I will beat you so badly that you will not be able to run," Buzzard said to himself, as he strutted into the feather-marked wrestling circle, holding his big arms in the air.

"Ready?" asked Bear Tracks. "Begin!"

Buzzard rushed at Storm Rider like an enraged bear. Storm Rider sidestepped, leaving Buzzard grasping at thin air.

"Ah-e, ah-e," yelled Speaks Twice, "Storm Rider is too quick for you, you big m-m-manatee!"

The combatants circled, one big, one small, one fuming, one wary. Buzzard repeatedly charged at Storm Rider. Storm Rider stepped out of his way each time. Other than a half-hearted attempt to trip Buzzard, it soon became obvious that Storm Rider was simply trying to keep from getting thrown.

"Why don't you fight me?" growled Buzzard. "Are you a scared mouse? You know I'm going to catch you eventually."

"N-n-not before you fall down from e-e-exhaustion," screamed Speaks Twice from the circle's edge. "Y-y-you cannot catch the wind."

Young boys jostled for viewing positions, some yelling for Buzzard, others for Storm Rider. Women pulled for Storm Rider. Warriors shouted, raising and changing bets, cheering first one, then the other. And one loud stuttering voice was heard above the others.

"Ah-e, ah-e, Storm Rider, Storm Rider. He's p-p-panting hard. You're w-w-wearing him out."

Buzzard rushed again. Storm Rider moved so fast that many spectators thought he passed through Buzzard's clutches like a hand through smoke.

"He is a mist," exclaimed a young boy.

"Or a ghost!" said his companion. "My cousin says some healers can change shapes."

Buzzard realized his mad rushes were not working, so he stretched out his arms toward Storm Rider hoping that the healer would take his hands in a show of strength. He would bend Storm Rider's hands backward and bring him to his knees.

Storm Rider extended one arm and gripped Buzzard's hand. For a moment, Buzzard was alarmed. Summoning all his strength, he still could not bend Storm Rider's hand, and his father's words exploded in his head: "He is stronger than you think." Slowly, Storm Rider's hand began to yield, but before Buzzard could gain the advantage and regain his confidence, Storm Rider yanked Buzzard toward him and grabbed him around the neck in a headlock.

Buzzard yelled and threw his arms around Storm Rider's waist. Storm Rider tried to throw Buzzard over his out-thrust hip, but Buzzard kept his balance. Buzzard lifted Storm Rider into the air, but still he would not let go. Buzzard picked up Storm Rider again and again but could not dislodge the healer who was attached to him as fast as a deer tick.

Buzzard bellowed again. He was wasting a lot of effort, and he was getting tired. His neck hurt. The healer was much stronger than he had imagined and much quicker than he. Still, he never doubted that he would prevail. He would wrestle all day and all night if he had to, but he knew Storm Rider would eventually make a misstep and he would have him.

In a burst of strength, Buzzard lifted Storm Rider off the ground by straightening his neck and head and gripping Storm Rider's arms, he pushed them upward and over his head with a mighty shout.

He was free at last, but both wrestlers lost their balance and tumbled to the ground with Buzzard still holding onto Storm Rider's arms. Buzzard fell on top of Storm Rider.

For a moment, both combatants lay there, gasping for breath. Bear Tracks ran over to see if they were hurt.

"Both wrestlers fell at the same time, but since Buzzard lands on top, I declare him the winner."

"Consider yourself lucky this time, pretend healer," Buzzard whispered in Storm Rider's ear as he rose to a bloody knee. "I'm going to hurt you next time."

"You are the one bleeding," said Storm Rider unfazed.

Pushing Storm Rider's head to the ground, Buzzard got to his feet drawing a chorus of jeers from the crowd. People knew the young men did not like each other, but few realized how much contempt Buzzard held for Storm Rider until the head-pushing incident. Even Buzzard's fellow bullies were embarrassed by his public display of outrage.

"D-d-disqualify him!" cried Speaks Twice. "He needs to be d-d-disqualified. He is a d-d-disgrace to himself and his clan."

"Speaks Twice, look how he holds one shoulder lower than the other?" said Spotted Fawn, wringing her hands. "Why did he have to wrestle someone so much bigger? He was bound to get hurt."

"Awh, he's okay. H-h-hurry, we need to find a spot so we can see the f-f-finish of the race," said Speaks Twice, pulling Spotted Fawn's arm.

Buzzard approached his father, expecting to be embraced, but Strikes Blows looked away from his son, disappointment on his face.

"My son, you have a long way to go before you become a leader of men. I hope you realize that soon. You cannot bully Black Faces."

A nerve under Buzzard's eye twitched, and his fists clenched.

"I beat him wrestling," Buzzard said defiantly.

"But you lost the people," said his father, wistfully.

"Who cares? They have always been on his side anyway."

Buzzard stomped away, but his shoulders were not as square as usual.

Storm Rider left the wrestling circle and made his way toward the blue jay whistle. Except for a few empty-handed warriors, people were smiling and patting him on the back. Storm Rider winced at one of the pats on his injured shoulder, noticed instantly by Spotted Fawn.

"I told you he was hurt, Speaks Twice. Go help him."

"Y-y-you worry too much. C-c-can't you see his crooked grin? N-n-nobody hurts the wind."

"He's in pain. Now go."

"Y-y-you did well, my friend," beamed Speaks Twice, "You held your own against that b-b-bully. Nobody's done that before. He did not beat you. He just f-f-fell on top."

"What is wrong with your shoulder?" asked Spotted Fawn, her face filled with concern.

"He was too strong. He kept picking me up, and I lost my grip on his head," Storm Rider said almost apologetically. "I felt it pop when we fell on it. Don't worry, I'll be all right."

Storm Rider put on a brave face, but his separated shoulder felt like a cypress tree had fallen on it. How was he going to race against his nemesis when he felt like he was about to pass out?

Bear Tracks called the young men to the starting line.

"What's the matter, fake healer," mocked Buzzard, "Did I hurt your poor shoulder, or are you trying to win the crowd's sympathy? That's the only thing you can win."

"My feet are well," said Storm Rider. "You will soon find out."

"All right, runners, that's enough," ordered Bear Tracks. "You two need to finish your discussion where nobody can hear you."

With a swift downward sweep of his hand, Bear Tracks started the race. Buzzard quickly lumbered ahead, while Storm Rider struggled to run fully upright. When the runners reached the far end of the plaza, it was obvious Storm Rider was in pain. He lagged further and further behind. By the time, they reached the landing, a surprised Buzzard was ahead by twenty paces, but as he snatched the red painted stick marking the halfway point in the race, he saw Storm Rider grit his teeth and grab his arm with his free hand to keep it from swinging. Holding his arm against his side, Storm Rider caught and passed Buzzard a half-dozen steps before crossing the finish line.

"I did not know your son could run so fast," said one of the gamblers.

"Not fast enough," grumbled Strikes Blows. "Besides, the healer was hurt."

Several warriors gathered around Strikes Blows to collect their winnings.

"Buzzard may not be as fast as the healer," said a Dog clan warrior, "but I would rather have him beside me in a Black Face village than a fast runner."

"Ah-e," said Strikes Blows. "Maybe being in a Black Face village would teach him to respect his opponent, or he would lose more than a race."

Strikes Blows walked dejectedly toward his lodge, his wife and daughters at his side. Seething with rage, Buzzard stalked off toward the lakeshore with his bully gang following behind.

Storm Rider moved through the crowd looking for his friends, but they found him first. They walked slowly toward his lodge, Storm Rider's good arm around Speaks Twice's shoulder and Spotted Fawn's arm around his waist.

"I am going to get your father," insisted Spotted Fawn, "He will know what to do about your shoulder."

"You f-f-fought him to a draw in w-w-wrestling and beat him in r-r-running," said Speaks Twice, "Y-y-you are a better man, but then he is not a man at all, he is a m-m-mean-spirited bully."

"I do not feel better," grunted Storm Rider. "My shoulder hurts."

"Thank you for bringing him home," said Father-of-Storm-Rider, "Take him over there under the tree so I can take a look at him."

"It's his shoulder," said Spotted Fawn.

"Ay-e, I saw when it happened," said Father-of-Storm-Rider.

"Is it bad, father?" asked Storm Rider, trying vainly to move his arm.

"Tell me where it hurts the most," said Father-of-Storm-Rider, pressing around the shoulder joint with two fingers.

"Everywhere," said Storm Rider, grimacing. "Ouch! Right there."

"It is not broken or dislocated. The swelling is too localized. Time is the only cure."

"Father, I do not want people to know I'm hurt. I am supposed to be a healer, not the hurt one."

"A shoulder tear is a difficult injury to hide," said Father-of-Storm-Rider. "You will have to wear a sling, and do not worry about what people think. Most will sympathize, and those that do not are not worth your attention."

"Will he be all right?" asked Spotted Fawn.

"Ah-e, gentle friend," said Father-of-Storm-Rider, nodding his head. "But he is going to be in pain for many sleeps."

"Y-y-you are one tough piece of l-l-leather," said Speaks Twice.

"I let all of you down—I could not hold on any longer."

"Let me tell you a story," said Father-of-Storm-Rider.

"Once there were two brothers, one wore red paint and the other wore white paint. The red-painted brother made fun of his white-painted brother. 'Brother, you paint your skin white like a clam. I think you have eaten so many that you are becoming one. If you ate red meat like me, you would be strong and brave. You carry firewood for old people, instead of a bow and arrows. You play with little children instead of running races and wrestling. People think you are a woman.'

"One day, there came a mighty roar and all the waters ran backward. A wall of water taller than a man rushed from the Big Salt Water and flooded the lodges. New lakes formed where there had been none. People ran around, first this way and then that way, not knowing what to do or where to go.

"They asked the red-painted brother what they should do. 'Keep your bows ready, the enemy approaches from the south,' he said. But they said, 'How can we fight when we are drowning?'

"So they asked the white-painted brother what they should do. He said: 'Get in your dugouts. Head for the high land along the Twisting Snake Water. There are plenty of oak nuts there to feed us, and cane for lodges grows tall and thick. We will survive until we can return home. My red-painted brother can watch for approaching enemies, while we rebuild our lives.'

"The people left the flooded land, and it was many years before they were able to return to their beloved lake. When they did, they were led by two brothers, one painted white, who was their Great Sun, and the other painted red, who was their war chief.

"The story of the two brothers is true. Buzzard is like the red-painted brother, always looking for the enemy. One day, he will find the true path. The people are going to need his strength. You are like the white-painted brother. They are going to need your wisdom and leadership."

"I h-h-hope he finds his true path soon, great healer," said Speaks Twice sarcastically. "And s-s-stays off mine!"

"Come into the lodge, my son. You need to rest your shoulder. I will make you a sling."

"We'll visit you tomorrow," said Spotted Fawn.

"Come every day until he recovers," replied Father-of-Storm-Rider.

8

Mourning Time

"I stay in the lodge today, son," his father said. "*Old Traveler* visited me last night and showed me how to fix a salve that will relieve some of the pain in your shoulder, but he had no cure for Buzzard's anger."

"I will stay and help," said Storm Rider taking his medicine pouch from his waist.

"I was hoping you felt well enough to go to Blue Hole and catch me a white perch. I am so hungry for white perch that I dreamed of them last night."

"I will go get Speaks Twice, and we will catch enough fish to feed the village."

"Two are enough," said the old man lying back on his sleeping mat. "Be sure to bring them after *Noon-Day-Sun* sets but not before."

"Strange request," Storm Rider thought as he walked swiftly toward Speaks Twice's lodge. "He always eats before sundown."

He thought his shoulder already felt better until he tried to raise it. Maybe his father would have the salve ready when he returned.

The fish were not biting in Blue Hole.

"They have decided this is not a good day to lie on the grill," fussed Speaks Twice.

It took the fishermen all morning and most of the afternoon to catch enough fish for their families.

"We must go, Speaks Twice. *Noon-Day-Sun* is setting."

"Wonder why your father wanted you back at sundown?" Speaks Twice asked.

"He and *Old Traveler* make the schedule," replied Storm Rider, suddenly growing very worried.

Storm Rider's aunt was waiting for him at the lodge door.

"Your father will not need the fish." Storm Rider's aunt said, her voice barely audible. "He did not wake up from his nap."

Storm Rider had known this day was coming soon, but still, it did not prepare him for the emptiness that drained his life force. He closed his eyes tightly against the stinging salt tears.

Storm Rider pulled the door flap aside and entered the lodge. For an instant, he thought that his father's outside shadow was flying around in the dimly lit lodge, but his racing heart calmed when he saw that it was only the lodge fire's reflection on one of his aunt's shiny black pots.

Without a word, Storm Rider and his aunt moved to Father-of-Storm-Rider's side and began dressing the body properly so the priests could carry it to the temple. Storm Rider lovingly placed the time-polished alligator-tooth necklace around his father's wrinkled neck. On his father's cheeks, he painted two intertwined rattlesnakes, one red and the other white, and along his side, he laid his father's medicine basket, walking stick, and blowgun.

Finally, he set his father's medicine-water bowl on his sunken chest and filled it half-full. The black locust thorn that he dropped in the water symbolized his father's awakening from death and the start of his new life in the Upper World.

"My brother has gone to the Upper World, but he will always live in my heart," she said. "We lived in the same lodge ever since our mother's lodge was burned when we were small children. I already miss his kind eyes and wise counsel. You must be strong for both of us, Storm Rider. I shall mourn his passing until I feel his outside shadow is happy."

She took a lump of charcoal from the ashes and painted her face black. Storm Rider blackened his face too. She cut off handfuls of her hair with her cane knife. Storm Rider put his hand on her trembling shoulder and then moved toward the door.

"I will get Turkey-Buzzard-Man," he said.

As soon as he let the flap down, a long wail rose above the routine sounds of the warm summer afternoon. People stopped what they were doing. They knew Father-of-Storm-Rider was dead, and they were sad.

Turkey-Buzzard-Man met Storm Rider at the temple door.

"I have been waiting for you," he said. "I heard little owl today. I knew he was calling your father."

Turkey-Buzzard-Man and three other temple priests followed Storm Rider back to the lodge. They bore a litter made of thick cane poles and covered with woven mats. White and black feathers fluttered from the ends. Before the priests entered the lodge, Turkey-Buzzard-Man dipped his fingers in the small pottery bowl he carried and sprinkled water on their heads. He gave each of them a small pinch of tobacco to put behind their lower lip and reminded them to keep their mouths closed while they were inside, else they opened a conduit for the outside shadow of the deceased to enter.

The priests moved Father-of-Storm-Rider's body onto the litter, covered it with a brightly painted deerskin, and placed his belongings on the litter. Storm Rider and his aunt watched silently as they carried his body to the temple, where it would lie in state for four days before being taken to the old abandoned village at Round Island on Big Cypress Lake where he was born. Turkey-Buzzard-Man beckoned for Storm Rider to follow the procession.

The priests slowly made their way to the temple, walking in practiced unison. They uttered a low drone, nearly drowned out by howling and wailing that grew louder as more and more of the village heard of the old healer's death. Even the curs joined in. Storm Rider had never heard such an outpouring of sadness before.

Speaks Twice and Spotted Fawn stood near the temple, heads bowed, tears streaking their blackened faces. Storm Rider nodded to them.

He was not allowed inside the temple, so he waited at the covered entrance. Turkey-Buzzard-Man and Fire Watcher reappeared a short time later.

"The body rests here for four sleeps," said Turkey-Buzzard-Man. "Then, we bury it at Round Island."

"Ay-e," acknowledged Storm Rider, "His nephews and cousins will want to help."

"I will send an envoy to Prairie Landing village to tell them of his death," said Fire Watcher. "I am sure that many there will want to join the cry."

"Crying mats will be set in front of the temple door," said Turkey-Buzzard-Man.

"You and your aunt should remove anything from the lodge you wish to keep," reminded Fire Watcher. "Always Frowning will burn it down four sleeps from now."

Storm Rider trudged back to his lodge, Speaks Twice and Spotted Fawn at his side.

"Lean on me," sobbed Spotted Fawn, her arm around his waist.

"H-h-he knew it was time for his inner s-s-shadow to cross the log to the Upper World," said Speaks Twice, sniffling.

"Ah-e."

"I k-k-know he is already busy h-h-healing," said Speaks Twice.

"In a strong, young body, too," said Spotted Fawn.

"Y-y-you can put your things at my house, until your new lodge is f-f-finished," said Speaks Twice.

"I will leave food and water at your door until you quit putting the empty bowls outside," said Spotted Fawn.

Storm Rider thanked them with a weak smile, as he lowered his lodge flap.

Loud crying woke Storm Rider from a deep sleep. The black moments before dawn found dozens of people already gathered in front of the temple steps, sobbing and wailing, and others were steadily making their way toward the mats. Most were Snake clan relatives, but there were many other villagers his father had treated.

Following custom, the mourners cried out their name and their relationship to the healer. A few told stories about his boyhood antics or his bravery during the Black Face attack, but most gave testimonies about how he had cured them or their loved ones. Great Sun joined the cry and praised Father-of-Storm-Rider's devotion to the well-being of the people and love of healing. Mourning went on until *Noon-Day-Sun* fully lit the plaza, and then started again at sundown and lasted until dusk. For four days, the people cried. Storm Rider knew people liked his father, but he never fully appreciated what affection they held for him. The old man had touched practically everyone in the village with his healing hands or his words, and they all came to cry.

On the eve of fourth day of mourning, Turkey-Buzzard-Man told Storm Rider to be at the landing at dawn on the following day.

"Tell the family we will be gone most of the day. Tell them not to eat anything. Only drink water. But they should bring bread to leave in the grave."

Five dugouts left the landing. Father-of-Storm-Rider's covered body rode in Turkey-Buzzard-Man's dugout, and family followed in the other four dugouts. As the canoes entered Big Cypress Lake, they were met by a half dozen dugouts from Prairie Landing village. The men, women, and children in those canoes bowed their heads and howled until the Grand Lake party landed at Round Island.

Turkey-Buzzard-Man asked Father-of-Storm-Rider's sister if she remembered where their old lodge had been, and she took him to the general area.

She walked around through the palmetto and found a small opening where the ground was covered with clamshells. She picked up a fragment of pottery vessel and studied the markings on it.

"I remember my mother making pots with this design. It is called Alligator-Entrails-Broken. See how a single line forms two interconnected scrolls. The circles inside the scrolls are called Big-Blackbird-Eyes, and the punctations surrounding the scrolls are Dots-Filling-In. The border is called Straight-Lines-Beginning. This could have been one of her pots."

"Do you think this was where your lodge was?" asked Turkey-Buzzard-Man.

"I cannot say for sure," said Father-of-Storm-Rider's sister. "I was only six winters old when we moved to Grand Lake village. Seems like I remember those two oak trees there, but there was a toothache tree in between where my brother carved his mark."

"Look," said one of Father-of-Storm Rider's nephews, "The ferns grow out of a rotten toothache tree. See the spiny warts on the bark."

"This must have been the old house site," pronounced Turkey-Buzzard-Man, "Let us take the corpse a blowgun-shot to the west. There, beneath the oak with the big limb touching the ground."

"Here, priest?" asked one of Father-of-Storm-Rider's clan brothers.

"Ah-e," said Turkey-Buzzard-Man. "Dig the grave deep enough to keep the raccoons from digging up the remains."

The grave diggers lowered the corpse into the waist-deep hole and covered it with the black soil from the old village area. Turkey-Buzzard-Man marked the temporary grave with seven red-painted clam shells—the number of sacred directions and the center—so he could find it a year later when he returned to retrieve the corpse for final burial.

"Before we leave we must thank *Noon-Day-Sun* for preparing his place in the Upper World," said Turkey-Buzzard-Man.

He asked the family to stand around the grave. From his woven shoulder pack, he withdrew a crème-colored ceramic pipe, the Pipe of the Dead. The pipe was about as long as a cane joint. The stem tapered. It was flattened at the mouthpiece, but beyond a collared flange, it slowly increased in diameter until joining a vertical cylindrical bowl. Both stem and bowl were decorated with the Broken Plaits design. Attached to the upper part of the bowl, facing away from the smoker, was a molded human skull with open holes for eyes and the nose and bared teeth. Molded arms and legs were attached, but they were of flesh, not bones. The hands rested on the pate of the skull, and the legs, bent at the knees, stretched out along the stem. The bowl occupied the position of the torso, the Broken Plaits design representing skeleton ribs.

Storm Rider stared at the pipe. How odd, the figure seemed to be a reclining person with flexed legs and arms, but it was half flesh and half skeleton. Then, he realized what was bothering him—the arms and legs faced the opposite direction from the way the skull faced, the arms and legs were backwards.

As he packed tobacco in the bowl, Turkey-Buzzard-Man noticed Storm Rider frowning at the pipe. In a few moments, he lit the tobacco with smoldering shavings from his fire drill, puffed, and passed the pipe to Storm Rider.

"Fire Watcher made the pipe. He said the 'burning stomach' idea came to him in a dream after he had eaten too much bloodweed," explained Turkey-Buzzard-Man.

The men all puffed on the pipe. The women abstained, but let the smoke drift through their hands and hair. The temple priest dumped the ashes on the loose dirt of the grave and replaced the pipe in his shoulder pack.

They boarded the dugouts for the long trip to Grand Lake. They paddled past several Prairie Landing canoes waiting for their return. Turkey-Buzzard-Man gave the greeting sign to the tall feathered warrior standing in the prow of the lead dugout. He returned the motion and howled, "Hou, hou, hou!"

"That was Red Club," announced Turkey-Buzzard-Man.

The trip home was long and sad. Even the beauty of the lake passed unnoticed in Storm Rider's sorrow. Everything reminded him of happy days gone by.

After burying his father, Storm Rider spent sad days sitting with his aunt in the dimness of their newly constructed lodge, their faces blackened. They rarely spoke. His aunt sobbed quietly, and he cried inside. They ate very little, occasionally sipping fish broth left at the door by his Snake clan aunts. Fresh drinking water was left daily in a polished black pot incised with a Worm-Tracks-Broken design that Storm Rider often had seen Spotted Fawn fill at the lake.

One morning during the Moon of New Leaves, Storm Rider awoke to find his aunt filling her carrying basket with dyed cane strips.

"Your father visited me last night in my dreams," she said smiling. "He told us to stop crying and to fill our days with sunshine. He said 'Sister, return to the arbor. Your friends have missed you long enough.' He said 'Send my son back to the people. They need his skills now that I am gone.'"

They left the lodge with Father-of-Storm-Rider's spirit touching their hearts.

Storm Rider filled his days with activities that would have pleased his father. There were few cures to perform, and Black Faces had not raided the village in two winters.

Joy slowly returned to Storm Rider as he remembered the happy days spent with his father. Speaks Twice helped him through his sadness. Just about everything Speaks Twice did or said was funny, and Storm Rider often caught himself smiling just thinking of his antics.

Like the time Speaks Twice had pretended to be a lost dog and had all the boys looking for the whining puppy in the palmetto. Only days later did he tell Storm Rider of the trick he had played. Until then, even Storm Rider did not know his best friend had learned to throw his voice. Another time he covered his face and body with mud and ran screaming through the brush arbor, scaring everyone half to death except old waddling woman, who threw a potful of water in his face, washing away the mud and revealing the mud monster's real identity. He told everyday stories with such wit that people stopped whatever they were doing and listened. Speaks Twice made people laugh. He still stuttered, but nobody made fun of him anymore. Storm Rider valued his friendship above all others.

Spotted Fawn comforted Storm Rider during the first dark days after his father's death, but during the last few weeks, she had been spending her days inside her lodge or under the brush arbor with the other women.

"S-s-she doesn't have time for us," remarked Speaks Twice. "She is learning woman m-m-mysteries, sewing, weaving, cooking, and how to keep us men c-c-confused."

"I saw her walking across the plaza two sleeps ago, but she never saw me or else pretended not to see me."

"Huh, l-l-let's go to her lodge and t-t-talk to her," said Speak Twice.

"I don't know, fisherman. What if she doesn't want to talk?"

"Well, t-t-then we'll know for s-s-sure she's mad at us."

They walked to her lodge, and Speaks Twice scratched on the door post.

"Spotted Fawn," called Speaks Twice, "C-c-come outside."

Spotted Fawn raised the door flap but did not step out of the lodge.

"I can't. It's not a good time. Maybe I can visit with you soon," she said, lowering the flap.

"I knew she didn't want to talk to us," lamented Storm Rider.

"W-w-what have we done to her? H-h-has she found new friends? M-m-maybe a warrior."

"Something is wrong," said Storm Rider. "Why would she give up her best friends? She has changed, and I don't like it."

"Ah-e, she's c-c-changed for sure," said Speaks Twice. "Have you n-n-noticed how tall she had gotten lately? How, ummmh, filled out everywhere?"

"I have eyes," replied Storm Rider.

In his heart, Storm Rider sensed that the Spotted Fawn he knew—his and Speaks Twice's childhood playmate—was gone forever, and it made his stomach crawl like it was full of tent-worm caterpillars. Spotted Fawn had just refused to talk to them, but amid his disappointment came a strange excitement.

"She's really pretty," said Storm Rider. "I never noticed before."

And she was. Her eyes were black pools, yet they sparkled like stars on a moonless night. Her nose was narrow and straight, and her lips were full. She had perfect white teeth that flashed when she smiled, but it was her smile that Storm Rider saw when he thought about her. It was slightly crooked, but when it took command of her face, it made crinkles in the corner of her eyes and dimples in both cheeks. Reddish highlights played in her black hair, which hung below her slender waist in two long braids. Her freckles endeared her to Storm Rider. Nobody noticed them anymore.

"S-s-sightless one, are you just now opening your eyes?" said Speaks Twice. "W-w-where have you been all these w-w-winters? She's just as p-p-pretty as she's always been."

"She seems different, fisherman, like a grown woman is wearing her skirt."

"Ah-e, that is true," said Speaks Twice. "L-l-looks to me like she has p-p-placed some kind of spell on you."

"Don't worry about me," said Storm Rider, heading toward his lodge. "Do you want me to help you run your traps tomorrow?"

"Ah-e, the b-b-blabbers are on the move. My traps will be heavy—I set them along their favorite trails. Maybe Spotted Fawn will come to her senses after she gets a good sleep."

As usual, Speaks Twice was right, about the fish anyway. All the traps except one had fish in them. But it was the empty one that drew most of his attention.

"L-l-looks like the father of the b-b-blabbers tried to get in," said Speaks Twice disappointedly, "but the entrance wasn't big enough, and he t-t-tore up the trap g-g-getting away."

"You'll catch him another time," promised Storm Rider. "Besides, you've got enough fish here to feed half the village."

After setting aside one basketful of fresh fish for their families, the young men split the remainder, threw the entrails to the hungry curs, and hung the halved fish on the smoking rack. They were repacking their gear in the dugout when Speaks Twice saw Spotted Fawn leave the arbor and head to her lodge.

He poked Storm Rider with his elbow: "Look who I see."

"Ask her if she wants to take a fish to her mother."

Speaks Twice whistled, like the blue jay. She looked toward the landing.

"W-w-would your mother like a fish to grill?" he shouted.

"She's coming. Don't be a fussy wren, Speaks Twice."

"Ay-e, she would like a white perch," said Spotted Fawn.

"Here, I caught this one just for you," said Speaks Twice, "Healer there helped. He put it in the basket."

"Ah, Speaks Twice, you are as silly as ever."

"We were afraid you were mad at us," said Storm Rider, summoning all his bravado.

"I was afraid you would think that. I am not mad. You two are my best friends. I have been working on something that I cannot tell you about, and I am trying to finish before *Pale Sun* disappears. My mother and aunts said I should start acting like a woman with responsibilities. My aunts said I do not have enough time to do all my work and run around with you two every time I hear a blue jay whistle."

"Aiyee, old people are the s-s-same everywhere. I know what you are g-g-going through. My uncles think I should spend my whole day r-r-running nets, knitting nets, making traps, c-c-cleaning fish, gathering firewood—doing everything they ought to be doing. I can hear them t-t-thinking: 'D-d-do not have fun, Speaks Twice. Fun is only for c-c-children and those with idle minds. D-d-do you have an idle mind, Speaks Twice?'"

"I see that you no longer wear mourning ashes," she said.

He shook his head, his throat as dry as his aunt's clay pots baking in the ashes.

There was so much he wanted to say, but he just stood there, gawking and swallowing.

"Are you all right?" she asked.

"No, I t-t-think he is g-g-getting sick," shrugged Speaks Twice, "He was acting c-c-crazy earlier. It may be the heat, but I do not think it is from *Noon-Day-Sun*."

"I wanted you both to know they no longer call me Spotted Fawn. My woman-name is Blackbird-Eyes-Shining or just Blackbird to my friends."

"W-w-when did you become a w-w-woman?" asked Speaks Twice, "Did it happen all of a s-s-sudden? Did it hurt?"

"Speaks Twice! I have to go now. Mother will be wondering where I am."

She touched their arms, and then she was gone. They heard the blue jay whistle just before she disappeared behind the lodge flap.

"W-w-what is wrong with you, Storm Rider? I've n-n-never seen you act this way before. She's still Spotted Fawn. She just has a new n-n-name."

"No, she's not the same."

"Is that an observation or a p-p-prophecy, healer? C-c-come, my friend, let's take these fish home before they s-s-spoil."

Storm Rider spent most of the next day walking the shores of Pond Lily Cove looking for medicine plants and charting their locations for future reference, but the young woman called Blackbird kept entering his thoughts. It took all his concentration to push her from his mind, but the instant he relaxed, she reappeared.

He thought of her frequently but saw her rarely during the following moons, usually when he was going to or coming from a healing or helping Speaks Twice at the landing. He caught a glimpse of her at the Feast of the Blackberries, while he walked in Great Sun's entourage, but she was hidden in the crowd, and as soon as the speeches and the smoking were over, she left, not staying for the social dance that followed.

He wanted to be with her but did not want to act like a clam around her again. He appealed daily to his snake guardian for the strength to overcome his sudden shyness around her. Until he found his inner strength, Storm Rider chose to avoid the places where he knew she would be, even though it meant not seeing her.

Despite having little healing to do, he immersed himself in his work. A broken bone to set and toothaches to treat were the main exceptions, although he was sought for the usual litany of aches and pains and complaints. He practically lived in the swamp, sometimes for days at a time.

Speaks Twice missed his friend's company and busied himself braiding new line and knitting fish nets. One day, while he was sitting in the shade of the big cypress repairing his damaged fish trap, Blackbird surprised him.

"I didn't hear you c-c-coming, mouse toes," he said. "H-h-have you finished what you've been w-w-working on?"

"Ah-e, almost. I hope you like it."

"W-w-what is it?"

"I can't tell you. It's a secret, but I didn't come to talk about that. Have you seen Storm Rider?"

"No. He's n-n-never at home anymore. He's been gone five s-s-sleeps this time. He says he needs to find all the m-m-medicine plants he can while the people are h-h-healthy. He says we will need them one day."

"He's never stayed gone so much before," said Blackbird. "Do you think he remembers that his father's grave digging approaches soon?"

"Ah-e, he r-r-remembers, Blackbird."

In his heart, Speaks Twice knew that Storm Rider's long absences were only partly due to his quests for medicines. He suspected his infatuation with Blackbird was the main reason, but he could not understand why he was deliberately choosing to stay away from her.

"Solitude helps free the mind of whatever is bothering you," thought Speaks Twice. "I know what you are doing, healer, but I wish I knew why."

"He needs to come home," said Blackbird.

"If he has not r-r-returned before *Pale Sun* sleeps, I will go look for him. L-l-listen, I think I hear your mother's c-c-calling. You better hurry home."

"Find him, fisherman," she said, running up the trail.

"I will," he called to her, as he inserted the new funnel to the mouth of the trap.

"If only my traps were big enough, I'd catch you too, healer," he said to himself.

Speaks Twice had been going fishing with his father and uncles since he was big enough to dog paddle. His reputation for fishing was growing as fast as his reputation for making people laugh. He was following in the footsteps of his father, Laughing Otter, who was well known for his fishing and his joking.

His most successful traps were cane-slatted cages with woven funnel-shaped entrances. They worked best when dropped among submerged limbs and turned to face into the current. They did not have to be baited, but when live red-bellied sunfish were placed in the cage, they attracted the best-tasting whisker mouth of all, the flathead, or yellow, catfish.

Speaks Twice caught fish when water was high or low, he caught fish when *Noon-Day-Sun* cooked the skin, and he caught fish when ice rimmed the edges of the lake. He took only what his mother needed and gave the rest of the catch away. Word of his generosity spread among commoners and nobles alike. The old, infirmed, and widowed loved him.

"He has a big heart," a woman told her daughter of fourteen winters as they pounded pond lily flour under the arbor. "He will make somebody a good husband."

"Listen to what your mother says," said her aunt. "I have seen older girls and even young women warm to his cute smile."

"Ah-e, if we don't have our woman's name yet, he calls us babies and tells us to save him a moonlight dance when we grow up," the daughter said shyly. "He could have his pick, and many are saying, they would not even mind being second wives. I hear married women talk crudely of how they would lie with him, if they could be sure nobody would find out."

"Did you know people have started calling him Red Legs?" said Bead-Basket's grandmother. "He catches fish like ibis, war chief of the fishing birds, and his legs are long and red too."

"Maybe they will make that his man-name."

"My husband says they will have his naming when the green wings return on the north wind. Niece, he would be a good catch. You better learn how to cook fish soon."

Speaks Twice finished repairing his trap and spent the rest of the afternoon looking for Storm Rider.

"Where did you go, my friend? Toward the Big Salt Water or up the waters of the Rain Tree? I would not be looking for you now, except Blackbird is worried that you will miss our sweat with the big buzzard and his broken-tooth nestling. You can't hide forever."

Speaks Twice glanced at the shady bank and instinctively reached for his hand line. Threading a fat earthworm onto the bone hook, he cast the bait into the shadows and began retrieving it with jerking motions. The fish struck viciously. The taunt line cut broad circles in the water. The fish pulled hard, sometimes very hard.

"This is not a giant whisker mouth," Speaks Twice thought. "I do not think it is a grunter either."

Finally, he pulled the tiring fish to the dugout, his fingers hurting from winding the line on his hand instead of the wooden spool. He picked up the last of the line and swung the fish into the dugout. He jumped back so quickly he almost overturned the dugout.

Lying in the bottom of the dugout was the strangest fish he had ever seen. It was thin and flat, brown on top and white on bottom. It had two eyes on the brown side and a mouth on the other. He dropped the fish into one of the open weave baskets that held his catch, tied it to the dugout, and lowered it into water. He paddled home as fast as he could.

"Get Bent Woman," one excited fisherman said. "She will know whether this is fish or abomination."

Nobody had ever seen anything like the oddity flopping before them. They decided it was a fish. It had gills, fins, and a tail like a fish, but it was flattened the wrong way, its eyes were not those of a fish, and the mouth was misplaced.

"I have seen this fish in my visions," Bent Woman said. "It is a flat fish. Its two eyes are on top of its head so it can always see *Noon-Day-Sun* and her husband, *Pale Sun,* from the bottom of the Big Salt Water where it makes its home. It is sacred. It must not be killed or eaten."

Speaks Twice turned the flounder loose, and Bent Woman sprinkled a pinch of tobacco in its wake.

9

Stone-Arrow-Point People

For days, the village talk was all about the flat fish. Concern was growing that the oddity might be a sign that the Mighty Wind was gathering in the Gulf.

"Bent Woman says the flat fish lives in the Big Salt Water," said an old woman, never raising her eyes from her basket weaving. "I think it is here waiting for the Mighty Wind to fill our lake with salty water."

"Ah-e," said her toothless friend, "My nephew says the clouds floating in from the Big Salt are taller and puffier than normal. He says they looked that way before the Mighty Wind came seventeen winters ago, the one that destroyed our village and brought us the young healer, remember?"

"Ay-e. It also carried away Great Sun's daughter. He was so proud of her, remember? And proud of her birthmark too! He said it proved that she was descended from *Noon-Day-Sun*."

"I saw the mark, and it did look like the sacred fire, all red with those three flames reaching out. I tell you, it scared me, and I got away from that baby fast. No telling what would have happened to this commoner, if I had touched it," said the toothless woman, her chin almost touching her long nose.

"I remember eating clams until our garbage heap grew so tall, we couldn't see the landing from our lodge," grimaced her companion.

"I still hate them," said toothless woman, pretending to gag.

"Me too, I would rather eat hot dog dung."

"Let me see your big basket. If it's water-tight, I might want to cover my head with it when the Mighty Wind comes."

"Hold your water, toothless one, you wouldn't even know it was raining unless your sleeping mat got washed away. You're too lazy to weave your own basket."

"You hateful old coot. Have you soiled the moss you wear between your legs?"

"Why don't you go find a hole and talk to a crawfish? You might find one that will listen."

"Why don't you go find one with a big pincher? That's your problem anyway."

"See, it's been so long, you can't even tell a pincher from a penis. Did you ever know the difference?"

"At least, my husband didn't marry a young girl."

"No, he died too quickly."

"Shush, women, women," said Storm Rider's aunt, raising her finger to her lips to silence the bickering. "Look, down the path. A stranger enters the village."

The village banter died, and all eyes watched the young man who was carrying a long white pole lined with white egret feathers and topped with a quartered sun disk. Four village warriors escorted him to Great Sun's lodge. Great Sun awaited him on his portico.

Villagers stopped what they were doing and moved toward the portico in small groups of twos and threes. The old women that had been fussing under the brush arbor pushed forward haltingly, amid much jostling and whispering. Fishermen hurried from the landing, slowing as they neared the chief's lodge, and the ranks of warriors encircling the lodge swelled, the polished handles of their war clubs gleaming in the morning bright. Even the dogs quit barking, realizing something unusual was taking place.

The young stranger approached Great Sun and bowed deeply. Great Sun asked the warriors who had escorted the stranger into the village to stand aside and motioned for the stranger to rise.

"Wonder what he wants?" whispered the toothless woman.

"Shuh, old Dog clan woman. If you'd be quiet, we might hear what they're saying," grumbled the old basket maker, ordering silence with a frown and a shake of her head.

Fire Watcher gave them a piercing look.

"What brings you to Grand Lake village, stranger?" asked Great Sun in a clear voice, reinforcing his words by putting two fingers to his lips and then quickly pointing to the stranger with fingers spread.

The stranger pointed to Great Sun, to himself, and then gripped his hands together tightly. Enunciating each word precisely, he spoke. Some of his words sounded vaguely familiar, but his language was foreign.

Great Sun tried to communicate with the visitor by using gestures but quickly realized that was complicating the effort. He said something to Fire Watcher, who then called for a young woman, wife of Shouts-At-Night, to approach the portico.

"Her name is Far-Away-Woman," said Fire Watcher.

She took a few unsure steps toward the chief.

"Come closer, young woman," ordered Great Sun, "Are you of the Thou-coue People, our brothers who live on the Great Water?"

"Ah-e, Great Sun."

"Some of the stranger's words sound Thoucoue," said Great Sun. "Are they?"

"Ah-e."

"Come under the porch and tell me what he is saying."

Frightened and confused, Far-Away-Woman moved timidly under the thatched shade.

"Great Sun, some words are familiar but not all. I do not understand everything he says. Great Sun, please do not ask me to translate when I might not get all his words right."

"Do not worry, woman, just tell us what you can."

Great Sun motioned for the stranger to speak. Understanding why the woman had been summoned, he spoke slowly, glancing at her frequently to see if she was following his words. He paused often, letting her translate for the chief.

"He is called Red-Clay-On-His-Feet. He is of the Anoy, the Stone-Arrow-Point People," said Far-Away-Woman, her shaky voice beginning to calm. "He lives on the water they call the Water-Runs-Red."

"Ah-e," nodded Great Sun. "I know of them. He is a long way from home. Ask him why he comes to Grand Lake village."

"I think he is saying that his people would like to come see Great Sun. They have gifts or, maybe, many frogs, I'm not sure which," related Far-Away-Woman.

"I do not think they would bring us frogs," laughed Great Sun. "Ask him when they would like to visit."

"He says in four sleeps."

"Tell him, we welcome the Anoy to Grand Lake village. Tell him to return with empty belly and his dancing sandals."

The young stranger listened intently as Far-Away-Woman struggled to translate Great Sun's welcome. His quizzical look passed, and he pointed to his sandals and rubbed his stomach. He smiled broadly at Great Sun, nodded to the young woman, and backed slowly from the portico. Once in the sunlight, he turned and ran swiftly to the landing. Warriors followed discreetly and watched while his dugout headed north in the direction of the Water-Runs-Red.

"Looks like another feast," said the old basket maker. "If those old wrinkled gourd heads only knew how much trouble feasts are for us."

"They don't care. They don't have to lift a finger. All they do is sit around and tell stories about how brave they were when they were young and how many young wives they can wear out," said her toothless comrade.

"Ah-e," agreed the old woman, "With their flapping lips, not their limp members."

The old women trudged back to the brush arbor, complaining like a pair of squawking coots.

Nobody was at the landing when Storm Rider pulled his dugout onto the beach, but the din from the plaza caught his ear, and he hurried to investigate.

"Why are people gathered in the plaza?" he wondered. "This is not a feast day. They do not carry their bows. Great Sun himself is on his portico, and why is Always Frowning waving his arms and squealing so loudly?"

He spied Speaks Twice standing next to his father. They were talking to Storm Rider's cousins, who had helped pull him from the bushes when he was an infant. Speaks Twice was motioning for him to approach. The men extended the palms-down greeting, and he returned the gesture.

"Hai, young healer," said Laughing Otter, "You missed our visitor."

"Ah-e, I did not know we were having visitors."

"M-m-maybe you would know if you s-s-stayed around more," said Speaks Twice.

"Now, fisherman," said one of Storm Rider's cousins, "the visit surprised everybody."

The older men resumed talking, and Speaks Twice nudged his friend with an elbow.

"Where have you been?" he whispered, pinching his friend's arm. "You've had us all worried."

"I'll tell you later, but first tell me about our visitor. Is there trouble?"

"He is an A-a-anoy," answered Speaks Twice. "His people are going to pay us a visit in four s-s-sleeps. We are giving them a w-w-welcoming feast."

"Who are they? They are not from the great swamp."

"We do not know much about them," said Laughing Otter. "I only heard about them from my grandfather when I was a yearling. He told me our peoples used to exchange visits back in the days when the Water-Runs-Red flowed into the head of the great swamp, but the visits stopped when *Old Traveler* changed the course of the river."

"Are they our brothers?" asked Storm Rider.

"No, I do not think so," replied Laughing Otter, "But they are distant relatives. They are brothers with the Thoucoue, the First Sun People, who are our brothers."

"W-w-why do they come to see us now?" asked Speaks Twice.

"I do not know, son," said Laughing Otter. "Sometimes, people like to make new friends or renew old friendships."

"Do you think they can be trusted?" asked Storm Rider, wrinkling his brows. "Maybe they are looking for an excuse to enter our village with hidden war clubs. Remember, the Red Sticks massacred a village of the Short-cut People, pretending to pay a friendly visit?"

"If they are not sincere, then their emissary took a big risk coming here. Put your confidence in Great Sun—he is astute and is not easily tricked. Even now he has warriors stashing their weapons where they can be reached at the first war cry."

Satisfied an attack was not imminent, the men walked toward the arbor where Storm Rider hoped to see Blackbird. She was not there.

"S-s-she's worn out her s-s-sandals going from the arbor to the landing, asking everybody if they've seen the healer. P-p-people are wondering if she's sick. I overheard one old woman t-t-talking about how round her belly is getting and s-s-saying that one of us is the father."

"So, the green flies have moved from the clam-cleaning beach to the brush arbor."

"Now, healer, w-w-where have you been? W-w-why have you been gone so long?"

"I needed to be by myself. I felt like my spirit was slipping away and taking my voice and my confidence with it."

"I n-n-notice your loss of words around only one person, healer."

"Ah-e, and I don't understand. I've never been struck dumb around her before."

"Huh, I think I know where your s-s-spirit is, and the thief is probably h-h-helping her mother get ready for the feast right now," Speaks Twice said. "T-t-they always bring b-b-baskets full of kunti bread. S-s-she adds the ground-up p-p-persimmons, especially for us. S-s-she knows how to please a man."

"Ahh, so you're a man now," said Storm Rider. "Did they give you your man-name while I was away collecting medicines?"

"I am one here," retorted Speaks Twice pointing below his belt, "A mighty one, too.

"Huh, one time in the grass does not make you a man. Real manhood is here," said Storm Rider, putting his hand on his heart, feigning a confidence he did not feel.

"S-s-speak for yourself, healer. Fish are waiting, and Great Sun is going to need all we can catch for the feast."

"My gear is in my dugout. I'll meet you at the landing after I let my aunt know I'm home," said Storm Rider, as he walked swiftly past the arbor and her lodge hoping to catch a glimpse of Blackbird.

He joined Speaks Twice, who was busy loading his loosely woven storage baskets in his canoe.

"Well, d–d–did you see her?" inquired Speaks Twice.

"No."

They pushed away from the landing and paddled directly across the lake.

"Why do we head across the lake?" said Storm Rider. "Your traps are in Pond Lily Cove."

"E–e–except for the one I r–r–repaired. I set it in the hidden pool you s–s–showed me. All the knots are doubled, and I added e–e–extra slats. Not even an a–a–alligator could get out—but then an a–a–alligator couldn't get in either."

"Why are we paddling so fast, fisherman?"

"I have a f–f–feeling."

They slipped beneath the low-lying branches that hid the pool and immediately noticed a big swirl where Speaks Twice had set the reinforced trap.

"H–h–hurry, Storm Rider, p–p–paddle next to the limb where the trap is tied, and I'll pull the trap into the dugout. H–h–hold on to me so I don't fall in."

Speaks Twice leaned over the side of the dugout but was unable to lift the trap from the water.

"It's h–h–hung."

"I can see a fish in it," Storm Rider said excitedly.

"G–g–grab that s–s–side and uhh, uhh, help me p–p–pick it up," said Speaks Twice.

The harder they tried to lift the trap, the more the dugout listed until it nearly turned over.

"H–h–here, hold my m–m–medicine bag," said Speaks Twice, "I'll get in the w–w–water and see if I can get it loose. W–w–watch that white-mouth snake l–l–looking at us and tell me if it drops in the w–w–water."

Speaks Twice had swung his legs over the side of the dugout when Storm Rider grabbed his arm.

"Wait, it is not hung. It is a giant fish."

The excited fishermen laced the trap to the dugout and paddled as fast as they could to the landing.

One of the fishermen smoking fish at the landing saw the rapidly approaching canoe and raised a warning. Red Stick raiding parties always approached from the east or south. Men dropped their cleaning knives and grabbed their bows.

"D–d–don't be a–a–alarmed, Grand Lake warriors," shouted Speaks Twice, "unless you are afraid of the b–b–biggest whisker mouth you have ever seen."

The men dropped their bows and waded out into the lake to help pull the trap onto the beach. The gathering crowd was amazed.

The head of the giant catfish was stuck in the funnel, held fast by its sharp, rigid fins. Its body was so large it could not pass through the opening. Speaks Twice and Storm Rider worked the fish free and struggled to hold it up as high as they could. It was longer than they were tall, and still, the fish's broad tail dragged the ground.

"Fishermen, you caught the father of all whisker mouths," one old fisherman announced. "I am glad he did not mistake you for red bellies, or he might have had a meal instead of being one."

Word of the huge catfish reached the village, and spectators hurried to the landing to see the fish. Even Great Sun and Sun Woman came to see the monster fish. Nobody could remember such a large fish being caught before.

"People of Grand Lake village," said Great Sun, *"Noon-Day-Sun* herself helps provide for our welcoming feast. She smiles on our best young fishermen. With this one whisker mouth, we can feed many mouths."

"Hummh," mumbled toothless woman, as she waddled back toward the arbor. *"Noon-Day-Sun* didn't have a thing to do with catching that fish. It was Speaks Twice."

Great Sun returned to his lodge, followed by his retainers and priests. Sun Woman lingered, talking with several women and rubbing the heads of the many children, who flocked around her.

Speaks Twice saw Blackbird coming toward them.

"Uh–ooh, h–h–here comes an angry she-bear."

"Glad you're back," she said softly. "The day of your father's bone-digging is near."

"I know," said Storm Rider, his confidence failing.

"W–w–where are your claws?"

"Hush, Speaks Twice."

"What about the t–t–teeth?"

"We missed you," she said, frowning at Speaks Twice. "We've got a lot to do for the welcoming feast, and then we have to get you two ready for the sweat lodge and the bone-digging."

"Ay-e, Speaks Twice has told me that Great Sun told everyone to put aside what they were doing and start amassing food and cleaning the village."

"You should have heard Always Frowning g–g–giving orders," giggled Speaks Twice. "You know, when he gets e–e–excited he waves his arms like he's t-t-trying to fly, and the more excited he gets, the more he s-s-shrieks like a woman."

"He has a lot of responsibility as Village Keeper, Speaks Twice. He's in charge of all the arrangements, he's got to make sure everything is ready for the feast or Great Sun will have his head," said Blackbird.

"Ah-e, but he's still a s-s-spectacle," said Speaks Twice. "Paint the war pole, re-thatch the arbor, s-s-sweep the trails, carry off all the f-f-fish heads the turtles haven't eaten. P-p-pick up around your lodges."

Speaks Twice whirled his hands around his head.

"D-d-dig fresh roots. Pound fresh flour. Fish and game taken during the next two s-s-sleeps belong to Great Sun. S-s-smoke them over oak wood. D-d-do not eat Great Sun's food. Use only your old s-s-stores or fast. Every clan must deliver six c-c-carrying baskets of food to the temple on the eve of the feast, t-t-three of fish, t-t-two of kunti bread, and one of f-f-fresh fruit and greens. Great Sun will keep any l-l-leftovers."

"Be quiet, Speaks Twice, he'll hear," said Blackbird.

"Now, w-w-women," Speaks Twice continued his animated impersonation of Always Frowning, pacing back and forth with his hands on his hips. "Be at the d-d-dance ground at first light on feast day. L-l-light your cooking fires. S-s-serve Great Sun and our guests when the dance pole's s-s-shadow reaches Great Sun's nose. A-a-after they are served, then the people can fight for a-a-anything that's left. Go! Get busy! D-d-do not rest until b-b-baskets are at the temple. I will be w-w-watching you."

"Fisherman, maybe you don't need to catch another big fish any time soon. It makes you delirious," said Storm Rider.

"Good to see you smiling again, Storm Rider," said Blackbird. "Come to our fire on feast day. I will have persimmon bread for you."

"Blackbird, oooh Blackbird, your aunt is c-c-calling you," said Speaks Twice in a mocking voice.

"I'll see you feast day. Storm Rider, I'm glad you're home."

Just like that she was gone, and he wanted to tell her so much.

"C-c-come on, healer. We've got a b-b-big fish to dress."

The morning of the welcoming feast day arrived warm and partly clear. The scattered clouds floating in from the Big Salt Water had flattened gray undersides, fair-weather clouds.

"They are like the hard bottom of a clay pot. No rain can get though," Storm Rider often heard his father say.

"Looks like *Thunderer* and *Lightning-Spirit-Bird* will not be visiting us today," murmured Storm Rider. *"Noon-Day-Sun* wears her bright robes. Now, where is Speaks Twice?"

Smoke wafted across the dance ground carrying the smell of baking kunti bread. Women were already cooking. Two old men were putting the final touches on the skin-covered bamboo seat where Great Sun would greet the Anoy chief. Vividly painted figures danced on the skins. Storm Rider recognized the panther and the bear and the other grotesque figures he knew represented the supernatural beings and forces that lived before the Earth Island and First People were created.

Storm Rider watched warriors as they carefully painted their faces and torsos and tied feathers in their hair and pierced ears. They slipped on so many bent-deer-rib armlets and anklets that a continual clatter arose from the dance ground when they moved about. Storm Rider also noticed warriors concealing cane knives under their breechcloths. Panther Claw, head war chief, sat impassively on a stool outside his lodge, while his wife tied the woodpecker-feather boa around his neck and his daughter placed the red-tufted, crow-feathered headdress on his shaved head. His war club leaned against his stool. He and the other five war chiefs were the only dignitaries, other than Great Sun, who were allowed to carry arms to a civic welcoming feast. War clubs were their badges of office, but their red color showed they had been used to kill an enemy, an ominous message to evil-intentioned visitors.

People began arriving, one family at a time. Each moved into its proper place—noble families lined the right side of the path the visitors would follow, common families the left. Great Sun's immediate family encircled his seat. They stood several strides apart from other families, as was the privilege of their divine birthright. They were direct descendants of *Noon-Day-Sun* herself. Storm Rider stood next to his aunt near the front of the Noble line. His aunt was Great Sun's cousin on her father's side and a confidante of Sun Woman.

Storm Rider spied Speaks Twice in the commoner line, and they exchanged the palms-up greeting.

"Glad you decided to come," mouthed Storm Rider.

Smiling broadly, Speaks Twice pointed to his hair and shook his head, making his warrior lock swing.

"Now I know what took you so long," thought Storm Rider. "You've been preening. I see your warrior lock, plaited with new white doeskin and adorned with the curly tail feathers of the green head. Which girl are you trying to impress, my friend?"

Speaks Twice thrust his chin in the air, quite pleased with his appearance, and started vigorously shaking his extended thumb, pointing down the line. He raised his eyebrows and grinned. Blackbird peered around her uncle and looked toward him. The realization hit Storm Rider like a potful of cold water in the face. Blackbird! She was the reason behind Speaks Twice's sudden concern with his appearance.

Blackbird lowered her eyes but not before she and Storm Rider exchanged furtive glances. She moved back in line and out of sight.

Always Frowning walked up and down the double lines of villagers telling them to be still and quiet and to look dignified in front of the strangers.

"So Speaks Twice has become like a male bluebird in the Moon of New Leaves," thought Storm Rider, jolted by the sick feeling in the pit of his stomach. "They are my friends. How could I have been so oblivious?"

He smiled weakly at Speaks Twice, and Blackbird would not show herself.

"Ooh, Blackbird," he silently pleaded, "Do not leave me alone. Do not empty my spirit. Do not condemn me to suffer the fate of my father, whose only love chose another."

"Why is your heart not singing, my nephew?" asked his aunt. "This is a day to remember."

"Ah-e. I will remember it."

All eyes turned toward Great Sun as he was carried into the dance ground. Dismounting from the bearers' shoulders, he stood in front of the painted chair and raised his arms toward the Upper World, silently speaking to the spirits. His magnificent headdress, feathered with tail plumes of the white egret, fluttered in the breeze. Family emblems and symbols of his heroic deeds woven into his short cape seemed to come alive with his movements. His pearl and shell-bead necklace caught the sunlight filtering through the low-hanging oak limbs. His bearing radiated divinity, but the stern expression on his deeply lined face portended no-nonsense deportment.

Great Sun lowered his arms. Fire Watcher handed him the white- and red-feathered pipe stem and his red-painted war club. He looked straight ahead. The deputation he had dispatched to escort the Anoy into the dance ground was returning, Red-Clay-On-His-Feet in its midst. Three steps in front of Great Sun, the entourage stopped, leaving Red-Clay-On-His-Feet to address the chief.

"Hou, hou, hou," he said, using the familiar acknowledgement heard everywhere along the Great Water. His next words were unintelligible, but he was smiling. He stooped and placed a small lidded basket at Great Sun's feet. Fire Watcher quickly retrieved the basket and handed it to Great Sun.

Great Sun opened the lid and removed one of the tiny stone arrowheads. He turned it around in his fingers, admiring its delicate but lethal lines—barbs that curved back toward the point made it virtually impossible to remove from prey by pulling or pushing on the arrow shaft. It would have to be cut out.

"Your gift pleases me."

Great Sun hoisted the basket over his head, and the people shouted their approval. He handed the arrowhead-filled basket to Fire Watcher and asked Far-Away-Woman to step to the front.

"He asks permission for the Anoy delegation to enter the village," she said.

"Tell him they may enter. We welcome the Anoy with happy hearts."

Red-Clay-On-His-Feet held up his arm, and the Anoy emerged from the live oaks at the edge of the dance ground, where they had been waiting. The people watched excitedly as the leader of the procession began to dance wildly, jumping, spinning, and flailing his arms, movements coordinated with the beat of a water drum. As the lead dancer leapt closer, Storm Rider realized that the feathered object he carried was not a baton but a pipe stem. About a dozen men followed behind the pipe bearer and drummer, single-file. They were clad only in their breechcloths and carried no weapons, at least none that were visible. Like the lead dancer, their faces were painted, some black, some white, and some half black–half white. They also moved to the sound of the drum—their steps were not exaggerated but were more like a shuffle. They bobbed their heads from side to side and often bent over like they were looking for something on the ground, all the while shaking gourd rattles. They reminded Storm Rider of turkeys searching for nettle seeds. Behind them came six women doing the shuffling step and singing. They carried brightly decorated cane baskets, which they periodically raised toward the sky and lowered toward the ground. Bringing up the rear were four lame men, obviously slaves, carrying heavy deer-hide bundles on their backs.

The Anoy pipe bearer stopped his wild gyrations before reaching Great Sun. With slow, deliberate movements, he rubbed the pipe stem all over Great Sun's head, chest, and back and then taking a step back, repeated the same motions over his own body. His drummer handed him the rolled deer skin used to suspend the heavy water drum. The pipe bearer unrolled it and carefully laid the pipe stem on it. From his waist pouch, he extracted an elbow-shaped, clay-pipe bowl and filled it with tobacco. He then inserted the pipe stem into the bowl and presented the pipe to Great Sun, holding a flaming stick to the tobacco. Great Sun puffed until the tobacco was lit, inhaled deeply, and released a cloud of smoke. He passed the pipe back to the Anoy pipe bearer who puffed. Then, while the pipe was passed to each male member of Great Sun's family and village officials, the pipe bearer clapped his hands, signaling for the gifts to be brought before Great Sun. One by one, the women placed their baskets at Great Sun's feet, and the slaves lay their bundles at his side. When the smoke was finished and the pipe returned to the pipe bearer, Great Sun rose and with a downward motion of his hands bade the people to sit. He then embraced the pipe bearer and gestured for him to speak.

"Hai, Great Sun, Sun family, Beloved Men, Esteemed warriors, and People of Grand Lake village, I am Flint Rabbit, eldest son of our Great Sun, who is in failing health and could not come meet our brothers, whom we have not seen in many winters. We are Anoy, or Stone-Arrow-Point People, as we are known to our friends. We smoke with you because our elders remember the long-ago times when our two peoples used to visit each another. We celebrated many marriages between our peoples, and your blood flows in some of our oldest families. Our elders tell us that our two peoples descended from the union between First Man and First Woman after Crawfish formed the Earth Island; thus in the dim time we were brothers and sisters. We bring presents in hopes of reestablishing those ties of kinship and friendship.

"Hai, gracious hosts, we desire only your friendship and your company on feast days, but we come with unsettling news. Marauders from the upper reaches of the Great Water have been raiding our friends on the Big Water and the Humped-Beast Water. So many warriors have been killed and women taken that injured tribes have begun seeking asylum with our brothers, the Thoucoue and the Little Thoucoue. We ourselves have taken in three fleeing families. We wish to renew our ties with the People of Grand Lake village, so both our peoples will be stronger. If we stand together, no enemy will be able to overrun our lands.

"I know you have difficulty with my words, as I do yours, but I hope the Thoucoue woman living among you understands them well enough to relay how serious the situation has become. I stop now and will let her talk my words to you before continuing with more pleasant subjects."

Flint Rabbit said something to Far-Away-Woman.

"What does he say?" asked the Great Sun, sensing the gravity of Flint Rabbit's words.

Haltingly, Far-Away-Woman related what she had gathered. She told of the threat posed by the northern raiders and of the Anoy's desire for an alliance. Concern filled her words, and the people listened and worried.

When Far-Away-Woman stepped back, Flint Rabbit continued with his speech, telling of the Anoy's epic history, their heroes, and their kinship with the Thoucoue, the Little Thoucoue, and the Many Waters People. The people understood very little of what he was saying and depended on Far-Away-Woman to give his words meaning, but his voice was pleasing and he smiled often, winning the trust of the people and Great Sun. Finally, he, too, stepped back and, pointing to the baskets and the bundles, gestured for Great Sun to open them.

"Gifts," he said clearly in the language of the Many Waters people, "Friends."

Great Sun opened each of the baskets himself, thanking Flint Rabbit each time with a nod and a smile. He took an arrowhead from one of the baskets and placed it on the deerskin in front of his chair. Then he passed the basket around the circle of family and village officials, telling the men to take some for themselves. He motioned for Fire Watcher and Always Frowning to distribute the remaining points among the people.

He opened one of the large bundles and was puzzled by what he saw. Firewood? The Anoy had brought him firewood!

"Maybe Flint Rabbit has been talking with Laughing Otter," said Great Sun without a hint of a smile.

Seeing the momentary confusion, Flint Rabbit rushed to diffuse what might have become a tense situation. Publicly embarrassing Great Sun was not a good thing, not for a fledgling friendship and not for keeping his head off one of the people's trophy poles. He grabbed a stick from one of the bundles and holding it vertically pretended to shoot an arrow. After the second imaginary arrow, Great Sun smiled and spreading his arms wide hugged Flint Rabbit, almost lifting him off the ground.

"Bow wood!" Great Sun exclaimed. "Our old people used to speak of this wood. It was given by *Old Traveler* to First People, but our ancestors used it all up, and they say that is why the sacred bow-wood trees now only grow in the land where great humped beasts drink from the Water-Runs-Red, many days from our land. The wood is so strong that it can send an arrow completely though a man."

Flint Rabbit and the people were visibly relived. Great Sun was smiling again.

"Far-Away-Woman," said Great Sun, "Tell Flint Rabbit how pleased we are with the gifts he has brought. We do not have flint stone to make arrowheads or bow wood to fashion our bows, so we accept the Anoy gifts with sincere gratitude. The spirit of the gift requires that we repay their generosity with gifts of our own. Tell him we will visit their village during the Falling Leaves Moon."

"He says your friendship is ample repayment," said Far-Away-Woman, "He wishes to formalize the promise of friendship with smoke."

"Tell him, the Beloved Men must unanimously approve our friendship before it can be affirmed by the sacred smoke. We will bring our decision to their village during the Falling Leaves Moon. Tell him, he has Great Sun's personal friendship. I have spoken."

Far-Away-Woman repeated Great Sun's words to Flint Rabbit, who managed to smile through his disappointment, but he knew his people would have done the same thing. No matter how much power Great Sun or his own father wielded, binding their peoples to each other with pipe smoke still depended on approval of the council of elders.

"Bring food," said Great Sun. "Our guests are hungry. Then the dancing can begin."

Roast dog was served to Flint Rabbit and each male member of the Anoy delegation. Afterwards came stews, pit-baked fish and lotus tubers, and kunti bread. When Great Sun, village officials, and guests were finished being served, Always Frowning signaled for the people to fill their food bowls, nobles first, then commoners. Serving lines quickly lost their class composition as relatives and friends commingled. Bowls filled, people moved under the shade of the huge oaks, where there was much talking, laughing, loud belching, laughing at the belching, but when the competitive farting began, many women moved back onto the sunny dance grounds and crowded into the small shade cast by the dance house, or House of Importance.

Speaks Twice found Storm Rider, sitting alone.

"Healer, your b-b-bowl is empty. D-d-did you eat anything? D-d-did you get a piece of Blackbird's b-b-bread?"

"I'm not hungry," said Storm Rider, barely able to suppress his resentment.

"Good, that leaves more for me. I'll be back. I'm going to get another piece and get her to come and sit with us."

"Speaks Twice, wait!" Storm Rider shouted after his friend, now rival, who was already running toward her cooking fire. He could imagine the two of them returning, arm in arm, smiling lovingly at each other. He should have stayed away, far from Speaks Twice, farther from Blackbird.

"Oh, no, she comes," he whispered, barely able to suppress his despair. "What can I say that will not betray my heart? Why didn't you choose me? We were always together in my dreams."

"Speaks Twice says you didn't get a piece of my bread, so, here, I bring you one," said Blackbird.

"Thanks, but I'm not hungry."

"I saved it just for you, Storm Rider. It's full of persimmons, just like you like it. Speaks Twice wanted it. He's already eaten the piece I saved for him. I've been waiting for you to come by our cooking fire."

"I, uh...."

"He is w-w-worried," interrupted Speaks Twice, "He f-f-fears our Anoy f-f-friends are insincere. I told him all he needs to do is have one of his v-v-visions so he will be able to tell for sure."

"Speaks Twice, you know visions don't work like that," said Blackbird, sitting down beside Storm Rider.

Storm Rider almost recoiled as her thigh pressed against his. Her warm fingers opened his fist and placed the warm bread in his palm.

"You need to eat something."

He took a bite, but the lump in his throat made it hard to swallow.

"What do you think of Speaks Twice's hair? He asked me to fix it. He wanted to look good so the girls would be impressed."

"Young girls already are g-g-giggly around me," Speaks Twice boasted, "but my fancy w-w-warrior lock is making young w-w-women turn their heads. I have noticed s-s-several flirting with me. I will dance with them to-night under the t-t-torchlight, and maybe they will ask me to dance with them under the m-m-moonlight."

"Humh, Speaks Twice," smiled Blackbird, "That's all you think about lately."

"Ay-e," said Storm Rider, joyously, realizing that Speaks Twice and Black-bird were not attracted to each other. They were as always, just friends, his friends.

"I must get back to our cooking fire. I see some big bellies returning for second helpings. Save me a dance, Storm Rider. Maybe we can dance under the moonlight, too."

She flew off to her mother's side. Storm Rider fell back on the ground, arms thrown back over his head, his temples pounding.

"Hummh, healer, so she would d-d-dance the m-m-moonlight dance with you. How do you get all the luck, when I am the best-looking? Oh well, I've got to help as many poor g-g-girls as I can. You'll have to take care of b-b-Blackbird by yourself, but if you need a-a-assistance, w-w-whistle like the jay, and I'll come running."

10

Cutting Cane and Gathering Dyes

The Anoy's visit was on everyone's mind. Men railed about the murdering northern raiders who did not fight for honor and revenge but conquest. Many young men took up their bows, anxiously trying out the new arrowpoints with the turned-down shoulders.

"F-f-fishermen, do not abandon your nets," fussed Speaks Twice. "Y-y-you know we cannot live off rabbits and s-s-squirrels."

Storm Rider was not worried about the hunters. He knew they would be back on the lake when the stews became thin, and wives complained. He hoped Great Sun and the council would chose him to be a member of the Anoy delegation—there was always the danger of snakebite—but every time he closed his eyes and tried to picture himself in the Anoy village, all he could see was Blackbird's smile and feel her warmth. So, he tried to put aside his profane thoughts by staying busy collecting and preparing medicines and thinking about his father's bone-digging.

Although the return visit was still three moons away, women started preparing. They had little choice. The morning after the Anoy left, Always Frowning stalked the arbor, making demands and giving orders. Sun Woman also paid a surprise visit to the arbor—she came to see Plaits Starting. After their brief conservation, Plaits Starting approached Blackbird and several other women.

"Blackbird, Sun Woman wants new baskets to carry our gifts to the Anoy. Would you come with me to gather the cane?"

"Ah-e, when?"

"Tomorrow, if it does not rain."

"Don't forget your cane beater."

"I'll be ready."

The gray morning turned unseasonably cooler and less humid after the late season front moved through during the night. Except for puddles trapped between exposed live oak roots, water drained quickly from the clamshell trail. Raindrop-beaded spider webs crisscrossed the path, ready to douse unsuspecting pedestrians. From the lime-water pond, spring peepers chirped in harmony with the locusts' shrill hum and the bullfrogs' basso. Seeing the women approach, the mother raccoon shepherded her litter into the waist-high palmetto, temporarily abandoning her hunt for the wary bullfrog.

The five women and the adolescent girl walked single file, Plaits Starting in the lead, followed by Bites-Him-Hard, Blackbird-Eyes-Shining, the girl, and two older women. Plaits Starting wanted more women to come, but she knew six would be able to carry enough cane to make many baskets. As the best basket maker in the village, she was the one everyone expected to organize and lead these cane-cutting expeditions. She knew where the best cane grew, when to cut it, and how to prepare it—an accumulated knowledge and skill passed down through her family for generations. She was faithful to the old tradition—her large collection of old baskets and mats made sure of that—but she also created new designs and forms. Children crowded around her at the arbor, trying to weave their little baskets just like hers. And she loved them. A Black Face arrow had taken away her chance of having children. It would have taken her life too, if the old healer had not stayed by her side for days during her delirium.

No matter how many trips she made to the tall canebrake on the Twisting Snake Water, Plaits Starting always felt a knot in her belly. She was responsible for gathering the cane and for getting everyone home safely. The Twisting Snake was the border of the people's land. Beyond were Black Faces, Black Hairs, and *Long Black Being.*

Blackbird sensed Plaits Starting's resolve. Blackbird was aware of the potential danger of a trip so close to Black Face land, but she needed the long cane for the bone basket she wanted to weave for Storm Rider's father.

The line of women moved along the trail well past the village. Blackbird's palmetto sandals and mulberry-bark skirt already were wet. A breath of air stirred the moss in the oaks, spreading goose bumps across her bare breasts and legs. She removed the deerskin-tote strap from her shoulder and wound it around her neck, affording a little more cover.

"It is cool for a Black Drink Moon day. I'm shivering," said Blackbird.

"Me too," agreed Bites-Him-Hard. "My pleasuring tips are so hard my moonlight-dance partners might mistake them for oak nuts."

"Huh," said the old waddling woman disgustedly. "No unmarried man in the village would make that mistake. They all know better, generous-spreader-of-legs."

"You old Spider clan woman," retorted Bites-Him-Hard, "You're just jealous because you haven't sat on a warrior's club since your breasts decided to lie down flat on your belly back in the dim time."

"Women, stop fussing!" said Plaits Starting. "Black Faces might hear you.

They have ears all along the Twisting Snake. Just remember, Strikes Blows' youngest sister was abducted from the same canebrake where we are going."

"Why do we have to go to such a bad place," asked waddling woman's granddaughter.

"The cane grows bigger and taller there," said Plaits Starting. "Sun Woman requests that we make as many waterproof baskets as we can before our delegation visits the Anoy."

"Granddaughter, do you forget? Cane must be at least two fingers wide and have joints as long as from your fingertips to your elbow. Anything smaller and we cannot weave the waterproof double baskets without the joint seams showing on the outside."

"Ah-e, I remember," said the adolescent. "So, why didn't warriors come with us?"

"They don't go with women to cut cane," said Plaits Starting. "Besides, we all carry cane knives and beaters, and, look, Bites-Him-Hard brings her brother's bow and arrows, while he fishes."

"I'd still feel safer if we had warriors with us."

"Huh!" said her grandmother, "They would be no help. Oak-Nut-Tips there would be keeping them busy in the bushes, instead of letting them watch for Black Faces."

"Enough!" demanded Plaits Starting.

The women stopped talking, losing their thoughts in the steady rhythm of their march. The cool morning gave way to bright, cloudless warmth. Birds were singing, and from a nearby hollow tree came the drone from a hive of honeybees.

"Ay-e, we are at the brake," thought Plaits Starting. "And no Black Faces."

The women plunged into the brake along a swath of downed cane. The cane was taller and bigger than Plaits Starting remembered. Some stalks were as big around as the arm, much too large for basket making, and were so close together that even Blackbird's lithe body couldn't squeeze between them. It was perpetually dark, and every noise made by the brake's many furred and feathered denizens resonated in hypersensitive ears.

"The bear was hungry," whispered Plaits Starting, "The tender leaves have been stripped and the stalks gnawed. Here is his track, a big one too."

"Look," said Blackbird, "The claw print is longer than my finger."

"Do you think he is still in the brake?" said the worried adolescent.

"No, granddaughter. Only birds and wood rats keep us company."

"Remember, talk in whispers and try to make as little noise as possible," said Plaits Starting. "If anyone hears us cutting cane, they will think the bear is eating."

The women split up, three moving along the bear's path and the others following a narrow intersecting deer trail.

The women were experienced cane cutters, so they went straight to work.

"Come with us, granddaughter," said waddling woman. "We'll show you how to cut cane. You can be our stacker."

Waddling woman extended her arms over her head and grabbed the rigid stalk. Then, she gave the stalk a vicious pull and dropped to her knees, riding the stalk toward the ground. Using her cane beater—a fire-hardened oak club with teeth carved on two faces—waddling woman's quiet friend struck the stalk where it bent the most, explosively shattering the stalk. Two sawing motions with the toothed club completely severed the splinters.

"Now what you need to do, granddaughter, is take your beater and hack off the flimsy limbs, right at the joints. Stack the trimmed cane over there, out of the way."

The women worked steadily, and shortly after *Noon-Day-Sun* reached its zenith, Plaits Starting asked the women to stop cutting.

"The piles are waist high. We have cut as much cane as we can carry. We need to break the cane into shorter sections for carrying."

The women sat on the piles of stripped limbs and began to break the cane into body-length sections.

"Sit here by me, granddaughter, I'll show you how to break the cane, but you'll probably have to help me get up after we're through. I get stiff when I sit."

"Huh! I always knew your tail was too fat for your bird legs to carry," said Bites-Him-Hard.

"Well, at least it doesn't look like a moth-eaten hide from all the pokes it has gotten," replied waddling woman.

"Women, I asked you to stop bickering while we are so far from home," said Plaits Starting angrily. "You can enjoy each other's company when you're back under the arbor, but here, you jeopardize our safety."

"Come here, granddaughter, pay no attention to Sand-In-Her-Crack. Watch how your grandmother does it."

Waddling woman grabbed a cane and pulled a body-length section across her lap. Leaving a gap between her hands, she twisted the cane in opposite directions and brought it down sharply across her thigh. The cane snapped loudly, and she deftly severed the frayed ends with her cane beater.

"See how easy. Now, you try," said waddling woman.

With all six working, the cane was quickly sectioned into carrying lengths and tied into bundles of manageable weight. Tote-lines were attached.

Plaits Starting finally breathed a little easier. They had gathered the treasured long cane, and now they were going home.

"Grandmother, wait, I need to make water."

The girl wandered down the deer trail and out of sight, even though she had only taken a few steps into the thick cane.

Plaits Starting was the first to notice.

"Shuuh! The birds have quit singing."

An eerie quiet fell on the brake. Plaits Starting picked up her cane beater and slowly rose to a crouching position. The other women were now alarmed. Arming themselves, they moved into a tight circle. Waddling woman had no trouble getting to her feet.

The girl emerged from the cane smiling and holding a spotted ball of fur. The wide-eyed women were aghast.

"Drop the kitten, now," whispered Plaits Starting.

The snarl of the big swamp cat shattered the quiet. She was close by, much too close.

"Grab your cane bundles," directed Plaits Starting in a low voice. "And run. I will face the swamp cat. Go!"

"I'm staying with you," said Blackbird, "Two cane beaters are better than one."

The brake erupted as the big cat crashed through the cane. Only the near-impenetrability of the brake stood between them and the fury of mother cat.

"Run! While we can."

Plaits Starting and Blackbird caught up with the fleeing women, just as waddling woman stopped and threw her bundle on the ground.

"I can run no farther," she panted. "Mother cat will just have to kill me here. Hurry and maybe the rest of you can get away while she takes out her anger on me."

"We will not leave you," gasped Bites-Him-Hard. "Who would fuss with me?"

The women encircled waddling woman, beaters and knives drawn. They waited. The only sound was each other's rapid breathing. Where was the cat? Was she stalking them? Was she behind or ahead of them, lying in wait?

Then, they heard the unearthly scream. The big cat was still at the brake with her kitten. The women were safe.

"That was scary, grandmother, wasn't it?"

Laughing through their tears, the women collapsed in a pile, embracing the girl and intertwining fingers. They all knew how close they had been to the world of shadows.

"Let's go home," said Plaits Starting, "And don't forget the cane."

The saga of the swamp cat and the cane cutting was told over and over that day. Villagers, young and old, listened intently. Warriors nodded and praised the women's bravery. The cane cutters reveled in their moment of fame, for they knew that hard work awaited them in the morning. The cut cane had to be prepared before it dried out, or their life-threatening journey would be for nothing.

Storm Rider and Speaks Twice caught up with Blackbird just as she was about to follow her mother into her lodge, away from the bustling plaza.

"Talk with your friends," said her mother, "You can speak with your grandmother later."

"I'm glad you're safe," said Storm Rider.

"H-h-how c-c-close was the cat?" asked Speaks Twice. "D-d-did she only have one k-k-kitten? Do you think she . . . ?"

"Speaks Twice," interrupted Blackbird, "I don't know about the cat. We were running too fast. I was scared, but I was not going to let Plaits Starting sacrifice herself for the rest of us. She is the brave one."

"Let us go, Speaks Twice. Blackbird needs to see her grandmother."

Blackbird hugged them and raised the door flap. Before she ducked into the lodge, she reached for Storm Rider's hand.

"I'll be at the landing when the sky fires begin to flicker."

She entered the lodge.

"H-h-huh, she didn't reach for my hand," grumbled Speaks Twice. "I guess it s-s-smells too fishy."

"Speaks Twice, don't act hurt. So many maidens are trying to win your attention that skunk smell couldn't keep them away."

"Ah-e, that's what I've been m-m-meaning to talk about with you. Rabbit-Tail-Wagging makes me laugh at e-e-everything she says, Afraid-of-the-Night laughs at e-e-everything I say, Smiling Eyes is p-p-pretty to look at, e-e-everywhere, Straight Legs knows the w-w-wild ways, and. . . ."

"I don't want to hear about your woman problems," interrupted Storm Rider, "You're going to have to work them out yourself."

"I t-t-thought that's what you'd say. Blackbird will give me g-g-good advice. I'll meet you two at the landing later."

"No!"

"Okay, then. D-d-don't get l-l-lonesome without me, and w-w-watch out for *Long Black Being*. S-s-see you in the morning, healer."

Stars filled the night sky, faintly illuminating the young lovers lying on the deerskin. Few words passed between them but what they shared was more powerful, more primal.

"Blackbird."

"I know. I feel the same way."

"When I get back from the bone-digging, I think we should talk to Fire Watcher."

"Let's see we how we feel then," said Blackbird. "Now, I must go, the basket makers start early in the morning."

Noon-Day-Sun awakened wearing a brilliant red cloak. Except for the girl, all the basket makers were sitting under the arbor when Blackbird arrived.

"Sit here," said Plaits Starting, pointing to a mat next to her bale of cane.

"Your eyes are especially shining this morning," said Bites-Him-Hard. "Did someone shine them for you last night?"

"I am just glad to be home."

"Ah-e," taunted waddling woman, "Don't tell her anything, Blackbird, or she will try to sample him for herself."

"Huh, I can see Big-Rear-End there has already taken her morning dose of stinging nettle leaves and black thorns," replied Bites-Him-Hard.

"Women, don't start your chatter this early," pleaded Plaits Starting, "My ears are already hurting."

Plaits Starting grabbed a cane with both hands, applied torque, and sharply snapped it across her deerskin-protected thigh, splitting the cane into five splints. The loud snap woke a pair of curs, which came to inspect the noise under the arbor. By midmorning, the women were surrounded by piles of arm-length splints.

"Oh, my aching leg," moaned Bites-Him-Hard. "I'll be so sore tomorrow, I won't be able to walk."

"That shouldn't be too much of a problem," said waddling woman, "Most of your work is done on your back anyway."

The women cleared the space in front of them for their water pots, tall, straight-sided, flat-bottomed pottery vessels filled with lake water. They dunked a double-handful of cane splints and, while they soaked, sang the song of Cane-Becoming-Basket.

"Ah-e, cane is cut, cane is cut."
"Ah-e, cane is quartered, cane is quartered."
"Ah-e, cane is peeled, cane is peeled."
"Ah-e, cane do not cry, cane do not cry."
"Ah-e, cane is not dead, cane is not dead."
"Ah-e, cane is aged, cane is aged."
"Ah-e, cane is dyed, cane is dyed."
"Ah-e, cane is woven, cane is woven."
"Ah-e, cane do not cry, cane do not cry."
"Ah-e, cane becomes a beautiful basket, cane becomes a beautiful
   basket."

Several women gathered around the singing basket makers, and some of the young children started playing with the limber splints.

"Tadpole," said a young mother, "Stop hitting your sister with the cane switch. Go put it back where you got it."

"Ah-e," said an old snaggled-toothed onlooker, "It holds the spirit of the swamp cat. It is too powerful for the child to hold. He could hurt his sister badly."

The frightened child dropped the splint and ran to his mother crying to be picked up. The snaggled-toothed woman retrieved the splint and threw it on Blackbird's pile, withdrawing her hand like she had been holding a burning piece of firewood.

"I'm afraid the spirit of the big cat will cause harm to anyone who touches the cane or baskets made from it," she said.

In two quick bounds, Plaits Starting jumped in the face of snaggled-toothed woman.

"Woman, you know nothing of spirits," said Plaits Starting, barely controlling her anger. "That is the dominion of prophets. I say the cane portends good luck—we entered the swamp cat's lair and returned without a scratch. She let us go with cane from her home. If she intended harm, we would not be here now. Go away and say no more about the cane."

Snaggled-toothed woman sulked away, mumbling under her breath and kicking clamshells at the cur dog lying in the shade.

"She knows nothing about cane or spirits," said Plaits Starting, returning to her mat next to cane pile. "And she scares little ones with her ignorance."

"Big ones, too, I'm afraid," replied Bites-Him-Hard. "Notice, several mothers moved their children to the other side of the plaza."

"Huh, let them go. They're all Panther clan women anyway, always finding danger in everything," said waddling woman, dismissing them with a sweep of her hand.

Plaits Starting took a wet splint from the pot and turned it so that the concave surface faced away from her. She notched the severed end with a flint chip. Biting the notched end with her front teeth, she peeled away a narrow strip of the hard outer shell. The pliable strip was about as wide as the quill in an ivory-billed woodpecker's tail feather, the width controlled by the spacing of the notches. It was as long as she was tall. Quickly, she peeled the rest of the splint.

The other women kept pace and before *Noon-Day-Sun* left the plaza, they had finished the peeling. Sitting among piles of strips and discards, only the tops of their heads were visible.

"You basket makers always make such a mess!" complained Always Frowning as he passed the arbor. "This simply must be cleaned up before you leave."

"Huh," came a voice hidden in the cane piles, "Clean it up yourself. Might help your disposition if you did some work for a change."

"Who said that? I will have your fingers broken," screamed Always Frowning.

Laughing Otter was delivering smoked fish to widow women when he overheard Always Frowning's tantrum.

"Village Keeper, you know Sun Woman wants new baskets to carry gifts to the Anoy. Would you have the basket makers stop their work to sweep the village? Sun Woman would not be pleased with you."

Exasperated, Always Frowning threw back his head and stomped across the plaza, every step splashing muddy water on his sandals.

"You did not make a friend," said Plaits Starting.

"Do not worry, I have other friends. Here, chew on a few of these," said Laughing Otter, dropping blackened fillets in every chamber. "They've been slowly smoked over cherry wood. I know you're hungry. Speaks Twice says you have not left the arbor since *Noon-Day-Sun* awoke."

"Great fisherman, you must have heard the bear in my belly," said one of the heads poking through the pile.

"Huh, old woman, I think the growling came from the other end," said another head.

"Women, enough! You hurt the fisherman's ears."

"It's not my ears, women, it's my innocence. My face is already the color of your brightest red basket, and I'm afraid if it gets any brighter it will make the rising *Noon-Day-Sun* look like her husband."

"Laughing Otter, it is Blackbird. Thank you for coming to our defense and for feeding us."

"You are welcome. Speaks Twice said he saw you before your cane cocoon got so high. Ah-e, I see the top of your head, and I hope to see the rest of you before long."

Laughing Otter made his way back to his smoking pit. Tomorrow, he would make his rounds again, leaving fish for the widows and the old ones.

"What a good man," thought Blackbird, "And Speaks Twice is growing up to be just like him. What a husband he will make, but my heart belongs to his shy friend."

"Basket makers," said Plaits Starting, "We have peeled all the cane. Take your strips home and spread them on your drying benches. Let them enjoy *Noon-Day-Sun* for one moon, and then bring them to the lime-water pit for dyeing on the day following the next feast."

The women emerged from their temporary chambers.

"I don't know how I can survive a whole moon without my joking sister," said Bites-Him-Hard.

"Just open your mouth and the dirty words will come, anywhere, anytime," grumbled waddling woman. "Humm, maybe not, you'll have to keep other things out of your mouth."

"We will see each other before then, basket makers," said Plaits Starting to the departing women. "Remember, make your strips lie in the dew for eight sleeps before we dye them or they will not welcome the color."

Turning to Blackbird, she continued. "Will you come with me tomorrow to gather the materials for the dyes? They must be fresh, or the colors will be thin and dull."

"Ay-e."

"Be at my lodge when *Noon-Day-Sun* awakens and bring your largest carrying basket. I will bring kunti bread."

"See you at first light," said Blackbird.

"Uuh, and Blackbird, tell your healer friend you have a busy day ahead."

"No need, he and Speaks Twice are setting fish nets tonight."

Morning found the village hidden by ground fog. The moist layer thickened as Blackbird and her mentor neared Pond Lily Cove.

"The black dye tree sits on the low ridge behind the dance house," said Plaits Starting.

"Ah-e, I have gathered dye nuts there before," replied Blackbird, pushing a damp strand of hair from her eyes. "My grandmother and I made the bone basket for her brother."

"We can still gather the nuts even though we can't see them. Our bare feet will be our eyes unless they find the white-mouth snake first."

Memory led the women to the black walnut tree, one of the few that grew off Twisting Snake ridge.

"My great-grandmother planted the tree, so her children would not have to walk as far as she did to gather black dye nuts," said Plaits Starting.

The women pulled off their sandals and swept their feet over the grassy ground feeling for nuts, to no avail.

"We are too early," said Blackbird. "They have not fallen yet."

"Then, we will have to climb the tree and gather them by hand," sighed Plaits Starting.

"I will do the climbing," replied Blackbird. "And drop them to you. Don't let them hit you on the head. They will make a big knot."

After a few minutes in the tree, Blackbird felt a slight breeze on her face, and like smoke from a doused fire, the fog lifted enabling her to see the nuts instead of having to feel for them.

The fist-size nuts clustered at the ends of limber branches. Blackbird inched along the sturdier limbs and pulled on the branches until she could reach the nuts, which were still encased in their thick green covering. Nuts soon covered the ground, and Blackbird scampered down the tree and helped Plaits Starting fill the basket.

"Is it too heavy?" asked Plaits Starting, rubbing her black-stained hands.

"Not if I attach the tote line and carry it on my back."

"Good, we have enough nuts to make the dye really black."

"Ah-e, look at our hands," said Blackbird. "People are going to start calling us Black Hands. They might mistake us for brothers of the Black Faces."

"It will wear off in time, especially if you scrub them with crushed bloodweed berries."

"Why don't you leave the nut basket here," said Plaits Starting, noticing Blackbird straining to lift the heavy load. "We can pick it up on our way back, and I can help you carry it since our other basket will not be heavy."

"Ah-e."

"Did you know my great-grandmother also planted the spiny-seed plants?" asked Plaits Starting, pointing to the shoreline behind the dance house. "Her brothers brought back the seeds from the waving grass, where the Twisting Snake meets the Big Salt Water."

"Huh, I always thought they grew naturally on Pond Lily Cove. Your great-grandmother had the wisdom of *Old Traveler.* No more long, dangerous journeys to get the dyes."

The dock plants grew profusely along the shoreline. The women pushed their way into the dense stand and quickly filled their basket with seeds and leaves.

"Ahhh," exclaimed Plaits Starting, "Our red and yellow dyes will be bright. Let's find some shade or *Noon-Day-Sun* will cook our skin."

"Put the basket down," suggested Blackbird, wading into dark water of the little cove. "The water is cool. We should swim first. My arms and legs are stinging."

The women splashed in the pool, until the alligator swam out to greet them.

"Uh, he goes under," said Plaits Starting, "Time to get out, or we will be his morning meal."

Scrambling to shore, they retrieved the seed- and leaf-filled basket. Plaits Starting hoisted it on her back, secured the tote straps, and the women returned to the black walnut tree to pick up the heavy basket. Each grabbed a handle, and they carried it between them back to Plaits Starting's lodge, stopping occasionally to rest their cramped hands and catch their breath.

"You should have asked Bites-Him-Hard to come. She could have helped."

"Ah-e," said Plaits Starting, "But then we would have had to put up with her man-stories."

"Do you think everything she tells us is true?" asked Blackbird.

"Judging by all the knowing smiles she gets, I believe so."

"Huh."

Plaits Starting and Blackbird carried the baskets to Plaits Starting's lodge and put them in the outdoor work area beside her lodge.

"My arm feels like I'm still carrying the basket," said Blackbird.

"Mine too. But at least we didn't have to make two trips. Thank you for helping, Blackbird. You know, I feel like you are my own daughter."

Touched by the sentiment, Blackbird smiled all the way across the plaza, much to the delight of the little boys tugging on her legs.

"Now, I have new dyes if Storm Rider wants me to weave the bone basket for his father," thought Blackbird, as she ducked into her lodge. "I must ask him soon. His aunt might be working on one, and the bone-digging approaches."

Blackbird helped her mother and sisters prepare for the upcoming feast, and whenever she could, she worked feverishly on her other creations. They had to be completed soon. There was no time to lose.

The Black Drink feast arrived. Prairie Landing and Grand Lake villagers celebrated together at the Pond Lily dance house.

"Why haven't we drunk the Black Drink with our brothers and sisters before?" asked Blackbird.

"My father s-s-says we used to s-s-share the drink before Prairie Landing's old Sun b-b-became chief," explained Speaks Twice. "B-b-but he and our old Sun had a f-f-falling out. They were b-b-brothers, but they wanted the same woman, and when she m-m-married our Sun, the young b-b-brother moved to Prairie Landing village and b-b-became Sun after Black Faces k-k-killed the old Sun, his uncle."

Storm Rider weighed the consequences of two men desiring one woman and thanked his snake guardian that Speaks Twice was happy with his many girlfriends.

"You are my friend, Speaks Twice."

"I k-k-know that, healer, and you are m-m-mine, but don't get any ideas about trying to s-s-steal my dancing partners. Aiyee, I might give you one or two, if Blackbird doesn't care."

"Ahh, I don't mind," teased Blackbird, "If he doesn't mind me dancing with some of the young men that watch me walk across the plaza. They are not looking at my spots either."

"Enough! I only dance with Blackbird."

Passing on Traditions

"Her belly hurts her all the time, and she has a fever," said Plaits Starting. "She says it feels like it is going to burst open. Will you take a look at her?"

"Ay-e," said Storm Rider. "I will come to your lodge tomorrow."

"Thank you, healer. Blackbird, do not keep him up too late. Have you finished the things we talked about?"

"No, but they should be ready in time," said Blackbird.

"We start the dyeing tomorrow at the lime-water pond," Plaits Starting reminded Blackbird. "Don't worry, healer, after your visit."

Plaits Starting walked back to her family, leaving Blackbird and Storm Rider at the dance fire.

"Ugh, my stomach doesn't feel good either," said Blackbird. "And I tried to drink only enough Black Drink to throw up one time. Once ought to be enough to renew my body and spirit, shouldn't it?"

"Depends how bad you've been," kidded Storm Rider.

"I think I'm going to be sick again. Awwh, and we haven't danced our favorite dance yet. My healer, I've got to go home. I don't feel good."

"That's okay," replied Storm Rider, feeling a bit sick himself but trying to keep the disappointment out of his voice. "I'll walk you to your lodge."

Next morning, still feeling the effects of the Black Drink, Storm Rider made his way to Plaits Starting's lodge and examined her ailing mother.

"She has a poison from eating food that's too old," said Storm Rider.

"Ah-e," acknowledged Plaits Starting. "I tried to get her to throw away those old garfish cakes, but she said they were her favorite and she hated to see them go to waste."

"I will make her medicine and perform the healing after it sleeps tonight."

"Thank you, healer," said Plaits Starting. "Can you give her anything now for the fever?"

"Let her chew this willow-bark shaving when she gets really hot and keep a wet doeskin on her forehead. I'll see her tomorrow."

The day was dreary and rainy, so Storm Rider remained in his lodge, stirring a boiling potful of fresh elderberry flower heads he had collected on the morning of the Black Drink feast.

"The flowers are cooked down enough," he mumbled to himself. "Father said to add two bloodweed leaves and let them wilt before pouring the tea though the strainer."

"Are you sure you are supposed to add bloodweed?" asked his aunt, who overheard him. "The stalks turned red a moon ago. They are poisonous now."

"Ah-e, Father said bloodweed makes the fever medicine more potent. But you can't boil the leaves very long and must pour off the tea quickly after they have wilted."

"Plaits Starting's mother must be very sick to need such a powerful tea," she said, looking up from her sewing.

"She goes about her work in her lodge, but her bloated stomach keeps returning every few sleeps," Storm Rider said. "Father told me that sometimes the illness hides from the medicine, and when the medicine wears off, it comes out again. I hope this will find all its hiding places."

"Please do not kill her, nephew. We are good friends."

"Don't worry," said Storm Rider. "She only needs to drink one swallow. The tea needs to rest for one sleep before she drinks."

"Listen, nephew, sounds like someone is outside the door."

"Storm Rider!" shouted a voice from outside the lodge.

He opened the flap to a drenched woman, shivering in the rain.

"Bent Woman sent me to tell you to come to her lodge."

"What does she want with me?" he asked.

"She did not tell me, but I would not keep her waiting," the woman said over her shoulder, running for shelter.

"You better go quickly," his aunt advised.

Storm Rider tied his short mantle around his neck, took off his sandals, and splashed across the plaza and down the trail leading to her lodge.

He scratched on the lintel, but there was no answer. He called out.

"Bent Woman! It's Storm Rider. I am here like you asked."

"Come in, Snakebite healer."

He lifted the flap and entered. It took a minute for his eyes to adjust to the dark. The dark was heavy and ominous, and he was chilled. Bent Woman was sitting around a small fire with eyes closed and lips moving as though she was talking to someone. He did not interrupt her. His father told him her prophecies always came right after her visits with the spirits, and her lodge seemed to be full of spirits. He waited patiently for her to tell him why she wanted to see him. To his amazement, he realized she was looking at him, even though he thought her eyes were closed.

"Ah-e, young healer, thank you for coming to see this woman. Your father asked me to tell you the tribal stories when I thought you were ready. 'Bent Woman,' that man said, 'I have filled my son's head with medicinal knowledge. Let him be free for a while before telling him the old stories.' That man knew that once you receive the ancient wisdom you can never return to the way you were before. You become a Tradition Keeper. Are you ready to receive the ancient wisdom, Storm Rider?"

"Ah-e, I am ready," Storm Rider said softly.

"Then we shall start today, and hereafter come to my lodge only when it rains," she said.

She reached into the fringed pouch around her waist and put the pinch of tobacco behind her bottom lip.

"The sacred tobacco purifies my words so I can tell the old stories faithfully. The words are heavy with age and tradition. Those who choose to hear them accept the responsibility of passing them on to the next generation. This is the way it has been since the beginning. This is the way it will always be.

"The traditions are the people. With them, we live forever. Without them, we wither and die like leaves after a hard freeze."

The rain beat a drummer's song on the palmetto roof. Bent Woman shed her woven cape and leaned closer to the fire. In the flickering light, her eyes shone like an alligator's in the torchlight and then blinked, becoming deep black pits.

She raised her gourd rattle and intoned the age-old Song of Passing on Traditions.

"Shoh dah dah dee ama-uh.
"Shoh dah dah dee ama-uh.
"Shoh dah dah dee ama-uh.
"Shoh dah dee dah.
"Shoh dah dah dee ama-uh.
"Shoh dah dah dee ama-uh.
"Shoh dah dah dee ama-uh.
"Shoh dah dee dah.
"Way hah, way hah."

She replaced the rattle in the red-, black-, and yellow-colored basket decorated with the Worm-Tracks design. Then, she spit tobacco juice on the coals sending a sizzling puff of smoke toward the darkened ceiling.

"In the beginning, there was only *Old Traveler*. He was not born like us. He was just there, always. He has no eyes or ears, yet is all-seeing and all-hearing. He knows everything because he has already lived the future and remembers what will happen.

"At first," Bent Woman continued, "there was only water. *Old Traveler* made crawfish and clams to live in the water. He sent crawfish to the bottom of the water and had him bring up mud to make the earth. But the earth was barren, and *Old Traveler* made men and animals so the earth would not be lonesome. He called the men the Many Waters People.

"*Old Traveler* gave the men laws, and for a while, they followed them, but after a while, they began to break the laws. The world became a bad place, and the men did not wish to live anymore.

"*Old Traveler* felt sorry for the men, so he made women and tobacco to make them happy, but the animals were jealous and mean-spirited. They made fun of the people because they did not have fur or feathers to cover their nakedness. The people begged *Old Traveler* to help. So, he gave the men bows and arrows and told them to shoot the animals, eat their flesh, and use their skins to make clothes.

"The world was cold and dark, so *Old Traveler* showed the people how to make fire by rubbing two pieces of wood together and how to cook their food. He made *Noon-Day-Sun* and *Pale Sun*. They were wife and husband. *Old Traveler* told them to bathe often so their light and heat would always be bright and strong. Wife obeyed, and to this day, *Noon-Day-Sun* has kept herself bright and shiny and lights the day. Husband disobeyed, and his dirty body gives off faint light or heat during the night, so we call him *Pale Sun*.

"*Old Traveler* created *Noon-Day-Sun* with his mind because there was no woman to lie with, but she is his daughter, and he loves her dearly. The people love and honor *Noon-Day-Sun* too, and she is always kind to them. Many times, she has stood still long enough for the people to defeat their enemies or finish an important undertaking, such as building a mound. Because he did not bathe, Great Spirit condemned *Pale Sun* to live alone, forever chasing his wife across the sky.

"Keep these words in your heart, Storm Rider. *Old Traveler* is the creator and the giver of all things. The people are here by his hand. We are what he allows us to be. Never think you are alone when performing a healing or seeing the future. *Old Traveler* helps the people through us. He is the ultimate healer, he is the ultimate prophet. Always humble yourself in his service and in your dealings with the people."

Bent Woman stoked the fire and added a branch. Flames licked around the wood, temporarily lighting her craggy face.

Storm Rider thought about the creation story, his mind full of questions.

"If *Old Traveler* is not like a man, what does he look like?"

"Nobody has ever seen him," answered Bent Woman.

"But if nobody has ever seen him, how do they know he has no eyes or ears?"

"He did not have human parents, so he cannot be like people. He has no parents. He has always been. He is without beginning or end. He is like the smoke that rises from the calumet or the wind that moves the water."

"But Bent Woman, if *Old Traveler* made animals for our food and clothes, why are some animals not supposed to be killed?"

"They are sacred. Let me tell you about them," she said, showering the coals with tobacco juice.

"There have been several great floods that nearly destroyed the people. In the first great flood, *Old Traveler* saved two good people in a big floating pot. Another time, *Old Traveler* appeared to six brothers and warned them to get ready because a big flood was coming. He told them to build a mud house like the crawfish and stay there until the flood was over. He said he would come back and tell them when it was safe to leave.

"The brothers did not want to live in a mud house, but they built it anyway. The flood came and lasted a long time, but eventually the water started to go down. The brothers had been cooped up so long that the youngest brother decided to go outside to see what damage the flood had done, but *Old Traveler* had not yet returned to tell them it was safe to leave. As the younger brother walked though the destroyed village, he turned into a screech owl and flew away.

"His brothers did not know he had turned into a screech owl, and they grew impatient. They thought younger brother had returned to the brothers' lodge in the village. So the second youngest brother went out to see if he could find his baby brother. He had not gone ten steps before he turned into a raccoon and ran away.

"Now, the other brothers grew worried. They were afraid that something bad had happened to their younger brothers. So, one by one the brothers left the safety of their mud house to look for their missing brothers. The third brother went out, and he turned into a bear. The fourth brother went out, and he turned into a white deer.

"The two remaining brothers realized that *Old Traveler* had punished their brothers for not waiting for his return. So, they waited and waited, but still *Old Traveler* did not come. The eldest brother decided that he had forgotten about them, so he went outside, and he turned into a hoot owl.

"That left only the next to oldest brother. He waited with his wife in the mud house, and in a few days, *Old Traveler* appeared to him.

"'I have been testing you and your brothers,' *Old Traveler* projected his thoughts into the obedient brother's mind. 'You have followed my instructions and did not leave your refuge until I returned. Now, you and your wife are the only people left. Go forth. You will be safe and prosper. You shall become the mother and father of all people to come.'

"'I have turned your brothers into animals because they did not obey me, but because they are your brothers, they must never be killed or eaten. From now on, screech owl, raccoon, bear, white deer, and hoot owl shall be sacred to the people.'

"Hai, that is the story of the sacred animals," said Bent Woman. "Now, go let your friend in before he drowns."

Storm Rider heard nothing but the soft rain on the roof, but he knew better than to question her.

Storm Rider raised the door flap, just as Speaks Twice was about to scratch on the lintel.

"Y-y-you scared me. Are you r-r-ready to l-l-leave?"

"She told me to let you in," said Storm Rider.

"H-h-how did she k-k-know I was here before I s-s-scratched on the door?"

"She just knows. Wait outside. I think we are through for the day," Storm Rider said, lowering the flap.

"Let him in, healer. I have one more story today, and then you will be through. The famous fish catcher may sit with us."

"T-t-thank you, high p-p-priestess. I do not mean to d-d-disturb you. I can wait outside. I t-t-thought you were f-f-finished and came to ask where Storm Rider went. Please, I shall w-w-wait outside."

"Sit!"

She shifted the wad of tobacco to her other jaw and spit into the fire.

"Open your ears. I tell you now about the Great Snake and how the Twisting Snake Water came to be.

"As you know, the snake is sacred," she said, "And he is very powerful, so powerful that one of our six clans, as you know, has adopted it for its totem. Great Sun is a member of the Snake clan, as are you, Storm Rider. Snakes are your protectors. They guarded you in the dugout that brought you to us.

"But they do not protect you, famous fish catcher," the old seer warned. "Lean on the man sitting next to you. He is your protection."

Bent Woman settled onto her sitting mat and related the story.

"Many, many winters ago, a giant snake lived in the great swamp. It killed many of our warriors. Tired of the threat, one of Great Sun's grandfathers struck the pole and assembled the warriors. He told them that they were going to have to hunt down the giant serpent so that the people would stop being afraid of going into the woods. Armed with bow and arrows and war clubs, the warriors hunted the snake. One war party found its head near the junction of the Little Oak Water and the Clamshell Water, and another party found its tail on the banks of the Beautiful White Water. The warriors and the snake fought long and hard. Many warriors were killed, but finally, they fatally wounded the snake. As the snake writhed in its death agony, its body wallowed out an impression in the ground that deepened and widened as its body decayed. The deep impression filled with water becoming the Twisting Snake Water.

"I have spoken," said Bent Woman, closing her eyes.

"Is s-s-she a-a-asleep?" whispered Speaks Twice.

"No, but she is through for the day. We should go now," said Storm Rider.

The young men moved quietly across the mat- and skin-covered floor. Speaks Twice reached for the door flap, when they jumped at the sound of her voice.

"Go catch this woman a white perch."

The young men sprinted across the plaza and stopped under the brush arbor.

"S-s-she scares me worse than the n-n-noise that follows me in the woods at d-d-dusk. She sees me with her eyes c-c-closed and knows what I am t-t-thinking," whispered Speaks Twice. "And I'm a-a-afraid she can hear me h-h-halfway across the village."

"Ah-e, I am nervous in her presence too, but, fisherman, she has a kind heart. I think she likes us."

"I don't p-p-plan to be around her l-l-long enough to find out," said Speaks Twice. "I'm glad you are going to be a T-t-tradition Keeper, not me. I would be so f-f-flustered that I wouldn't r-r-remember a word she said."

"Let's go to my lodge. It's starting to drizzle," said Storm Rider.

"I was c-c-coming to get you to h-h-help me mend my fish net, but now it looks like it's g-g-going to rain all day, so I g-g-guess I'll go home. Mother b-b-baked me some garfish cakes. See you t-t-tomorrow, healer."

The rain was falling harder, and it was getting dark. Storm Rider welcomed the rain. He had a lot to think about. At his father's request, Bent Woman was passing on the tribal lore to him. She deemed him worthy to become a Tradition Keeper. It was a lot to shoulder coming so soon after his naming ceremony—a Snakebite healer, a Tradition Keeper. Would he be able to live up to everyone's expectations of him? Was he worthy?

Two days later, Storm Rider dashed to Bent Woman's lodge while *Noon-Day-Sun* shined briefly through the drizzle. Pulling the flap aside, he ducked his head and entered the dark interior. His eyes took a second to adjust to the dimness, but he held his excitement until he was sure that Bent Woman was not visiting with the spirits.

"Bent Woman, Bent Woman," he said excitedly, "Wren is perched on your door post, singing the 'chuee' warning. Something bad is going to happen. What does it mean?"

"Wren has appeared three sleeps in a row. I have talked with the spirits, but they have not revealed the nature of the warning. But the sacred Rain Tree keeps appearing in my dreams, so I know that it is somehow involved. I will tell you the story of the Rain Tree, and maybe Wren's warning will become clear in the telling.

"Hear my words.

"Long ago, our ancestors were gathered at Rain Tree mounds. They had just finished burying their beloved chief's bones in the big mound, and the funeral ceremony was over. Our ancestors were loading the dugouts for the long voyage back to Grand Lake village, when suddenly a young man appeared on the bank, running so fast he left a bright glowing streak like a burning stick waved in pitch dark. When the man reached a tall cypress tree, he stopped and waited, as if he was listening to something. Only then did our surprised ancestors realize that the stranger had a beautiful face that shone like *Noon-Day-Sun*. Our ancestors heard the shouts of people chasing him, but instead of running, *Golden Face Man* waited by the tall cypress tree, and when the screaming mob was almost on him, he began climbing. His enemies began climbing the tree too, one after another, until his foes clung to every limb. Higher and higher they climbed until they reached the top. Our ancestors watched helplessly knowing the man had nowhere left to go. Just as *Golden Face Man* was about to be caught and thrown to his death, he stood on the topmost limb and, raising his arms above his head, rose into the clouds.

"His pursuers were dumb-founded. They looked at each other and then climbed down the tree so fast that many fell into the water, splashing it onto the trunk. As soon as water splashed on the tree, the skies opened, and it started raining so hard that our ancestors could not see the tree. They could not see *Golden Face Man's* pursuers but heard them running back the way they had come, shouting something about magic and evil spirits. As soon as the shouts quieted, *Noon-Day-Sun* came out and shone brightly, even though it was still pouring.

"Our ancestors believed that *Golden Face Man* was the Rain Spirit. To this day, when we need rain, we go cut a small limb from the sacred tree and bring it back to the village. We are careful not to splash water on the tree or let the limb fall in the water, because rain and waves might swamp our dugouts before we get home. Once at the village, Fire Watcher wades into the lake, swishes the limb around in the water, and hurries back to the temple before the rain starts.

"Small twigs bring showers, branches bring downpours, and limbs bring storms with wind and hail. It will rain for as long the limb is left in the water. We are always mindful of how much rain we need, so we know how big the limb must be and how long to leave it in the water.

"It is the same with water splashed directly on the tree. A drop or two will bring a gentle rain, a handful, a downpour, and a double handful, a storm.

"That is the tradition of Rain Tree, as I learned from my grandmother," said Bent Woman. "But I do not know why the Rain Tree and *Golden Face Man* keep appearing in my dreams. This I do know. My dreams do not raise false alarms, and you should always pay attention to Wren's warning. Keep the story of the Rain Tree in the front of your mind."

That night Storm Rider went over and over the story of the Rain Tree. It seemed like any other story. Yet, it knew it was more. Bent Woman dreamed of it, and Wren had delivered her warning.

Bent Woman continued to pass on the ancient stories during the hot moons. Storm Rider had heard his father tell some of the stories before, but he listened intently to every word. He never interrupted, and only when she finished telling a story and made sure the story's message was clear would she ask if he had anything to say. She welcomed his words, knowing that a questioning mind grows out of attentiveness and interest. Storm Rider asked many questions, and Bent Woman answered every one.

"To be a good healer you have to know what makes people sick and how to treat them," said Bent Woman. "You have been trained by the best healer the people have ever had, but also you have been chosen by *Old Traveler* to be a prophet. And to be a true prophet, you must know the ancient traditions and what they mean. Knowing the traditions enables you to know the thoughts of the people and to recognize the signs that reveal the future.

"When you leave my lodge today, Snakebite healer, go with the knowledge that I have taught you all that was told me," Bent Woman said one gray morning. "We finished the stories just in time. I saw a pair of green wings yesterday. The hot moons are over, but your training is not yet finished. Your father wanted me to send you to the temple when your days at my fire were over. Fire Watcher is expecting you. I talked with him yesterday."

"Thank you, Bent Woman. Your words will be in my heart always. Though we cannot say his name in death, I will send smoke to my father for bringing me to your fire."

Storm Rider opened the lodge flap. The drizzle had stopped, and bright sunlight flooded the lodge.

"*Noon-Day-Sun* smiles on you, Snakebite healer," said the old woman.

12

Nobles and Commoners

"The r-r-rains must be over. The Snakebite healer himself w-w-walks through the village without his m-m-mantle," kidded Speaks Twice. "A-a-all this time, I t-t-thought you were learning how to become a p-p-prophet. Now, I can see you were only learning to f-f-forecast rain—when you go to Bent Woman's lodge w-w-wearing your mantle, it rains; when you don't go to Bent Woman's and don't w-w-wear your mantle, t-t-there is no rain."

"It is good to see you have not changed, catcher of small fish," Storm Rider kidded back. "You know that Bent Woman told me to come to her lodge only on the days when it rained. Now, I will finish my training with Fire Watcher at the temple."

"S-s-seems like you have been training forever. Why did you have to be a healer and a prophet, too? Y-y-you need to go fishing with me. I hear fish t-t-talking all the time. They say: 'Why don't you b-b-bring the Snakebite healer fishing with you anymore, so we won't have to w-w-worry about getting caught?'"

"It will not be much longer. Fire Watcher told me to lay out four sticks and throw one away each time I come to the temple."

"Can you count that high?"

"Ay-e!" said Storm Rider, as he walked toward the Fire Temple.

The temple was built on a low mound made of dirt. It was larger than lodges in the village, even larger than Great Sun's lodge. Unlike round village houses, the temple was square, and its mud-plastered walls were topped by a separate roof thatched with dried grass cut from the lake's edge. Tall red posts stood on either side of the low entrance, and the red ridgepole supported carved wooden birds painted in bright colors, red, black, white, and yellow. His father once told him that they were great ivory-billed woodpeckers, whose loud cries warned of enemies approaching through the swamp—perfect guardians for the fire temple, the holiest of holy places.

Fire Watcher awaited Storm Rider at the entrance. Storm Rider had never set foot inside before, and he reached for his medicine bag as he stooped to enter the low door. Village gossip claimed that people with impure hearts or who were not born of the people would die if they entered its powerful interior. Storm Rider knew his heart was pure, but he was not born to the Many Waters People. Yet, he knew his father and Bent Woman would never have sent him to the temple if they believed he would die. Neither would Fire Watcher be holding the door open for him to come inside. He stepped through the door without a backward look, and he did not die.

The temple was a foreboding place. It was both shrine and bone house. As his eyes grew accustomed to the smoky, dark interior, he saw the sacred fire burning in a large clay fire pit in the center of the large room. It was fed by four arm-sized logs pointing in the cardinal directions. The priest sitting cross-legged by the fire seemed unaware of his presence. Storm Rider noticed his long curving fingernails—it was Turkey-Buzzard-Man.

Baskets full of bones of nobles sat on shelves in the side room, awaiting burial in Rain Tree mound. In front of the baskets was a waist-high clay platform where Turkey-Buzzard-Man performed his grisly duty of stripping the flesh remaining on year-old corpses before storing their bones in burial baskets. Even in the dim light, Smoke Rider could make out strange, colorfully painted figures on the sides of the bone-cleaning platform. Garlands of fresh cedar hung from rafters, their strong fragrance helping to cover up the smell of death and their power protecting temple occupants from dark forces. Still, a dank, musty odor hovered just above the hard clay floor and lingered on Storm Rider's mantle and hands until he washed in the cleansing waters of Grand Lake.

Spirits were said to hide in temple corners and fly around the ceiling on whiffs of smoke from the eternal fire. Priests who spent most of their lives in the dark interior had a paler skin than everybody else, and their eyes seemed wider and blacker. Storm Rider was thankful he was a healer and prophet instead of an ashen temple priest.

"Welcome to the temple," said Fire Watcher in a voice that sounded suspiciously like the hairy beast at Storm Rider's naming ceremony. "You know your father was my clan brother and cousin. I hope to repay his many kindnesses to me and my family by instructing his son in our laws, customs, and history.

"Before your father died, he asked me to speak with you about these things, because he feared that a man without knowledge of the people's most basic rights and privileges would only be half a healer, one likely to turn to witchcraft to make himself more powerful.

"We will have four sessions," said Fire Watcher. "Each day you will sit facing a different direction, thereby respecting the sacred quartered circle of *Noon-Day-Sun's* passage. Today you face east."

As he settled onto the woven mat, Storm Rider wondered what Fire Watcher was going to tell him that he didn't already know. He was, after all, raised among the people. He was aware of tribal codes of behavior and customs. Ever since he was small, his father had taught him to watch people closely, to pay close attention to what they said and, more particularly, what they did.

"Words and deeds are keys to people's beliefs and feelings," his father often said. "How well people follow the code of conduct and how faithfully their words represent the truth often provide clues for diagnosing sickness and prescribing treatments. Often, a person's future can be seen in what he thinks and does."

Fire Watcher studied Storm Rider's face and seemed to reach into his thoughts.

"You are probably wondering what I can tell you that you don't already know about our people. You may be familiar with most things, but have you ever thought of them all together as *Old Traveler's* plan for the Many Waters People? To truly understand the people, you cannot see only individuals. You must see us as one people, a people unique among all others living in the great swamp."

"How did he know what I was thinking? I thought Bent Woman was the only one in the village who could hear thoughts. I must try to keep my mind clear next time, try to think only of his words."

His regard for the priest soared. He understood now why his father sought Fire Watcher's counsel on so many matters. Fire Watcher had the insight.

Fire Watcher sat on his mat, casually resting his arm on a flexed knee.

"Hear my words," he said, throwing a pinch of tobacco in the sacred fire.

"You should know what I do as a temple priest. It will help you understand why your father wanted you to come see me after his death. You probably think my only jobs are to keep the sacred fire burning and to stand next to Great Sun at ceremonies, but actually I have many duties.

"I keep track of the movement of *Noon-Day-Sun* and *Pale Sun,* so that we will know when to schedule our feasts and retrieve our dead for final interment in the temple or Rain Tree mound. This is a responsibility that comes down from the dim time, when the Many Waters People were one with the Thoucoue, the Little Thoucoue, the Anoy, the Cowah, and the Yoron.

"I keep our laws and history in my head, so I can advise Great Sun and the Beloved Men when disagreements or challenges arise. Only this morning, I reminded Great Sun that Howling Wolf's family owns first rights to the fishing grounds at Blue Bank, because his grandfather had prior claim over

Big Hand's family. Big Hand did not like Great Sun's decision but accepted it because the history was explained to him. Of course, Big Hand has rights of usufruct, as we all do, when Howling Wolf or his family members are not fishing. Knowing history and the law not only keeps us from making mistakes but provides us with an accepted basis for judging everyone fairly.

"I also keep the people's genealogy, here," he said, raising both hands to his head. "Many disputes can be resolved simply by reciting the birth order in our families, even those from previous generations. We are a people founded on kinship, and the tie that binds us all together is the degree of relationship to First Man and First Woman. I am Great Sun's brother, but he is Great Sun because he was born first. I was born last. Always Frowning was the middle brother. So, Great Sun is closer to First Man and First Woman, Always Frowning is closer than I. Birth order also determines what positions we hold in the village, that is, if we are fit to hold those jobs.

"Another thing about being the genealogy keeper is that every couple has to consult with me to make sure they are not too closely related to marry. No one more closely related than the grandchildren of first cousins are permitted to marry.

"So you can see, Snakebite healer, I actually work for my kunti bread. Go now and come back tomorrow when you see Turkey-Buzzard-Man awaken *Noon-Day-Sun*."

Storm Rider walked swiftly across the plaza. When he reached the landing, he waded out waist deep in the lake, splashing cold water over his face and hair. He stood in the water until the clean smell of lake water replaced the temple smell in his nostrils, and, shivering in the cool wind, he hurried to his lodge for a dry breechcloth.

That night, Storm Rider dreamed fitfully, chased by plumes of swirling black smoke with faces that disappeared when he tried to look at them. He woke hungry, long before he was due at the temple. He rummaged around in the dark until he found the bread basket and quickly swallowed two pieces of kunti bread, which he sopped in the still-warm rabbit stew, which his aunt left in the pot sitting in the ashes of the lodge fire.

"Hungry, my nephew?" asked his aunt, awakened by his stirrings. "I am baking garfish cakes today. They will be in the ashes when you return."

When Storm Rider arrived at the temple, Fire Watcher was waiting for him. Storm Rider's mat was on the north side of the sacred fire. Today, he would sit facing south.

"The direction of good luck and warmth," Fire Watcher said casually. "But it also sends us the Mighty Wind."

With a pinch of tobacco and the usual admonition about listening to his words, Fire Watcher began his instruction.

"Long ago, *Old Traveler* divided the people and their Thoucoue brothers into two classes, nobles and commoners. He did this to keep from diluting his divine blood. Only his direct descendants whose bodies carry his blood can become great suns or village chiefs. They are our nobles. Our Thoucoue brothers keep the noble bloodline pure by letting only sons of Great Sun's sisters become chiefs—the next Great Sun always being the oldest son of Great Sun's oldest sister. They say the mother is always certain, even if the father is not, but Thoucoue nobles all marry commoners. Our people keep succession completely pure. The oldest son of Great Sun always succeeds his father as chief, so both his parents must be nobles.

"*Old Traveler* created this noble-commoner division long ago when our people were as numerous as the waves on Grand Lake. Now, we are not as many, and keeping our noble bloodline pure is becoming a problem for our young nobles seeking noble husbands or wives. Great Sun's own son, Little Sun, has chosen not to marry because he has not found a noble girl he wants in the village. We have invited our brothers from the Lower Twisting Snake, the Clamshell, and the Persimmon to our next Black Drink dance, hoping he will find a wife. If not, the line of chiefs in Great Sun's honored family will end."

"Honored priest, what if Little Sun were to marry a commoner?" asked Storm Rider.

"It would not affect him. He could still become Great Sun, but his son could not succeed him. Many young people who are not in line to be chiefs or town officials pay no attention to the class distinctions. They marry whomever they please or, should I say, whoever pleases them, but their children are always commoners and are not allowed to hold any village office. When mixed marriages occur, children always belong to the class of the lowest ranking parent.

"I have noticed that you are attracted to a girl of a commoner family. If you and that girl were to marry, there would only be joy and celebration, since you are not in line to be a Sun or village chief, but remember, because she is a commoner, your children could never become ranking officials. They could, of course, be healers or prophets or warriors, wherever their destinies take them."

"I understand that I am noble, only because my adoptive father was noble," said Storm Rider. "But since there are so many people more closely related to Great Sun than there are offices in the village, the matter is moot anyway. I am happy to be a healer and seer. I have never spoken with Blackbird about this, but I know she is content with who she is. She has no aspiration to be someone she is not and cannot hope to be."

"I've never heard anyone grumble about not being able to hold an office that their class prevents, but I have heard older commoners gripe about having to use formal terms of respect for noble children, when, they say, that children should show respect for adults regardless of class.

"There have always been those grumblings," said Fire Watcher. "Yet, it is only a salubrious formality that recognizes the divine blood of *Noon-Day-Sun's* earthly relatives, and it has been so since the dim time."

Fire Watcher gently pushed the fire logs closer to the center of the sacred fire, making the hot coals glow brighter.

"The fire seems pleased that you are here, Snakebite healer. Tomorrow, face the west."

Storm Rider emerged from the dark temple, shading his eyes from *Noon-Day-Sun*. He didn't understand why being in the temple made his stomach growl like an angry bear, but he remembered his aunt telling him that there would be garfish cakes in the ashes. He was nearly running before he realized how fast he was walking, drawn by the thought of the delicious cakes.

"No, no, go wash," objected his aunt. "You smell like old rotten meat and cedar."

His dip in the chilly lake water was short, but he carried a dried poultice of bloodweed to wash away the odor.

Later, when Storm Rider was telling his aunt what Fire Watcher said, it occurred to him that he had never seen his father treat commoners any differently from nobles.

"Why do you think my father never asked his patients what class they belonged to?"

"That man already knew their class," his aunt replied. "He knew everybody's family tree as well as Fire Watcher, but the real reason that man never asked was because class made no difference to him. He treated everybody the same."

Next morning at dawn, Storm Rider was waiting in front of the temple. He watched Turkey-Buzzard-Man coax *Noon-Day-Sun* into opening her eyes and paint the morning sky with blazing streaks of red and blue. A flock of snowy egrets flew toward Bird Island, dotting the waking sky with white.

Morning ritual completed, Turkey-Buzzard-Man started for the temple door. Without ever looking at Storm Rider, he said: "Fire Watcher waits for you inside."

As was his custom, Fire Watcher fed the fire a pinch of tobacco. Storm Rider took his seat on the floor, facing west, and respectfully waited for Fire Watcher to begin.

"Everyone in the village belongs to one of six clans. Clans are the oldest family lines. They began in the dim time when people and animals were able to talk with each other. The animals encouraged every family to pick one of their number as protector and confidant.

"'Always talk to us,' the animals said. 'Carry a small piece of our fur or a tooth in your medicine bag, so we will always be close. We will warn you of danger and bring you good luck. Call on us when you are hurt or sick or lost and we will help you, but do not misuse our powers because they cannot be restored.'

"'Because some of us were brothers in the dim time, we made rules preventing members of the same clan or brother clans from intermarrying. To have allowed such marriages would have resulted in distant relatives marrying relatives.'

"These were the true words spoken by the totem animals—Wolf, Bear, Dog, Panther, Snake, and Spider," said Fire Watcher, "I pass them to you, faithfully.

"In the old days," he continued, "There were more clans than we have now. Then, some clans were only for nobles and some only for commoners. People of the Wolf, Dog, and Panther clans were discouraged from marrying each other. So were people of the Bear, Snake, and Spider clans. Intermarriage between the two clan groups was encouraged. Such preferred marriages prevented even distant relatives—people who might have shared a common ancestor as far back as the dim time—from marrying. They also maintained the pure successions required to name our chiefs, but as our numbers thinned, the old rules were forgotten. Today, there has been so much intermarriage among clans that all have noble and commoner members.

"Maybe you have noticed the painted figures on the bone-cleaning platform," said Fire Watcher, thrusting his chin toward the sacred altar. "Clan totem animals. These spirits carry the corpse's outside shadow to the Upper World so it will not harm or frighten the living.

"Brothers and sisters belong to their mother's clan, but their father does not. He belongs to the same clan as his brothers and sisters and his nieces and nephews. Remember, a person always inherits his clan through his mother.

"You are an exception, Storm Rider. Your real mother and father were not of the Many Waters People. When you were adopted, you became a member of the Snake clan, because that was the clan of your adoptive father."

"I became a Snake because my father was a Snake. Does adoption always take precedence over normal inheritance?" asked Storm Rider.

"Only when the real parents are unknown, like yours," replied Fire Watcher. "When the real parents are known but are dead or have thrown away the child, and the child is subsequently adopted, the child remains a member of the birth mother's clan. Adoption changes nothing. Since no one knows who your mother was, your adoptive father thus became the only means for you to gain entry into one of the people's clans.

"As you can see, we are a people divided—we belong to different classes and to different clans," said Fire Watcher. "Yet, we are one people. Our government sees to that, and so does the feeling we have here."

Fire Watcher placed his fist over his heart.

"*Old Traveler* gave us our government, too. Through his daughter, *Noon-Day-Sun*, he passed down the laws to First Man and First Woman, and, ever since that time, they have been handed down through his sun descendants. But because *Old Traveler* is all-knowing, he never intended for his laws and means of governing, though sacred, to be put into effect exactly the same way by all the people. He gave people the ability to choose what was best for them, and thus our government differs from that of our brothers and our enemies. What does not differ among us and our brothers, the Thoucoue and others, is that each of our tribes is led by an earth-bound god, following divinely sanctioned laws.

"Every village has a sun chief. Chieftainship passes from father to son unless the old chief has no son, and then their wives or sisters become chiefs temporarily until a new male leader can be chosen by the council. The Persimmon People are led by a female sun to this day. She was so beloved by her people that their council voted her chief for life.

"Chiefs must be men or women of integrity and impeccable principles. The people depend on them to keep the village running smoothly. They settle disputes, carry out justice, and make sure everyone has enough to eat, especially old people and widows. They oversee funerals and ceremonies and lead affairs with other villages and tribes. Along with the Beloved Men, the council of elders, they have the final word in matters of war and peace. Their power is absolute because it is their divine right."

Admitting a blinding white light though the door, Turkey-Buzzard-Man entered the temple, walked directly toward Fire Watcher, and whispered in his ear.

"Great Sun wishes to see me," said Fire Watcher. "I must go. Tomorrow, you face north."

Storm Rider hurried from the temple headed for Speaks Twice's lodge, but the fisherman's mother told him that he and his father were fishing and would not return until after dark.

"Puhhwee! Healer, you need a bath," said Speaks Twice's mother. "You smell just like that dreadful temple."

He bathed in the lake and followed the aroma of fresh venison roast and kunti bread to his lodge.

"You're soon going to have me looking like Big Round Belly's son," said Storm Rider, gobbling down a piece of bread.

"I know how hungry you get sitting in that dark temple," said his aunt. "Must be something over there that makes you want to eat."

"Ah-e, I think it must be looking at all those skinny priests. Looks like they never get anything to eat."

"I do not know about that. Your father used to say he had never seen anyone eat as much as temple priests. They are always asking for food."

"Maybe I should carry Fire Watcher some bread tomorrow. It is my final day. Then, I can go fishing with Speaks Twice, unless someone needs me to perform a healing. Has anyone asked for me?"

"No, everybody seems to be doing okay. Waddling woman complains about her rear-end hurting, but she always hurts somewhere. Far-Away-Woman's little girl had a nosebleed, but it stopped. One of the curs did bite off part of another one's ear, but all 'Half-Ear' did was yelp a bit and then went back to eating fish guts."

Storm Rider put the new leister and strong braided line that Speaks Twice made for him in his basket along with his other fishing gear.

"There, everything's ready in case I get to go fishing tomorrow," he thought. "If we get through at the temple before the shadows leave the plaza, I know where to look for Speaks Twice—he'll be running his traps either at the big dead oak or the hollow stump. Will he be surprised!"

"Aunt, is there enough bread to take to Fire Watcher in the morning?"

"Ay-e, I'll wrap up a few cakes in leaves from the Peeling-Bark tree and put them in your basket. You are just like your father. He never visited Fire Watcher in the temple without carrying him something to eat."

Storm Rider fell asleep listening to the leaves whistling and, in the morning, trudged disappointedly across the plaza. The air was cooler and a breeze blew steadily out of the east.

"The north wind came through last night," he thought. "The fish will be sleeping today. No use trying to wake them. The north wind must have known I would be facing north today."

Storm Rider followed Turkey-Buzzard-Man into the temple and resumed his seat at the perpetual fire. He remained silent until Fire Watcher finished his short opening ritual and then handed the thin bread cakes to the priest.

"Ay-e! I was hoping you could read my mind, prophet," he said smiling. "Your father used to bring some of your aunt's bread when he came to see me, and it is the best in the village. I hope she shares her recipe with her future daughter-in-law."

"Ah-e, good, but the best, I don't know," Storm Rider thought. "You've never eaten Blackbird's kunti and persimmon bread. Now, that's good, too."

"It is your last day at the sacred fire, so I will try not to be windy. I see you have plans for later since you brought your fish basket. I hope whisker mouth awakens. You know they always sleep late after a north wind blows through.

"Yesterday, I was telling you about our government and our chiefs when Great Sun sent for me, so I will resume there.

"Knowing what chiefs do does not always mean that men and women who hold that office make good leaders. Grand Lake village has been fortunate to have had two of the best leaders the Many Waters People have ever known. Great Sun and his father, the Great Sun before him, always have ensured that our storage bins were filled with oak nuts, pond lily and greenbriar roots, and other foods in season. They redistributed surplus to everyone instead of keeping it for their family and friends or wasting it on extravagant feasts. They returned to the old ways by sponsoring feasts every new moon and restored the meaning to the Black Drink ceremony, which had degenerated into an irreverent spectacle and wild orgy for both young and married people. Their war clubs helped save the village when Black Faces slipped past our sentries and burned our lodges. The old Sun gave his life in that battle defending his people. Your own father saved the village on another occasion.

"Great Sun has several people who help with village duties and advise on matters of state," continued Fire Watcher. "Sun Woman, his wife, is his main advisor, but she does not hold an official position in the administration. Yet, I know personally that he seeks her guidance on every important matter that affects the village and often on everyday matters, too. In the old days, the people used to have an assistant chief, who carried out Great Sun's wishes, saw to the routine jobs, and scheduled feasts, dances, and foreign visits, but since we no longer have as many people, Always Frowning and I now share those duties. Always Frowning is the Village Keeper responsible for maintaining the grounds and public buildings and for seeing that all arrangements are in place for our ceremonies and feasts. Because I am a temple priest, I am not officially in the village administration. You already know what my duties are, but what you may not know is how important the sacred fire is to the welfare of the people—so important that, in the past, negligent fire watchers who allowed the fire to go out were put to death.

"I thought my shadow was bound for the Upper World when the Mighty Wind put out the sacred fire the day before you came to us," Fire Watcher said. "I even offered to tie the cord around my own throat, but Great Sun said no, that I did not have to die when it was *Old Traveler* himself who put the fire out. He said that *Old Traveler* had a reason for extinguishing the flame and that none of his earthly descendants could have prevented him from carrying out his plan. Good thing fires at Prairie Landing and Red Earth villages still burned, because I was able to secure the sacred coals to relight our fire. It has not gone out now in seventeen winters."

Storm Rider empathized with Fire Watcher and was glad the priest had not been killed. He understood why his father liked the fire's guardian. He did, too.

"As you know, Great Sun, Always Frowning, and I are brothers. Great Sun is the oldest, and I am the youngest. Brothers usually make the best village leaders because they grow up together and know each other better than anyone outside the family. Yet, if there is any jealousy or friction between Great Sun and us, another member of the sun family will be appointed in our place. None exists between us, although I wish Always Frowning would be more sensitive when he tells the villagers what to do. He did not have good people skills growing up, and he has only gotten worse with age, but he is a good person.

"Great Sun enjoys absolute power among the Many Waters People. His word is final in all matters of state and property and person. We his brothers serve at his behest. We have no power that is not sanctioned by him. But you know the people are also served by a council of elders, the Beloved Men, which shares authority with Great Sun, and although Great Sun could act unilaterally on any matter—it is his divine right—I have never heard of any of our suns ever exercising that right. Great Sun and the council always come to agreement, always unanimous, and always in the best interest of the people. There is a story of long ago that one of the young suns, who defied the wishes of the council and the people, prematurely died under mysterious circumstances, so it seems that, even if a wayward sun does come to power, *Old Traveler* still manages to keep the best interests of the people at heart.

"The Beloved Men are our elders. They are not all nobles, although four of the six sitting members are. They are chosen by their respective clans for their wisdom, experience, oratory, and ability to compromise. Their authority is nearly equal to that of Great Sun but comes to us in a different way—by consensus, not decree. Great Sun not only listens to words of the Beloved Men, he will not act without their approval.

"I know you are getting anxious to see if you can wake the fish, healer," said Fire Watcher. "This is why I saved the longest instruction for your last day. Whisker mouth will not be as sleepy tomorrow."

"Nor I."

Fire Watcher smiled, or so Storm Rider thought.

"I hope he knows I was joking," he thought.

"Not much longer now. Here is some water. Drink. It will help you swallow my words.

"Each of the lake villages has four or five war chiefs. We have six, but Grand Lake is the largest village and also the capital of all the people. Unlike civil chiefs, war chiefs earn their positions by being great warriors and leaders of men. Class and birthright make no difference. There are always more war chiefs than civil chiefs because of the danger they constantly face. If we only had one or two war chiefs and they were to be killed in battle, we would be at the mercy of Black Faces and Red Sticks.

"We are a peace-loving nation," proclaimed Fire Watcher, "But we defend our borders and our people with the fury of the big swamp cat protecting her kittens.

"You already know about the position we priests and healers hold in the village. We are keepers of the ancient traditions, the genealogy, and the history of the people. We watch the sacred fire. We heal wounds and illnesses and dream of things to come. The people's government would only be a half government without us to counterbalance those who would rather make war than live in peace. Although we do not hold government offices, like the priests of old, we are the religious leaders of our people and spiritual advisors of Great Sun. He has let it be known that his door is open to us at any time of the day or night. Not even the Beloved Men or the war chiefs enjoy such open access to him.

"Every village on the lake has its own sun. Many of those suns are uncles or cousins of mine. Divine blood courses in their bodies just like it does in ours, but not as strongly because we—Great Sun, Always Frowning, and I—are closer kin to *Old Traveler*. Each village has its own Beloved Men and its own government and acts according to its own laws and wishes. No village counsels or interferes with any other, with one exception," explained Fire Watcher. "Revenge raids are the sole prerogative of every village, unless a village asks for our help. As you know, Great Sun is the supreme sun of all the villages of the people throughout the great swamp. When we receive such a request, Great Sun and the Beloved Men meet in council to consider the proposal. Their approval must be unanimous before our warriors will join the war. Only Great Sun on advice of the Beloved Men can approve or avert general warfare. Only Great Sun and the council have the power to divert food from our food bins to help other villages in need.

"That, young healer, is the basis for our government. Hai, I have spoken."

The priest stood, gathered his doeskin mantle around him, and disappeared in the side room where the burial baskets were stored. When he returned, he handed Storm Rider a small quartz crystal.

"This is my gift to you, Snakebite healer. Hold it up to *Noon-Day-Sun* when you need protection or counsel. It holds her healing power even in dark places. Hold it up at the bone-digging. Go now while her light shines. My debt to your father is paid."

13

The Bone Basket

No fanfare awaited Storm Rider when he left the temple that bright fall day. The shadows were already long, but he found a sun-bathed spot and held up the crystal toward *Noon-Day-Sun*. Rainbow colors refracted through the flat faces on the crystal as he turned it around in his fingers, but they conveyed no vision, gave no counsel—they were silent.

"Maybe I am not meant to see visions," he thought to himself. "I have never seen the future. I have never foreseen enemy raids, floods, or mighty winds. Only Bent Woman can do that. I have trouble figuring out what my friends are going to do the next minute, especially Speaks Twice."

He peered at the crystal again, halfway expecting to fall into a daydream or a trance, but nothing happened.

"Father always told me that the people recognize true prophets by their ability to see the future," pondered Storm Rider. "So, why do they judge me by the circumstances of my arrival and how I look? Being delivered by the Mighty Wind and protected by rattlesnakes does not open my eyes to the future. Bearing *Lightning-Spirit-Bird's* jagged mark in my hair and possessing different colored eyes do not show me what will happen. I cannot see the future, not even with this magic crystal, and the people will find out soon enough."

He remembered Speaks Twice making a big fuss about his uncanny success in the shell game.

"Y-y-you see the pebble through the c-c-clamshell," said Speaks Twice, after watching him correctly pick the right shell ten times in a row. "Y-y-you have the vision."

"You know I cannot see the pebble," objected Storm Rider. "All I do is watch the shuffler closely, and then I guess. A little luck helps, too."

"Huh! And crows do not eat d-d-dead fish either," said Speaks Twice. "P-p-people say I am lucky, and I c-c-chose the right shell half the time. You already k-k-know where the s-s-shuffler is going to leave the pebble before he does."

Yet, prophet or not, Storm Rider still considered himself fortunate. Very few young men and women—never before an orphan—were chosen to be Tradition Keepers. He thanked his father for sending him to Bent Woman and Fire Watcher. They were patient teachers and exceptional people. Their love of and pride in the Many Waters People's way of life came through in everything they did and said.

He tucked away the crystal into his medicine bag and watched the darkening sky. Huge, cold drops splattered in his face, and he took shelter under the brush arbor as the heavens opened. Women were running for their lodges, except for waddling woman and her quiet friend, who never stopped peeling lotus roots, even as puddles collected around them. Blackbird was already gone.

The thunderstorm moved off as quickly as it had come. Storm Rider watched as it rolled across the lake transforming the water into the same dark gray color as the cloud. The only way to distinguish lake from cloud was by the whitecaps on the lake. Lightning lit up the boiling cloud layers, and Thunder could be heard after the sun returned and turned shivering cold into a cool damp blanket.

Just as he started for his lodge, he heard a blue jay whistle. He looked around, expecting to see Speaks Twice, but it was not Speaks Twice coming toward him.

"Blackbird!"

"Your aunt told my mother you finished your instruction in the temple," she said. "Congratulations. I know your father would be proud of you."

"Thanks, Blackbird."

"I have been watching where *Noon-Day-Sun* awakens and know the time nears when your father's bones must be returned to the temple before his burial in Rain Tree Mound."

"Ah-e. Turkey-Buzzard-Man says we go to Round Island five sleeps from now. Speaks Twice is going with me, but he also asked Buzzard and Broken Tooth to go, and I do not understand why. Buzzard never liked my father. I asked the priest why he was sending them with us, and all he would say was that it would take all four of us to find the shells marking the grave."

"You can be sure he has some purpose in mind," she said, flashing her heart-melting smile. "He knows you and Buzzard would not dare kill each other while you are digging bones. Maybe he thinks you will become fast friends by the time you return."

"Makes no sense to me."

"If you want me to make the basket for your father's bones, I would be honored," said Blackbird.

"Ah-e. I would like that. I know my father would be pleased, too. He always thought of you like a daughter."

"And he was like a father to me," she said. "I miss his warm smile."

"The sweat starts in the morning."

"Ah-e, I know." she said, hugging him tightly and nuzzling his neck.

"Come by my lodge later. I have something for you and Speaks Twice."

She walked quickly to her house, while he stood as stiffly as a lodge post, watching her until she disappeared inside. With his heart pounding in his ears and his skin on fire, Storm Rider walked briskly to the lake and waded out waist-deep. He dove into the cold water and swam underwater until his lungs felt like they would explode, surfacing with a shout.

The shout awakened an old man, napping under the shade of a big live oak tree at the landing.

"Are you drowning?" the old man inquired. "Have you seen enemy dugouts? Or do you shout because life is good, healer?"

"Life is good," he said, running past the old man who already had resumed snoring.

Covered with goose bumps, he ran to his lodge, finding it empty. His aunt had rejoined the other women under the arbor. He kicked off his wet breechcloth and tucked a dry one between his legs and pulled it over his belt. He rubbed his arms and legs vigorously and fastened the lodge flap to the lintel, letting the brightness stream into the dark interior. It was not cold enough for a fire, and he was beginning to warm up. He pulled a few dried leaves from the strand of willow hanging from a rafter and began crushing them in his cypress medicine bowl.

His thoughts drifted to Blackbird, the upcoming sweat, and the trip to Round Island.

"Family and friends always dig their loved ones' bones, so why are Buzzard and Broken Tooth coming with me and Speaks Twice?" he wondered. "Turkey-Buzzard-Man must have good reason to put us together, when everyone knows that we do not like each other."

What he did not know was that before his death, his father asked Turkey-Buzzard-Man to send the four of them to find his grave.

Although participating in the bone-digging rite was considered a high honor, it brought the living into potential contact with the shadow of the deceased and was very dangerous, requiring protection from ghost sickness. Members of the bone-digging party were required to spend four days in the sweat lodge before going and four after returning. They could drink water and eat grilled venison at night when they went home to sleep, but they could not eat acorn cakes, greenbriar-root dumplings, or fish. Fish and plant food made the body weak and susceptible to ghost sickness.

Storm Rider put up his deer antler pestle and bowl and went looking for Speaks Twice. He found him on the lake bank, cleaning two large catfish.

"I-i-if I had known you were c-c-coming, I would have s-s-saved you a whisker mouth to clean," said Speaks Twice.

"I'll forgive you this time."

"Healer, I'm h-h-honored to be going with you to dig your father's bones, but I am not l-l-looking forward to s-s-smelling Buzzard sweat for eight days. I hope b-b-bone picker has a good reason for t-t-teaming us with them."

"Come by my lodge in the morning," said Storm Rider. "Before sunrise."

"Okay. S-s-should I wear my smelly b-b-breechcloth or the bright-colored one I wear to dances?"

"Why? Are you planning to dance with Buzzard? Doesn't matter anyway, we won't be wearing anything inside."

"Do you mean some l-l-lucky maiden might get to see me n-n-naked? I think I'll just leave my b-b-breechcloth at home and walk through the village without any c-c-clothes. No, I better not. I'd be k-k-kidnapped before I reached the plaza."

"Sorry, woman pleaser. Nobody but waddling woman is up at dawn, and I don't think she can run fast enough to grab your man club."

"Uugh! T-t-that thought makes me want to wear my b-b-bearskin coat. See you tomorrow. I've got to get these fish to my aunt before it's too d-d-dark to see."

Storm Rider watched his friend trot across the plaza. He saw him stop and pick up a crying toddler. Whatever he said to the unhappy child stopped her tears, and by the time he put the child down, she was laughing and babbling. Speaks Twice had that effect on everyone, young and old. Well, almost everyone—and two of the ones that were immune to his charisma would be sitting in the steam with them in the morning.

Storm Rider headed back to his lodge. He didn't tell Speaks Twice that Blackbird had a gift for him, but he'd already made up his mind to carry her gift to the fisherman in the morning. He planned to wait until black dark before he went to see Blackbird.

Blackbird was happy Storm Rider wanted her to weave his father's bone basket. She had been collecting materials since her trip to the tall cane brake in anticipation, but even if a relative was making the old healer's bone basket, she still needed cane and dye for the sitting mats she was making for the sweat ceremony. Those mats were now finished, and she would give them to Storm Rider tonight.

She wanted everything to be perfect, so she carefully followed old tradition. She let the strips absorb the dew for eight days before dying them. For black color, she boiled the strips in a watery mash of crushed black walnut hulls. For yellow, she boiled them in a decoction of mashed broadleaf dock leaves and roots. For red, she used the same dock dye, only she soaked the strips in the lime-water pond for four days before boiling them in the dye. The strips accepted the dyes perfectly. The colors were brilliant.

"The blacks are like crow feathers, and the reds are shinier than red seed," her mother said.

"I spent so much time weaving the sitting mats that Storm Rider and Speaks Twice thought I had forsaken them," she thought. "When they see them, they will know what took so long."

She chose to decorate them with the blackbird-eye design, her namesake. Unlike the alligator-entrails design she planned to use on the bone basket, the blackbird-eye design was fairly simple to produce. Warp-and-weft was perpendicular. She created the outer border of the eye by running a yellow warp strip over one red strip, under two red and one black strips, over two black strips, under one black strip, over two black strips, under two black strips and one red strip, over one red strip, under three red strips, and finally over two red strips. This pattern was started again after running under twenty yellow strips. For the touching warp strip, she lengthened or shortened the number of weft strips that she ran over or under as needed to form the diagonal eye—always counting, always watching which strip needed to go over or under. The work took intense focus and nimble fingers. It also took its toll on fingernails, and her fingers bled constantly from many tiny cuts inflicted by the razor-sharp edges of the cane.

"If Storm Rider only knew how many times I had to take out the strips and start over, he would say I had the patience of a heron waiting to spear a minnow," she thought. "Speaks Twice would say I was a blue jay drunk from eating too many elderberries."

Her deft hands had already formed a double-hand-size section of the bone-basket bottom since she had entered the lodge. She planned to weave a lidded, trunk-shaped funerary basket as long as her arm and two hands wide. Plaits-Starting lent her an old bone basket from her collection to copy, and she had been studying the warp-and-weft pattern for many sleeps, memorizing the counting and the over-and-under sequence.

"One red warp strip goes over five yellow strips, under two, over five, under four, over one, under four, over five, under two, over one, under six, over one, and under six. The first black warp strip touching the red strip goes over five yellow strips, under two, over five, under two, over one . . . ugh, I forget," Blackbird lamented. "I'll just keep the old basket in front of me."

"When are you going to give Storm Rider his sitting mat?" asked her mother. "I thought his sweat started tomorrow."

"He's coming later."

"After dark?"

"Ah-e."

"I do not guess he will be coming inside then," said her mother knowingly.

"No, I will give them to him outside."

"Tell him we will be thinking of him at the bone-digging, and watch out for prying eyes, daughter. I think I hear scratching on the lintel. Better get the mats."

The couple walked into the inky blackness under the moss-draped, low-limbed live oak beside her lodge. They embraced.

"What do you have in your hands?" asked Storm Rider.

"Sitting mats for the sweat tomorrow, for you and Speaks Twice."

"Thank you. I never thought about mats," said Storm Rider, pressing his nose against her cheeks and touching her lips with his.

"You need to get your rest, but I wanted to wish you luck," said Blackbird, "And remind you what awaits you after your father's bones are returned."

She placed his hand on her breast and nipped his ear with her teeth. Then she was gone, and he could not see her until she opened the lodge flap and waved.

Storm Rider stood for a long time, marveling at his good fortune and wishing his upcoming ordeal was over. The wait would seem like forever.

He tried to get her crooked smile and warm body out of his mind, as he headed through the dark silhouettes of the lodges. He tripped over a scurrying raccoon and was jolted back to the trial ahead of him.

"I worry what Speaks Twice might do or say after being cooped up with Buzzard for eight days," he thought. "At least, we will be in the sacred sweat lodge where nobody would dare harm another and risk incurring the wrath of Great Sun. I hope Speaks Twice holds his tongue, it can hit as hard as a blow from a war club."

His aunt was smiling when he entered the lodge.

"Hungry?" she asked.

"No."

"It is hard to believe that our loved one has been gone for nearly twelve moons," his aunt said. "Tomorrow, you begin purifying yourself so you will not catch ghost sickness at his grave. I know how hard this is going to be for you, but do not let your feelings toward Buzzard cloud what is most important."

"It is not me I worry about, aunt."

"Can you control Speaks Twice or Buzzard?" asked his aunt.

"No."

"Then you must not worry about what you cannot do anything about."

His aunt began putting away the shell beads she was stringing.

He took the quartz crystal from his medicine bag and turned it over and over in his fingers. He thought about tomorrow and the next few days.

Bent Woman's words filled his thoughts.

"Your father's two shadows must be reunited before the transformation to spiritual life is complete," she told him. "His inner shadow has already made the journey to the Upper World, but his outer shadow lingers in this world, never straying far from his bones. This is why we bury our loved ones in hidden graves far from our homes. For as long as his outside shadow remains on earth, there is always a danger that people who cross its path will get ghost sickness—ghost sickness causes people to go crazy and die screaming.

"You will lead a bone-digging party to Round Island to find your father's grave and mark it so the bone pickers do not have to look for it. The next morning, Turkey-Buzzard-Man will dig up your father's remains and bring them back to the temple. His remains will be safe to touch then because his outside shadow leaves for the Upper World when his bones are exhumed, if it has not already made the journey.

"At the temple, Turkey-Buzzard-Man cleans his bones with his long fingernails and places them in a new cane basket. He puts the basket on a shelf in the anteroom until the Dance of the Dead is held at Rain Tree mound. Then, his bones along with those of all honored dead who have died since the last dance are buried in the mound in one big funeral. This is our way. This is the way it has always been."

The Dance of the Dead was still two moons away.

"The dark is heavy, nephew. My eyes are heavy. I will wake you in the morning."

"I will be awake. Sleep well, aunt."

He lay on his mat, listening to the swamp sounds. They seemed louder than usual. The chirping of the crickets and the croaking of the tree frogs blended in wild, unrehearsed song. The deep "ouar-ouar-ron" of the bullfrogs and the "who-whoo-who-whoo-who-whooaw" of the hoot owls joined in. The bellowing alligators in Pond Lily Cove and the howling wolf pack on Fish Island added their voices to the chorus. It was as if every animal in the swamp was trying to outsing every other.

He loved the music of the night. It always cleared his thoughts and made his troubles small. His father always told him to listen to the animals. "The creatures are wise," he said. "They know what is important and what is not. They never lie or mislead."

The voices of the animals all said the same thing—the upcoming days were to be devoted to honoring the memory of his father. His quarrel with Buzzard was unimportant by comparison.

Suddenly, he was startled by a fluttering in the lodge. The dreaded screech owl lit on his arm. How did the bird get in the lodge? He had shut the door flap. Strange, he could see its big yellow eyes in the dark, but he could not feel its sharp toes digging into his arm.

"Why are you here, tonight of all nights, messenger of death and misfortune?" he wondered. "Am I dreaming?"

Though it was pitch black in the lodge, he could see the little owl plainly. He watched it puff its feathers and turn its head around backwards. Its eyes grew larger and larger, and suddenly he realized those large eyes were his. He was seeing what owl already had seen.

He saw two overturned dugouts, and *Long Black Being* carrying three limp bodies in its huge hands. He watched the creature leave the swamp and wade through the Waving Grass taking its meal to its filthy lodge in the west.

Then, the Rain Tree materialized, and there on the top branch was *Golden Face Man.* Just as *Long Black Being* reached for *Golden Face Man,* ice started falling from the sky, and the tree disappeared in a thick mist.

He heard the voice of Blackbird-Eyes-Shining calling to him.

"I am coming, Blackbird."

She put her hand on his shoulder and gently shook it.

"Wake up, Storm Rider," said his aunt, shaking him again. "Open your eyes. Blackbird is not here. Time to get up. Your sweat starts soon."

"I must have been dreaming," he said, putting his medicine bag around his neck. No use frightening his aunt by telling her he had seen the screech owl on the very day his father's honoring ceremony was to began.

"May your guardian protect you," she said, as he rose to leave. "And brush that feather from your arm."

14

Ambush at Round Island

If looks drew blood, there would be four bodies in the sweat lodge. It was apparent that Strikes Blows and Laughing Otter had warned their sons about the consequences of dishonoring the memory of the old Snakebite healer. Neither Buzzard nor Speaks Twice spoke for four long days, but then they did not need to speak. Their glares did the talking. The only time Buzzard looked away from Speaks Twice's face was to stare at Storm Rider. Storm Rider knew Speaks Twice had gotten under Buzzard's skin with his caustic comments, and it was easy to see that Buzzard was having a hard time restraining himself from lashing out physically at the fisherman. Nobody ever insulted Buzzard before, and Speaks Twice was relentless. Buzzard never encountered anyone like these two men, who were not afraid of him, did not cower before him, or slink away during his rages.

Storm Rider and Broken Tooth barely acknowledged each other's presence. They had no quarrel with each other, and their mutual dislike was brokered by the intensity of Buzzard's hatred of Storm Rider and Speaks Twice. Speaks Twice, on the other hand, considered Broken Tooth a smaller version of Buzzard and a worthy candidate for his barbs and pointed looks.

Sitting in the hissing steam, drenched in sweat, Storm Rider tried to concentrate on the happy days spent with his father and on his future life with Blackbird-Eyes-Shining. Sometimes when Buzzard's and Broken Tooth's conversations interrupted his daydreaming, he would shut his eyes and try to empty his mind of all thought—focusing on the effort to achieve complete mindlessness, to enter into a state of nothingness. He never completely succeeded, but on his third day in the steam, he was startled when Turkey-Buzzard-Man touched him on the shoulder and told him it was time to go home. The day's sweat was over, almost as soon as it began, it seemed. He could not account for any of his thoughts since early in the morning.

That night, while lying on his sleeping mat, he mulled over his unusual experience that night, wondering if he really emptied his mind or if he merely slept all day, sitting up.

"Did you dream?" his aunt asked.

"No, I don't think so. At least I don't remember dreaming," answered Storm Rider.

"Well, then, it does not matter whether you put yourself in a trance or slept. The effects were the same—your mind was empty," said his aunt.

"I guess so," he said, lying back on his sleeping mat.

"Your father told me that Bent Woman is able to bring on sleep in the blink of an eye. One minute she is wide awake and the next in deep sleep. It does not matter where she is or how many people are around, and she can be standing or sitting down. He said her eyes flutter wildly like she is watching something moving very fast, and when she awakes, she often says she has been visiting the spirits. Her prophecies usually come right after these spirit visits," said his aunt.

"I remember nothing, so it must have been sleep and not a trance."

"Seems to me like you opened your mind, but *Old Traveler* simply had no message for you. Now rest. You need your strength. You are so thin that you could squeeze though one of the openings in your fish basket."

"A day of your cooking will make me as fat as I was before."

Storm Rider and Speaks Twice were waiting at the entrance to the sweat lodge when Buzzard and Broken Tooth arrived.

"Our last day, finally," said Buzzard, placing his hand on Broken Tooth's shoulder. "Then maybe we can get away from the bad smell."

"I'm afraid not, it c-c-comes from your rear-end," said Speaks Twice.

"Shuh," cautioned Storm Rider, "Here comes Turkey-Buzzard-Man."

The priest extracted three or four dozen hot clamshells that were heating in the fire outside the sweat lodge and placed them in the swept-clean, puddled-clay pit in the center of the small, temporary, bent-pole building. The young men dropped their breechcloths and took their seats around the pile of shells. Turkey-Buzzard-Man poured a pot full of water on the shells, instantly filling the shelter with sizzling steam. Beads of sweat broke out on their bodies.

Storm Rider closed his eyes. He remembered the screech owl that visited him on the eve of the sweat. Where did the feather come from? He began to think he must have imagined the whole incident—it was too improbable, finding an owl feather immediately after he had dreamed about the evil little owl. Perhaps the owl was not evil at all but an omen. The bird had come to him at night, the time when owls normally are awake, hunting, hooting, courting. The evil owl that foretells death and misfortune comes during the daytime, when real owls are sleeping.

He considered the rest of his dream—*Long Black Being*, the Rain Tree, and *Golden Face Man* rising into the clouds. If the owl was only his mind playing tricks on him, then everything else must have been a confused nightmare. Still, it worried him. He told no one about seeing the owl or about his dream, not even Speaks Twice. He wanted to talk first with Bent Woman. She would know whether it was a bad dream or a vision, but speaking with anyone except the others in the sweat lodge or his immediate family was forbidden during purification rites.

He slept the remainder of the day, a dreamless sleep, and awakened to Speaks Twice's voice.

"The p-p-priest is here to c-c-commute our sentence. Healer, let us leave this m-m-miserable hut."

"That's right, go play with curs. Come on, Broken Tooth, at least we have a little time before we have to see these fleas again," taunted Buzzard, freed momentarily from the etiquette of the sweat bath.

"H-h-have you been feeling all right, healer?" asked Speaks Twice. "You've hardly s-s-said a word for the past two days."

"I have been practicing sleeping, tall catcher of fish"

"Uh-huh! I hope p-p-practice is over now. W-w-we've got a long way to go tomorrow, and I'm going to need some h-h-help paddling."

"See you at the landing."

At dawn on the eve of the one-year anniversary of his father's burial at Round Island, Storm Rider and Speaks Twice arrived at the landing, paddles in hand, and climbed into Speaks Twice's dugout with the tall sides designed for carrying lots of gear and fish baskets. When Laughing Otter hollowed out the dugout, he left seats at both ends of the canoe, essential for sitting effortlessly when deploying or running nets and traps or stringing or casting lines.

When Speaks Twice asked why his father had left the seats—none of the other dugouts had them—he laughed and told his son that he would find out soon enough. And he did. After returning from his first all-day fishing trip in the swamp without having raw knees and an aching back, Speaks Twice marveled at his father's foresight.

Buzzard and Broken Tooth got into Buzzard's brand new dugout with its low sides, narrow bottom, and polished and oil-coated exterior—a war canoe, built for speed and stealth. They kept dipping their paddles in the water, until Turkey-Buzzard-Man raised his arm and told them to listen.

"Find the seven red shells," he said, "If they are still in line, dig seven small holes two hand spans apart and seven hand spans deep along the line. If the shells are scattered, dig seven holes in each of the cardinal directions leading away from the shells. Remember, if you have to start a new line of holes, always dig seven holes, no more, no fewer. Seven respects the sacred directions and the center.

"When you find the bones, refill the hole, and set out these seven turkey buzzard feathers around the remains. Hold vigil at least seven steps outside the circle of feathers, until I arrive tomorrow.

"Remember, do not speak unless absolutely necessary and then only in whispers," warned the priest. "If the corpse's outside shadow is still hovering nearby, it might hear you and try to invade your bodies hoping to unite with your shadows. Hopefully, the corpse's shadow will have journeyed already to the Upper World, but it may have been too frightened to go by itself and could be waiting for *Old Traveler* to personally accompany it to the Upper World when its former body is exhumed.

"May your guardians watch over each of you," said Turkey-Buzzard-Man, as the two dugouts pulled away from the landing.

As the voyagers paddled past the last hut, Storm Rider smiled at Speaks Twice sitting in the stern.

"Yes, I h-h-heard," said his friend. "The blue jay w-w-whistle."

"She lets us know she goes with us."

The dugouts pulled out into the big part of the lake avoiding the many sunken limbs in the shallows. The water was clear and cool, and schools of fish could be seen in the depths. Thin, feathery clouds floated in from the north riding on the light breeze. They would turn into a high, gray blanket by afternoon.

"If we do not get a s-s-strong head wind, we should reach Round Island before *Noon-Day-Sun* t-t-travels halfway across the sky," Speaks Twice said, pulling hard on the paddle in an effort to keep up with Buzzard and Broken Tooth, who already were several canoe lengths ahead.

They stroked in unison—a practiced motion that came from years of paddling together all over the lakes and waterways in the swamp. Their strong strokes sent the dugout across the wrinkled surface of Grand Lake like an arrow shot from a bow. Yet, they were no match for Buzzard's sleek war canoe or his powerful back and muscled arms. With Broken Tooth helping, the dugout seemed to fly above the water. The unacknowledged competition was over before the dugouts reached Pond Lily Cove, which was just out of sight of the village.

"What is the matter? Are you slugs tired all ready, or do you always paddle like girls," taunted Buzzard, his voice carrying over the water.

"W-w-well, Buzzard, it's good to see you are s-s-still a Buzzard," replied Speaks Twice. "D-d-do you think it could be w-w-what you eat that makes you so pleasant, or c-c-could it be gas pains? Hey, healer, do you have a c-c-cure for gas?"

"Stop baiting him, Speaks Twice. We are pledged to honor my father's bones."

"Tell him that, my friend."

"He knows," said Storm Rider. "He makes his own choices. We should not let him make ours for us."

Buzzard's dugout continued to pull ahead and, thankfully for Storm Rider, out of earshot of Speaks Twice's continual barrage of name calling and taunting.

The big orange disk of *Noon-Day-Sun* peeped through the cypress trees. Flight after flight of ibis, egrets, and herons flew overhead. Storm Rider wondered where these birds went during the day. He and his father saw many wading birds on their medicine-gathering trips but never as many as filled the skies at dawn. A flock of teal—the first he had seen since the oaks dropped their acorns—swooped low over the dugouts, their rapidly beating wings whistling in the wind. Buzzard stopped paddling long enough to take a shot at the little ducks with an imaginary bow and arrow. Garfish slapped the water with their tails, and a flock of squawking vultures fought over the remains of a deer that had strayed too close to the swamp cat's lair.

The boys paddled steadily into the bright gray glare of morning. They entered Big Cypress Lake, the wide left-hand arm of Grand Lake fed by Little Eagle Lake and Rain Tree Water. Alligators lined the shore, and raucous coots swam in and out among lily pads, diving for underwater plants in the shallows. Gray squirrels hidden in the thick drapery of moss fussed noisily at the canoes as they passed. The voyagers startled a mother bobcat and her two half-grown cubs fishing for crawfish along the muddy bank. The mother cat screamed her displeasure before she and her cubs vanished into the dark shadows beneath the trees.

They heard the sound of rushing water before they could see the black water pouring out of the chute at Bird Island. The black water drained the huge cypress swamp hidden behind the lakeshore. The swamp was once part of Long River but had been cut off when the river shifted eastward. As long as Big Cypress Lake was lower than the water level in the swamp, the swamp water emptied into the lake, but when the lake was higher, the flow reversed and filled the swamp.

"The lake and the swamp p-p-play a continual game of back-and-forth," said Speaks Twice. "I wish we were fishing. W-w-watch, Storm Rider, the bugs disappear the instant they reach the mixing water. If I had my s-s-spool line and baited hook, we could catch all the big mouths we could eat before any of them realized what was happening to their friends."

"Too bad the chute lies in Prairie Landing village's fishing grounds," said Storm Rider.

"M-m-maybe you could ask Red Club if we could fish here. You two seem to be g-g-good friends now."

Speaks Twice abandoned his fruitless argument and returned to his paddling, casting one last wistful look at the largemouth bass noisily devouring the silver-sided shad caught in the swirling water.

To Storm Rider, the chute was a landmark. Round Island lay directly across the lake, and he and Speaks Twice paddled hard to reach the water-locked section of lakeshore before Buzzard's canoe. Buzzard, realizing he had already passed the island, dug his paddle into the water spinning the light craft around and paddled furiously, water flying, drenching Broken Tooth, but Speaks Twice and Storm Rider were already pulling their dugout onto the bank when Buzzard nosed his canoe into the reeds lining the muddy bank.

Speaks Twice glanced at Buzzard but did not say a word. He merely thrust out his chin and grinned.

Buzzard fumed under his breath—he did not want the ghost of the old Snakebite healer entering his shadow. As they got out of the dugout, Storm Rider saw Buzzard squinting at Broken Tooth, and Broken Tooth cowering, as usual, accepting the blame for Buzzard's dugout not winning the informal race to the island.

A thick canebrake had claimed the island after the old village was abandoned. The men collected their deer shoulder-blade hoes and sharp digging sticks and headed into the cane.

"Turkey-Buzzard-Man said to look first under the big live oak tree closest to the old landing, the one with limbs touching the ground," whispered Broken Tooth, who was also mindful of the island's resident shadow.

"Looks like they all have limbs t-t-touching the ground," observed Speaks Twice, frowning.

"Me and Broken Tooth will go this way," said Buzzard, pointing with his digging stick. "You two go that way, if you are not afraid."

"Wait!" Storm Rider said, growing uneasy. "I have a strange feeling. Something is not right. No birds are singing."

"What! Now, we are supposed to wait for birds to sing? You have lost your head. Come on, Tooth, we have bones to find so we can leave this place and present company."

"You might want to look at these footprints before you lose your head for real," said Storm Rider, pointing to the tracks leading into the cane.

"Footprints? A shadow does not leave footprints," said Broken Tooth, growing uneasy.

"Let me see these so-called tracks," exclaimed Buzzard, squatting for a closer look.

"Someone has tried to rub them out with a leafy branch. See, you can tell the branch has not been broken long. The sap oozes," said Buzzard, as he read the signs in the mud. "The weaving on the sandal print is not one of our patterns."

"Shuuh. Be q-q-quiet," Speaks Twice whispered. "Y-y-you three better come here and t-t-take a look."

Quietly, the men walked to where Speaks Twice stood, staring at four large dugouts hidden in the bushes. They had been hastily covered with limbs, and the paddle used to hack off the limbs lay beside the nearest canoe. The end was flat unlike their pointed paddles.

"Smell that?" Buzzard asked. "Rotten alligator oil. My father says Black Faces use it to keep away mosquitos and deer flies."

"Black Faces!"

The canebrake erupted with blood-chilling war whoops. Warriors—their faces and bodies painted black—rushed out of the cane, filling the air with arrows. Broken Tooth screamed and fell to his knees, an arrow sticking completely through his left bicep. Buzzard saw his friend go down and, bending low to offer less of a target, rushed to his side. He bulled over two of the war club-brandishing attackers with his shoulder and headed for two bowmen who were dragging Broken Tooth toward their dugout. They were so surprised by Buzzard's fearless rush that they let go of Broken Tooth's hair and stepped out of the way. The tall one hit Buzzard on the back with his bow, breaking the bow in two, while the other tried to nock an arrow so he could shoot this crazed bear. Buzzard swatted him aside like he was a pesky deerfly.

Grabbing Broken Tooth's uninjured arm, Buzzard lifted his wounded friend and draped him across his shoulders. When he reached his dugout, he slid Broken Tooth off his shoulders and with a mighty shove, pushed the canoe into the lake as far as he could. He turned to face the on-rushing Black Faces with his bare hands. An arrow dug into his thigh. Another entered his forearm as he threw up his arm in defense. He never saw the heavy blow that struck the back of his neck and sent him into a dark and empty world.

When the attack started, Storm Rider and Speaks Twice ran to their dugout after their bows. They saw Buzzard race through the enemy warriors trying to save Broken Tooth and watched as he was felled by the war club swung by the fierce Black Face leader.

"Buzzard has fallen," shouted Storm Rider. "Shoot the Black Face standing over him. He is going to club him again."

The men released their arrows at the same time, bringing a howl from the short, heavy warrior who happened to step in front of the Black Face leader at just the wrong moment. One arrow passed completely through his hand,

and the other opened a gash as it caromed off his shoulder. The arrows diverted attention from Buzzard. The fierce leader rushed Storm Rider and Speaks Twice, his followers on his heels, all wild-eyed and yelling at the top of their lungs.

Storm Rider and Speaks Twice did not have time to draw their bow-strings for a second shot before the shouting mass of Black Faces was upon them. Speaks Twice was knocked off his feet by three men, who pinned his arms in the mud. He kicked vainly at the Black Face trying to grab his feet just as the leader's club caught him high on the forehead, and he went limp, blood pouring from the nasty cut.

Storm Rider ignored the searing pain in his side where the cane knife sliced the skin across his rib cage. He tried to swing his bow, but there was no room. Using it like a parrying stick, he warded off blow after blow from his attackers. His enemies seemed to be moving in slow motion, while his own movements were much faster. It was like he could anticipate their thrusts and see their swings beforehand.

He held his own for several moments against the overwhelming odds, until one of the Black Face warriors grabbed his bow. He jerked frantically, trying to free it when he felt the enormous blow at the nape of his neck followed by a brilliant white flash and then nothing, absolutely nothing. He fell face first into the soft mud.

The Black Faces crowded around the fallen young men, shouting and waving their weapons. Their victory celebration went on for several minutes, until their leader raised his arm, stopping their frenzy.

"Something is wrong," he growled. "The swamp sounds stop. Somebody watches."

A cool wind brushed across their flushed faces and moved the cane and moss hanging from the oaks. The intruders immediately fell silent, filled with dread. The wind came out of the west, the direction of sickness and death.

"Lake People's spirits are unhappy and vengeful. We need to leave this place quickly."

15

Cannibal Beasts

Buzzard, Speaks Twice, and Storm Rider awoke with throbbing heads, hands tied, and a rough plaited cord looped around their necks. A Black Face warrior with a leering smile held the end of the cord and kept jerking it. His antics amused the other fighters at first, but they were not in a laughing mood, their brows wrinkled with worry. The cool west wind was gone, but the swamp was still too quiet, and the silence clearly unnerved the Black Faces.

"W-w-why didn't they k-k-kill us?" asked Speaks Twice, running his hand over the bloody knot on his forehead.

"They are Black Faces," said Buzzard, grimacing. "They are saving us to cook and eat. Did either of you see what happened to Broken Tooth?"

"N-n-not after you put him in the dugout. M-m-maybe they forgot about him," said Speaks Twice.

"They did not forget," said Storm Rider. "Two Black Faces waded out to the dugout and overturned it, but I did not see Broken Tooth."

Buzzard's empty stare was fixed on the ground. The pain came from his heart, not his wounds.

"I was not able to save my friend," he mumbled. "Why did death not take me instead? I am a warrior, ready to die a warrior's death in the glory of battle. Yet, here I sit, tied up like a mad dog, while my friend is gone."

"W-w-we don't know that he's d-d-dead," said Speaks Twice. "He may have g-g-gotten away and warned the village. We aren't far from P-p-prairie Landing village."

"He could not have swum with his injured arm," Buzzard reminded the others.

He turned away and dropped his chin on his chest.

"My father's bones. We never got a chance to find them," moaned Storm Rider.

"F-f-fire Watcher will find them tomorrow," said Speaks Twice, "a-a-

and if he doesn't, we will d-d-dig them when we get away from these b-b-beasts."

"When you're cooked and eaten, long legs, you don't get away," said Buzzard.

"They are not going to eat us here, or we wouldn't be tied up," said Storm Rider. "We're too close to Prairie Landing village, the smoke would be spotted."

"Maybe they don't always cook people. Laughing Otter sometimes eats raw clams," said Speaks Twice.

"I think they're going to take us to their village in the waving grass," said Storm Rider. "At least, that's what *Long Black Being* did in my dream."

"These are real men, Storm Rider, not imagined spirits," reminded Buzzard. "If we are here tomorrow when Turkey-Buzzard-Man comes, we need to warn him that Black Faces await him."

"H-h-he will know s-s-something is wrong when we don't g-g-greet him from the bank," said Speaks Twice.

"If he approaches anyway, we should start yelling as loud as we can, even if they kill us," said Buzzard. "At least being killed with an arrow beats being cooked and eaten."

"Ay-e," agreed Storm Rider.

The Black Face leader walked into the captives' midst. He kicked Buzzard in the stomach and dragged Speaks Twice away from the others. He jerked Storm Rider's noose and placed his hands over his ears.

"I don't think he wants us talking anymore," said Storm Rider.

The Black Faces intended to raid Prairie Landing village when luck delivered the bone-digging party into their hands. They were retaliating for Red Club's sack of their village three winters before, when two warriors were killed and the village burned.

"Red Club's village will burn another day," promised the Black Face leader. "But we will burn three of their young warriors, and our dead warriors' families will be avenged."

The Black Face raid was well planned and executed. It took two days for the attackers to cross the Big Salt Water bay and paddle up Dead Cypress Water, their progress slowed by caution. They brought four dugouts. Each carried three men. The warriors took turns sleeping in their canoes—two always paddling while first one, then another, slept. At the head of navigation in the Dead Cypress, they lifted their heavy dugouts out of the stream and shouldered them more than twenty arrow shots to Twisting Snake Water. The Dead Cypress Water did not run into the Twisting Snake. No stream did. Twisting Snake Water flowed down the center of a broad ridge, formed by an ancestral course of the Great Water, which prevented local streams from entering it.

Once the raiders were in the Twisting Snake Water, they sent out scouts but encountered no enemies and ascended the stream without incident. They pulled their dugouts out of the Twisting Snake and carried them down the high ridge until they reached the head of Rain Tree Water. Here, they lay in wait for their scouts to give the all-clear signal before paddling down Rain Tree Water and along the brushy southern shore of Little Eagle Lake, searching for a staging area for their attack on Prairie Landing village. They found the perfect hiding place, the thick canebrake at Round Island.

The Black Faces did not know that their hiding place had once been a village of the Many Waters People or that a bone-digging party was headed straight for it at that very moment. And they did not know the old village was haunted.

The accidental encounter with the party saved them from having to attack Red Club's village, where fighting would have been heavy and deadly. *Spirit Being* smiled on them by sending them young men to fight instead of seasoned warriors. Still, the Black Faces knew they had faced a worthy enemy.

The Black Face leader admired the bravery and strength of the young warrior with the big arms and the quickness of the small one with the strange-looking hair and eyes. Even the tall one with skinny legs had stood his ground without fear. Only one of the enemy warriors fell quickly— going down in the first salvo of arrows. He had either drowned or gotten away because when his men capsized the canoe he was in, he was nowhere to be found.

Because the enemy combatants were so brave, the leader decided to take them back to Redfish Point village as examples for his people's own sons. He knew the captives would endure the fire and die without crying or begging. By eating their flesh, his warriors and their sons would acquire their prisoners' bravery and prevent their shadows from reaching the Afterworld where good Black Faces would have to fight them again. Before his village could sing of their great victory, he had to make sure his war party got home, safe and sound.

He, Shark Killer, leading warrior of the Redfish Point Black Faces, earned his reputation by being their fiercest fighter and ablest war-party leader. He had come to the great swamp as many times as he had fingers and never once had any of his braves been killed or captured. Yet, this time he worried. The signs were bad, and his men were still deep in enemy land.

"Whose hand stilled the swamp?" he wondered. "Enemy warriors or evil spirits? The cool death wind touched all our faces. Who would it claim? None of my men are seriously hurt. Death must still be lurking."

Shark Killer had a bad feeling. He was afraid of no man, but he feared spirits. Without prisoners, he would have withdrawn immediately. Prisoners would slow his retreat, and if one should escape and warn Red Club's village, he knew he and his men would be killed, forever dooming their shadows to wander the great swamp, unable to return to the sea that had given them birth. So, he posted sentries and waited for dark.

Night came, cold and still. Dugouts were launched without making a splash. Black-painted faces and bodies and full body tattooing blended so completely with the inky blackness that paddles seemed to move by themselves. Dawn found the warriors resting on the banks of Dead Cypress Water—safely in Black Face land.

Shark Killer tasted the salt in the air. He thanked *Spirit Being* for delivering his men without serious harm. Their wounds would heal. Those bad signs must have been meant for his enemies—after all, they had fallen into his hands.

"One more day in the dugouts, then home," he said, twirling his war club over his head. "Our dead are avenged. Their shadows can now enter the sea. Honor songs await you, my braves, and eating the captive warriors will make us stronger and braver than ever."

The captives could not understand what the leader was saying. Some words sounded familiar, but one was unmistakable—the word for eat was the same as theirs. There was no longer any question what fate awaited them at the Black Face village. They looked at each other, understanding each other's thoughts without saying a word. They were going to be cooked and eaten. They had to escape.

Shark Killer motioned for the dugouts to be put in the water, and the crews dragged them down the bank and across the soft mud flat lining the stream's shallow end. Their trails through the carpet of needle rushes looked like water slides of giant otter.

The warriors threw the captives roughly in the dugouts and pulled the dugouts through the shallows into deeper water. Once headed downstream, the Black Faces began talking and laughing. Storm Rider caught himself imagining these happy-faced men as friends and fathers going to a fun-filled ball game or social dance. The image vanished when the snaggled-toothed warrior in the front of the boat grinned at Storm Rider and rubbed his belly, drawing howls of laughter among his companions.

"Cannibal beasts! You are not real men!" Storm Rider cried out. "Do you eat your own young too like bull alligators?"

His outburst earned him a paddle slap in the back.

He drew into himself trying to ignore the throbbing cut on his ribs. Despair flooded his spirit. He was on the verge of giving up and resigning himself to his fate when he imagined he saw his father's face in the thunderhead looming ahead. His father was smiling and was speaking to him without moving his lips. His words rang in Storm Rider's mind like rumbling thunder.

"You are destined to be a great healer and prophet. You and Buzzard will lead our people in the days to come."

His father's face vanished, and a familiar whistle entered his consciousness. It too came from the magical cloud. Hidden in the whistle was the voice of Blackbird-Eyes-Shining.

"I miss you, and Speaks Twice, too. Hurry home, I will be waiting for you."

The vision healed his spirit. It gave him hope when hope was nearly lost. He grew alert, watching for landmarks, observing turns, and trying to gauge distances. He did not know how or when, but he knew they must try to escape from the Black Faces and their horrible cooking fires.

The dugouts passed the last of the dead cypress trees lining the bayou—casualties of the prolonged dry spell that turned the freshwater stream into a tidal channel. They entered a vast expanse of marsh grass, the waving grass. Rosseau cane and rattlebush fringed the bayou banks, but otherwise the monotony of the waving grass was interrupted only by clumps of live oaks growing out of ancient beach ridges and shell garbage heaps left by ancient Black Faces. Occasionally, alligators slid from the narrow banks, and muskrats scurried for cover when the voyagers glided by their feeding grounds—places where the big rodents had eaten the vegetation to a stubble, a testament to their voracious appetites.

In the shallows, Storm Rider saw his first blue crabs walking on their spidery legs. It did not take him long to find out what their large pinchers were used for after his tormentor grabbed the largest one he could find and threw it on Storm Rider's bare lap. His tormentor's gleeful howls drew everyone's attention, including a frowning Shark Killer. That stopped his raucous demonstration, but his torturer did not remove the crab and kept glancing back at Storm Rider to see where it would pinch next.

Storm Rider quickly saw that his efforts to dislodge the crab were only causing more distress and pain. He stopped wiggling and trying to buck it off his lap. It took all his resolve to keep from moving when the crab burrowed between his tightly clasped legs only inches from his exposed penis. He spread his knees slightly, and the crab dropped onto the floor of the dugout and scurried backwards under the Black Face's arrow quiver, putting an end to his tormentor's fun.

When grassy banks appeared, the Black Faces ran the canoes along them and dragged their hands in the water. At first, Storm Rider thought the per-spiring men were trying to cool off, but he soon realized that they were catching something to eat—handful after handful of tiny grass shrimp. The clear-bodied creatures looked too much like dragonfly nymphs to suit Storm Rider's taste, but the Black Faces obviously relished them, shell and all. Most important, the shrimp were superabundant and would make excellent sur-vival food when they escaped.

The captives were placed in separate dugouts so they could not talk to each other. The lead canoe was Shark Killer's, then came the one Speaks Twice was in, next Storm Rider, and last Buzzard. The dugouts kept enough distance between them so the captives could not make eye contact. Still, Storm Rider managed to catch sight of his friend and Buzzard as their dug-outs rounded bends in the stream. Speaks Twice seemed to be all right, but Buzzard was obviously hurting—the broken shaft of the arrow sticking from his thigh was attracting swarms of deerflies.

As if in answer to Buzzard's misery, a driving rain swept over the canoes, soaking everything. The storm passed as quickly as it had come, leaving the water misty and the air heavy and hard to breath, but it took away the deer-flies and gave Buzzard some relief.

When the rain moved off, Storm Rider realized they were no longer in the narrow stream but had entered a great salty bay. The marsh fell be-hind quickly. It seemed that an endless hill of water lay in front of them—everywhere he looked, the water seemed higher than their canoes. Their shallow draft dugouts were meant for sluggish bayous and smooth lakes, not for the rough waters of the bay.

During the brief downpour, the dugouts pitched and rolled on the white-caps, and spray drenched the boats each time they cut through a wave. Cap-sizing seemed imminent, and Storm Rider knew that with his hands tied, he would drown.

"Better to drown than be eaten," he thought, almost welcoming a watery grave.

But Shark Killer and his men were experienced in handling their canoes in rough open waters. Instead of heading into the waves or along them, they turned the dugouts around and ran with the waves until they overtopped them. Riding the waves relieved the sickening motion but jarred everyone's insides when the dugouts shot over the crests and fell into the troughs be-tween waves. The jarring ride was over as soon as the storm-agitated waters calmed.

The dugouts resumed their course across the wide bay toward their desti-nation. When Storm Rider saw smoke on the horizon, he knew Shark Killer had guided them straight to his village without any landmark to guide him.

"Black Faces say they came from the sea," remembered Storm Rider. "Maybe they recognize watermarks like we do landmarks. Maybe their great spirit lets them remember the trails they took to their villages when they first climbed out of the sea."

A shout from Shark Killer brought the canoes to anchor. The Black Faces smeared their faces and bodies with fresh black paint—a paste made of charcoal and alligator grease. They blackened their teeth. They donned necklaces made of seashell beads and wolf and alligator teeth and brushed their hair with garfish-jaw combs. They tied red feathers to the long tresses on the sides of their heads, a hairdo only worn by proven warriors. Now, they were ready to enter their village—as warriors returning from battle bearing spoils.

The sentry spotted the approaching canoes and alerted the villagers. The mob gathering at the landing began shouting and waving their bows and clubs. The rabid Black Faces quickly deployed into two ragged lines about two body lengths apart.

"What are they doing?" wondered Storm Rider, his dread deepening. Several men jumped into the water and pulled the dugouts onto the shore, beaching them at the mouth of the screaming, wavering lane. A chill gripped Storm Rider as he watched two men drag Speaks Twice toward the lane. They raised him to his feet and prodded him with sharp canes—drawing fresh blood from many small cuts. Speaks Twice kept turning around, trying to fend off their jabs with his hands, which were still tied together, but the greasy-face man holding the cord around his neck kept jerking him into the lane. It was then that Speaks Twice and Storm Rider and Buzzard understood what these heathens were doing—they were trying to force him to run between the two lines of screaming men, women, and children, which converged on a large hut sitting on the highest part of the shell heap.

Speaks Twice threw his bound arms over his head and started running. The greasy-faced man gave the cord a fierce jerk, almost spinning Speaks Twice completely around, and then, with a mighty shout, flung the cord into the air. Speaks Twice was beaten unmercifully with canes and sticks. Bloody whelps crisscrossed his arms, stomach, and legs, and clam- and oyster-shell missiles raised raw contusions all over his blood-streaked body.

"Run! Speaks Twice, run!" Storm Rider yelled, feeling his friend's pain. "Don't give up. Don't let them beat you."

"Ignore the pain," yelled Buzzard. "Just a few more steps. You can make it."

Finally, painfully slowly, Speaks Twice stumbled toward the end of the lane and collapsed in front of the portico of the large hut.

"He's not dead," Buzzard called to Storm Rider. "Hurt, but not dead."

Storm Rider was next. Shark Killer himself pulled the healer to the mouth of the whipping lane and gave him a hard push and a kick. Ducking and dodging, Storm Rider ran the gauntlet. When he emerged at the porch of the large hut, the shouting died and clapping began. People looked at each other in disbelief. Nobody before had ever run the gauntlet without being hit anywhere but on the arms. One hag accused Shark Killer of capturing ghosts instead of men that bled real blood. Undaunted, a small, frowning girl walked up to Storm Rider and began switching him with a limber cane switch, bringing a roar of laughter from the gathering.

Buzzard was last to enter the whipping lane. Three men dragged him from the dugout. He could barely stand. Storm Rider saw the fire in Buzzard's eyes and watched him walk slowly, unbelievably slowly, up the whipping lane. He never cried out or limped despite the torrent of fresh blood streaming down his leg. Blow after blow stuck him, especially on his face and bleeding thigh, but he never once raised his arms to ward off the blows, he never flinched, and he never showed signs of pain.

Storm Rider could feel the terrible beating that Buzzard was ignoring. Even Speaks Twice raised his head, watching Buzzard's punishment. Blood ran into the big man's eyes, blinding him, but he did not wipe them. Blood streamed from his lacerated nose, but all he did was spit and snarl at the Black Faces.

"You stink like dog dung. Your faces look like rotten meat covered with blue flies. Is that as hard as you can hit, you clams?"

Buzzard insulted them all and saved the last for the alligator-skin-draped man standing on the portico.

"Bite my hard ass, alligator man, if you have any teeth."

Buzzard stepped out of the whipping lane, barely recognizable under his bloody mantle, but standing and smiling at the man on the portico.

Storm Rider and Speaks Twice were overcome with admiration for the man who, until now, had been their biggest nemesis. They had never seen anyone braver than Buzzard. They knew at that moment that they would live or die together, because they would never try to escape without Buzzard.

16

Captives' Sentences

After the beatings, the Black Faces gathered around the grass-thatched hut atop the shell heap. The building was the temple and also home to the old shaman. It was slightly larger than common residences and had a porch and a better view but otherwise was undistinguished. From here, the shaman would pronounce the captives' sentences.

Black Face warriors tied Storm Rider and Speaks Twice together, their backs to each other. Buzzard was tied spread-eagle to a square driftwood frame, which ominously spanned a large ash-filled hole. The boys expected to die, and Speaks Twice and Storm Rider made up their minds to follow Buzzard's example. They wanted their inside shadows to journey to the Upper World with heads high and smiles on their faces. They would show the hated Black Faces how Many Waters People died.

The people anxiously awaited the old shaman to light the cooking fire that would slow-roast Buzzard who had already started singing his death song.

The shaman stepped off the porch and into the sunlight. The crowd quieted. Buzzard sang louder. But the shaman carried no torch. Buzzard would not burn today.

The old shaman made a frightful figure. He wore an alligator skin as a mantle, and both ears were missing—courtesy of a Chestnut Eater warrior from the Water-Runs-Red in the land of the Piney Woods. That man's bleached white skull now hung from the honor pole in front of the temple, his ear-biting teeth knocked out. His charred thigh bone dangled from the shaman's belt.

Speaking in a high-pitched falsetto voice, the shaman addressed the crowd. He spoke for several minutes and then paused and summoned an old woman from the back of the crowd. Slowed by arthritis, she limped painfully through the crowd supported by a young woman who looked to be about seventeen or eighteen winters old. Both wore rags and never raised their eyes, even when the shaman spoke directly to them. What did the shaman want with beggars? Storm Rider was not even sure they were Black Faces. The old woman had red dots bordering the elaborate black-line tattoos on her forehead and upper arms like nobles among the Many Waters People. The young woman did not have any tattoos but did have a prominent red birthmark on the back of her shoulder that resembled a tattoo. Another word from the shaman and the women faced the crowd, still without raising their eyes.

Buzzard's singing stopped, and Storm Rider and Speaks Twice sat up straighter. The shaman said something to the women again and then addressed the people.

"Pointed Tooth, there, is head man of Redfish Point village," said the shaman, pointing with his thigh-bone trophy. "I am Smoke Hand, shaman of the Redfish Point People. You already know Shark Killer. We have decided what to do with the three of you."

Slowly, the tattooed woman began to speak, her words deliberate and hesitating but unmistakable—she was speaking the language of the Many Waters People. This woman was one of the Many Waters People. She was a Black Face slave.

"Strong Man without Fear, you will be roasted and served to our young warriors who have not struck blows, so they will gain your bravery. The feast will take place when little night sun grows completely round."

The slave woman waited for the shaman to pause before translating Speaks Twice's sentence.

"Tall Man, you will be given to the widow, Painted-Face-Woman. You will provide food for her cooking pit and gather fuel for her fire. So that you cannot run away or escape by canoe, you will have one of your hamstrings severed and a hand cut off."

Continuing to stare at the ground, the slave woman translated Storm Rider's punishment.

"Strange Man That Moves Like the Wind, you will spend one moon with Smoke Hand in the temple. At the feast of the Strong Man, you will be blinded, so that your blue eye cannot see into the hearts of the Sunrise People and your brown eye cannot show you the way to escape. After that time, you will be free to go and come in the village. If you try to run away before then, you will be tied in the Sinking Grass for the red wolves to eat, but no Sunrise person's hand shall take the life of one painted by *Spirit Being*."

Smoke Hand dismissed the slave woman with a wave of his arm. Her young friend helped her to a small grass hovel behind the temple, and they crawled inside. Pleased with the verdicts, the people began to disperse, except for several boys and young men who lingered near the captives, discus-

sing what they had just witnessed. These lake warriors were the most unusual
captives Shark Killer had ever brought to Redfish Point village.

"Nobody has ever run the gauntlet without being struck," said one of
the Black Face men. "Did you see how he caught all the blows with his
hands?"

"Yes, he could have plucked our arrows out of the air," said another. "I
wonder if Shark Killer captured the strange man while he slept?"

"Shark Killer will tell us at the feast of the Strong Man."

"Strong Man bleeds, but he did not feel pain," said an amazed young warrior. "Our strongest warrior would have fallen from so many blows. He did
not even run. He did not cry out once."

"What makes these lake warriors so different?" asked a wide-eyed youth.
"How can we defeat them?"

The young Black Faces knew Shark Killer would tell them that their
bravery was measured by the valor of their enemies. Yet, they knew that
glory and honor came from fighting, no matter who the foe. And there were
so many enemies—the Chestnut Eaters, the Flat Heads, the People of the
Rocks, and the tall brown-headed Mosquito Slappers of the western sand
coasts. The Black Faces were not sure they were ready to die at the hands of a
tribe of supernatural warriors, like these Lake men, before they had a chance
to earn their first warrior tattoos.

Storm Rider, Speaks Twice, and Buzzard were taken to separate locations
in the village where they would be held until their sentences were carried
out. Buzzard was moved to the far end of the shell ridge, where smelly clamshells and rotting fish guts were thrown. There, he was bound to a twisted
live oak tree with only the shade of its gnarled evergreen limbs to protect
him from the burning sun and pelting rain. Speaks Twice was tethered to the
doorpost of Painted-Face-Woman's hut, and a braided leash long enough to
reach inside the hut was tied around his neck. Storm Rider was taken to the
shaman's hut where his feet and wrists were tied and a muskrat-skin blindfold put over his eyes. He was secured to a heavy water-worn stump that
took four warriors to drag inside the hut.

Tied up and fed only clam broth and scraps, the boys spent long days
and even longer nights suffering the humility of captivity. Buzzard suffered most. For days, small boys pelted him with shells and switched him
with limber canes, but when their repeated attacks failed to elicit a response
of any kind, they shifted their mock battles to sunning turtles and cowering dogs.

Smoke Hand cut the arrow from Buzzard's thigh and wrapped the ugly
wound with wet moss sprinkled with powder from a red root. He pushed
the broken arrow shaft protruding from Buzzard's arm all the way through

the arm and cauterized the bleeding wound with a glowing ember. Buzzard gritted his teeth but did not utter a sound.

Smoke Hand took a clamshell from his medicine bundle and untied the cord holding the valves together. Buzzard turned his head away from the powerful stench. Rotten meat! Smoke Hand kept pointing to the decaying meat and then back to the thigh wound. Buzzard thought the shaman was trying to tell him his leg was going to rot, until he saw white larvae crawling in the meat—blue fly maggots.

"That old man is going to put maggots in my wound to eat the pus," Buzzard laughed under his breath. "Even cannibals do not like to eat bloodshot or rotten meat."

Speaks Twice's neck was raw and bleeding from Painted-Face-Woman's constant jerking. She would pull him inside her hut, jabbering and pointing. When he failed to understand what she wanted, she would throw a screaming fit, beat and kick him unmercifully, and push him back outside. Her anger had no bounds, and Speaks Twice knew her dead husband was in a better place, even if he was wandering in the Wasteland.

From his first moment in the shaman's hut, all Storm Rider thought about was escaping. With his eyes blindfolded, he depended on sound, smell, and touch to show him around in his world of light and dark shadows. In a few days, his other senses told him where everything was inside the hut and gave him a general idea about the layout of the village.

He continually pulled on his knots and the heavy stump.

"No use," he thought, "Too tight! Too heavy!"

The old earless shaman wasted no time opening Storm Rider's basket, which the raiders confiscated from Speaks Twice's dugout. Storm Rider heard the contents being emptied and moved around on the hard clay floor. Then the mumbling started as the old man realized what he was seeing.

He listened closely as the shaman rose from his cross-legged position, walked five steps to the entrance, lifted the flap, and descended the shell heap—one, two, three, ten quick steps down the slope. Almost immediately, he was out of hearing distance, and that could only mean he had to be walking in the direction the wind was blowing. If he had turned into the wind, Storm Rider would have been able to hear his footsteps in the shells until he reached the landing, where he could hear a dugout being dragged onto the shells. Since the wind always blew off the ocean during the day, he knew the old man had gone north. That meant he was not going to see Pointed Tooth, whose hut was south of the landing. Who then?

He listened to the steps returning—the shaman's and two others of softer footfall. When he heard them talking outside the door, he was mad at himself for not figuring out who the old man had gone to see. The old man wanted to talk to him. He wanted answers. He had gone after the slave women.

He felt his blindfold being untied, and a nimble, calloused hand brushed his cheek. It was the young slave woman. She looked him straight in the eyes before returning to her place by the old woman's side.

As his eyes adjusted to the dim light, he confirmed what his nose and fingers had already told him—the smells of death were all around. There were dried snake skins, muskrat skins, and strands of souring seaweed hanging from roof poles. Bones and teeth of muskrat, otter, and many other small animals were heaped in piles around a driftwood bench next to the back wall. On the table, he saw skulls and more bones, but they were human. Black sockets in the skulls stared back at him, and the teeth were bared in an eternal grimace. He wondered whether they belonged to revered ancestors or cannibalized victims. A fire pit lined with clam shells lay at his feet, and its grease-soaked ashes told of horrible, unspeakable meals.

"The old frog wants to know why you have medicines with you," said the old slave woman. "He asks if you are a shaman."

"Old frog!" Storm Rider thought. "That proves he does not understand a word of the Many Waters People's language or he would have her skewered and cooked for dinner."

"Tell him yes," he said.

"He wants to know what happened to the experienced shamans. The Sunrise People would never make shamans out of nestlings."

"Say that I was sent by *Old Traveler* to heal the sick and dream the future."

"He says *Spirit Being* would not entrust such duties to a nestling."

"Then ask him how he thinks I got the mark of *Lightning-Spirit-Bird* in my hair and why my eyes are of two colors. Ask him why he covers my eyes. Is he afraid I can see at night, afraid I can see the blackness of his spirit?"

"Careful, young shaman, let him ask the questions," the old woman warned.

"He says he has seen people with light-colored hair living on the sand islands to the west, and he says that eyes of different colors can be put out the same as normal eyes."

"He wants to know your name and the names of the other two captives."

"Tell him I am Storm Rider. The big man is called Buzzard. Tall man is Speaks Twice."

"He says you have funny names. He will give you and tall man proper names after the warrior feast. The big man will not need one."

"Tell him how happy I am. I always wanted a Black Face name."

"He calls himself Smoke Hand, but I call him Old Frog. He says to tell you that he is the most powerful shaman that has ever lived."

"I am not interested in his boasting," said Storm Rider. "But I would like to know your name, you and the young woman. I can tell you come from the great swamp, but does she?"

"I am Cane Basket," said the old woman. "I am of the Bear clan. Young woman is just called Woman. She is from the great swamp too, but she does not remember her family or clan. She was only an infant when warriors brought her to Redfish Point village."

"Where were you taken captive?" asked Storm Rider.

Smoke Hand's raised arm stopped their conversation.

"Shuh! He wants to know if you have ever healed anybody."

"Tell him I have healed many people. Tell him I heal people bitten by the white-mouthed snake and the snake with rattling tail."

"He says nobody knows how to cure white-mouth snakebite. He wants to know about the other medicine."

"Ask him what makes him think I will tell him my secrets," said Storm Rider defiantly. "They were passed down from my father and his clan father before him."

"Let me tell you why, fool-hearted man," warned Cane Basket. "If you refuse, you will be fed to the wolves, and your friends will be cooked."

"Hand him the leaf with three lobes. Tell him it is good for sore gums and bleeding."

Cane Basket translated his words, picked up another plant and turning it around in her hand, pretended to be asking about it.

"I come from Prairie Landing village on Big Cypress Lake," Cane Basket said, while the shaman was busy studying the leaf. "I was fifteen winters old when Black Face monsters captured me and my sisters while we were gathering oak nuts on Twisting Snake Water. Now, I am old and worn out."

Storm Rider told her of his dream about *Long Black Being* carrying three limp bodies to its lair in the marsh—a premonition that had come to pass.

"Let me tell you," said Cane Basket. "Short Black-Face beings or *Long Black Beings,* it makes no difference. They are all the same."

Cane Basket picked up a piece of shredded willow bark and raised her eyebrows.

"Tell him that the yellow medicine comes from the inner bark of the tree with many narrow leaves that grows along sandy stream banks. A tea brewed from it helps headache and aching backs and legs."

"Let me talk to him about the medicines," said Woman. "He will think I am passing on what you two are saying."

While Woman went on and on about the bark—what aches and pains it remedied—Cane Basket and Storm Rider resumed their conversation. Cane Basket smiled at Woman's words.

"She makes up stories about all the people the medicine has helped. I told her to be careful and not get too carried away. Stories are easy to forget when they are untrue."

"Why did the Black Faces not cook you?" Storm Rider asked.

"These vermin only eat warriors, the bigger the better. They think it makes them strong and brave. They make slaves of women and children and use them for barter."

"You mean slave trading?"

"No, to get things they want. My two sisters who were captured with me were both traded to Mosquito-Slapper beachcombers for alligator-oil jugs—pottery jugs. Clay! They traded my sisters for mud."

"You were not traded, were you?"

"No. I was claimed as a second wife by an older warrior, who is now dead. I was young and pretty then, and his first wife liked the watertight baskets I made. After he was killed, she kicked me out of the lodge. These generous people let me live on the edges of the village like a dog, eating bones and sleeping under bushes, but when some hag needed a new basket, they always came looking for me."

"Woman, show him that bark scale next to your foot," said Storm Rider. "It is from the toothache tree. It is chewed for toothache and sore gums."

Woman looked at the bark scale like she was admiring a pretty basket and gave the shaman an extended discourse on its many uses.

"Woman was brought back from the swamp by warriors who captured her in a raid on her village," Cane Basket continued. "She was adopted by a Black Face family whose own daughter was stolen by the Chestnut Eaters a few weeks before. It did not take the foster parents long to decide they did not want her. Even though she barely knew how to walk, they threw her out anyway. I guess it was too much trouble to drown her. When I found her a few days later, she was eating scraps at the garbage dump. I started looking after her—only fitting, huh? Two swamp girls stolen from their homes, destined to eat Black Face scraps together."

"Cane Basket has been the only mother I have ever known," said Woman. "She saved me from becoming alligator bait when I was small and from Black Faces penises after I grew up. She showed me how to make myself so filthy and ragged that even these filthy and ragged murderers would feel sorry for me and throw me a bone. She taught me how to weave watertight baskets and speak the language of the Lake people—skills she knew would make me too valuable to kill or trade. I had rather eat scraps with her than grilled alligator tail with them."

"I am glad your paths crossed. *Old Traveler's* hand is in your fates," said Storm Rider.

"I think *Old Traveler* stays away from Black Face land," said Woman. "He did not create these vermin—they grew out of blue fly maggots."

"Old Frog here is so excited about the new cures that he is about to come out of his breechcloth," said Cane Basket. "He keeps asking where he can get these strange plants."

"Tell him they do not grow in the waving grass, but he can find them around the salt springs on the high islands. He does not even have to leave Black Face land to collect them."

"Cane Basket, hand me that twig with the red berries," said Woman. "What is it used for, Tied-Up Man?"

"Purifying the stomach. Boil the leaves and berries until the water turns black and then drink large quantities. It is called the Black Drink Bush"

Smoke Hair took the twig from Woman and turned it around and around in his hands trying to memorize the details. Woman talked incessantly about its healing magic.

"Where did Shark Killer capture you?" Cane Basket asked.

"At Round Island."

"The old Round Island village was near my home. I am from Prairie Landing village," she said. "We heard stories about a famous snakebite healer who was born at Round Island but moved away. Was he called Cloud Bringer?"

"Ah-e," said Storm Rider. "We were going to dig his bones when we were captured."

"I did not know he was dead or I would not have spoken his name," replied Cane Basket.

"I don't think it matters, now. We are too far from his bones for his shadow to hear."

"Old Frog grows restless with your long conversation," said Woman, frowning at Cane Basket. "He says that next time we must shorten our words. I told him that Lake people's words are not as clear as Black Scum words and that it takes many of them to say what can be said in a few words in a superior language like his. I also told him that it requires a long time to understand what you are saying because we think you are slow minded."

Smoke Hand rose, abruptly ending the conversation.

"I go to Crying Eagle's village now to treat his pregnant wife," he croaked. "Their young shaman was killed by the Chestnut Eaters last week, and they have no shaman to look after her. Tell Cloud Man there that we start at first light tomorrow."

"Okay, great shaman," said Woman.

"Leave his blindfold off. He cannot spy on souls when there is nobody here. Make sure his knots are tight. Do not let me find them loose, or I personally will hang your heads and flayed pelts from the honor pole."

"As you wish, mighty one."

"And clean my toilet pit before you leave. There might be some greasy bones you can suck on."

"Oh, thank you," beamed Woman.

While Smoke Hand collected his medicine bag, blood lancets, and alligator-skin cape, Cane Basket and Woman emptied the foul-smelling pit into a snapping turtle shell and set it outside the door. They would dump it in the lake on their way back to their hovel. They threw a handful of charred clamshells and tufts of dried marsh grass into the pit and set a small fire.

"Why do you burn the pit?" whispered Storm Rider. "The smoke!"

"Shell ashes hide the smell, at least until he uses the pit again."

"And he uses it a lot," said Woman.

"Tell Cloud Man I want him to show me the treatment for snakebite in the morning, and, then, go crawl into your burrow but make sure you are here before the squawking coots wake the village," ordered Smoke Hand, as the women fled the smoky lodge.

"We will be here," replied Cane Basket.

"And I wish your cape was made of blue crabs," said Woman in the language of the Many Waters people, with a sweet smile on her face.

Having deliberately left her walking stick inside, Cane Basket stepped back into the lodge and dropped a piece of wet deerskin in Storm Rider's lap.

"Cover your face after we have gone," she whispered.

Storm Rider kept his face buried in the wet rag, but the choking, burning smoke lingered for a long time in the closed lodge.

Despite being tied to a heavy stump in an enemy temple waiting for his eyes to be put out, Storm Rider was thankful—he finally was alone. Thoughts flew through his mind like migrating pigeons darkening the sun with their numbers, but they were only about one thing—escape. He did not yet know how or when, only that they would. They must. And Cane Basket and Woman would have to help.

17

Remembering Bent Woman's Teachings

Next morning, Storm Rider performed a mock snakebite-healing ceremony. Smoke Hand watched intently. The shaman memorized the vocables of the healing song quickly but grew frustrated trying to cause the snake fang, which would be used in a real ceremony, to magically jump from Woman's body into his knotty hand.

"This is lake people's magic," he said. "Not for us Sunrise People."

"I wish you would hurry up and get it right," complained Woman, speaking in Black Face tongue. "I grow tired lying here resting."

Smoke Hand thought that was funny, his yellow toothy grin reminding Storm Rider of cypress knees after beavers stripped the bark.

Days dragged by. Smoke Hand practiced and practiced until finally he mastered the fang trick.

"Now, I am ready for a healing," said Smoke Hand. "If only I had snakeroot."

"Let me find it for you," pleaded Storm Rider.

Smoke Hand pretended not to hear.

For several days, Storm Rider kept asking Smoke Hand to let him search for the anti-venom, and Smoke Hand kept ignoring his requests.

Finally, the shaman admitted that his apprentice could not find the plant, and Storm Rider intensified his pleading.

"I would not run away," he promised. "I would never leave my friends. Keep me tied up, send a dozen warriors with me, but just let me go look for it."

Storm Rider was sure the plant did not grow in the marsh. He knew it only grew in the dry woods, but he needed firsthand knowledge of the terrain in order to plan a getaway. All he knew was that the great swamp lay in the direction of the rising sun on the far side of the bay, but he had no idea which of the many streams or lakes offered the best escape route.

As much as Smoke Hand wanted snakeroot, he refused to let Storm Rider leave the temple. He was shrewd enough to know that Storm Rider wanted to scout the terrain.

"He says if you ask him to go look for the plant one more time, he will cut off your little finger and eat it in front of you," said Cane Basket, wrinkling her face. "I think I will ask him again, so you will be able to see for yourself whether or not the old man eater thinks you taste good."

Storm Rider laughed at her wit, but the laugh was shallow. Deep down Storm Rider felt helpless and scared.

Smoke Hand scowled and snapped at her.

"He does not like you laughing when he says nothing funny. He does not think I am translating his words faithfully, and he says if it does not stop, he is going to let Woman do the translating from now on. He thinks I am giving you information that will help you escape."

"I knew he was worrying about us talking so much," said Storm Rider.

There was a scratching on the door flap, and Woman opened it to Shark Killer. The scarred warrior did not enter but waved Smoke Hand outside. The men walked around to the edge of the porch where they could not be heard.

"Dung Breath says he sees no signs of you being slow minded and that even stupid lake people would not put up with a dim-witted healer. I told him how much I love Redfish Point village and have enjoyed serving him for the last forty winters. I told him it makes me sad for him to think I would encourage anyone to run away from such a wonderful place and such fine people."

"Do you think he believes that?" asked Storm Rider.

"No, he is not completely stupid, but he says I am lucky to live with the Sunrise People. I might have wound up with cruel Chestnut Eaters or, worse, with crazy Mosquito Slappers."

Storm Rider shook his head.

"He is right about one thing," said Woman. "He never says anything funny."

"I think I will keep talking a lot, so he will let Woman do the translating. She has won his trust with her gift of gab and her fake smile. She gets around so much better than I, and besides, he lets her carry clam broth to your friends every other day, so they will not starve before Buzzard dies."

They heard the men returning, and their last words revealed they had been talking about Buzzard's execution.

"Seems as though they are going to invite Crying Eagle's village to dine on poor Buzzard and watch you and Speaks Twice receive your punishment," whispered Woman. "If you are planning to escape, you better do it soon. *Pale Sun* has changed from almost empty, when you arrived, to nearly half full. If you wait until it fills up completely, it will be too late."

Smoke Hand opened the door flap and sat down cross-legged across from Storm Rider.

"Old woman, tell Cloud Man I do not think snakeroot grows in the sinking grass. After we put out his eyes so he cannot run away, he will come with me and Shark Killer to High Island to get snakeroot."

"Ask him how I am supposed to find snakeroot when I'm blind?"

"He says he knows what it looks like," said Cane Basket.

"Then why does he need me to go with him."

"He says it is your medicine, and he wants you there when he digs it up, so snakeroot won't withhold its potency when it sees itself in strange hands."

Smoke Hand pointed his trophy thigh bone at Storm Rider.

"Accept your fate, Cloud Man. You will not leave this village until you are blind, and we will say no more about it."

"He understands, wise shaman," said Woman.

"Shark Killer wants me to find snakeroot soon," said the shaman dejectedly. "Two of his warriors fell to snakebite during the Moon of Redfish-Running. One lost the use of his foot and can no longer seek glory in battle. That man was my nephew. The other man waded into a nest of white-mouth snakes. He did not last through the night but died screaming, his face so swollen and purple that even his family did not recognize him. Worst of all, his spirit died too. *Spirit Being* tells us that people who are eaten and those who die from snakebite cannot return to the sea. There is no more terrible death than to die of snakebite."

Storm Rider almost felt a tinge of sympathy for the old shaman. He knew how he would feel if the two victims had been Many Waters People. After all, he still was upset about Broken Tooth.

"I hate to see anyone suffer and die when they can be helped."

"I am not going to translate those words for him," shot back Cane Basket, quickly erasing his weak moment. "I do not believe you will feel too sorry for these cannibals when you see them eating Strong Man. You see that old man-eater sitting there? He will be the one that cuts off chunks of Strong Man's flesh while his heart still beats, just to see if he is cooking thoroughly. Remember, Black Faces do not suffer the terrible double death from cannibalism—death of the body and death of the spirit—because they do not eat their own kind."

Storm Rider's sympathetic moment passed, and worry lines creased his forehead. Time was running out. They had to get away, and they had to leave soon.

Woman kept Smoke Hand busy talking. She had been flattering him for days, and he was directing more and more of his conversation toward her.

"He likes me," whispered Woman. "But he does not trust you two."

"I can tell. He does not even let me look outside the temple," said Storm Rider in a low tone. "I guess we will just have to take our chances on finding a waterway that leads back to the great swamp. I will ask my Snake guardian to show me the way."

"No need to ask your guardian spirit when you have me," said Woman.

"First, you better figure out how you are going to get away," said Cane Basket. "They have started posting a sentry outside the temple day and night, and they have doubled the number of guards at the landing. I think they are expecting the lake people to come for you."

Smoke Hand's stomach grumbled, and he went to the pit in the back of the temple. He could be heard releasing wind and grunting, and soon a fetid odor pervaded the temple.

"I know all the canoe trails," Woman said, leaning toward Storm Rider. "I will show you which ones to take."

"You two women cannot go with us. It will be too dangerous, and besides, we have not gotten away yet," he said. "When we do, we will have to move fast."

"Smooth your forehead, Storm Rider. This old woman will not slow your flight. I am not going with you, and Woman can keep up better than your two friends. At least, she does not have holes in her leg and arm or a bloody neck. You need her strength, and you need her to show you the way across the sinking grass."

"They will kill you two just like they will us if they catch us trying to escape," argued Storm Rider.

"We are ready to die. At least, our lives in the Upper World will not be spent as slaves to smelly Black Faces," replied Cane Basket.

"No more excuses. You hurt my ears," said Woman. "I am coming with you."

Storm Rider saw her narrow-eyed look. Woman was coming.

"I must get word to Buzzard and Speaks Twice," said Storm Rider. "They have to know what we are planning."

"Your friends have been doing some planning on their own," said Woman.

"How do you know?"

"We talk a little when I carry them their food. Their guards are not as fastidious as yours, and besides, the guards are young and smile when I smile at them. Tall Man's watchman starts smiling when he sees me coming. His wife was stolen by Chestnut Eaters last moon, and he is in a bad way. I smile big at him and pull my skirt up high when I bend over so he can see plainly what he lusts for."

"What are they planning?" asked Storm Rider.

"They asked me to loosen their bindings," said Woman. "So I have been replacing hard knots with slip knots, but I place a small twig through the knot, so that it feels tight when the guards check. Tall Man can now pull his hands free completely. I gave him a stingray spine to use as a weapon in case he is discovered. Strong Man will be loose when the sky turns red today. He hides a deer-bone knife in his breechcloth. His leg is well enough to walk a few steps, but he cannot run without opening the wound again. I will steal a dugout. He cannot make it wading through the sinking grass."

"Why did you not tell me what you were doing?" asked Storm Rider.

"I had to see how closely the Black Faces were watching," she said. "If I had been caught, you would have been able to say you knew nothing about escaping. The old man would have believed you because he says when healers lie, they die."

"But, you should have. . . ."

Their conversation was interrupted by the shaman returning to his seat on the hard-packed floor.

"What were you saying to him, Woman?" asked the shaman.

"I was telling him about the sights of High Island—how it towers above the sinking grass, how its ponds are salty like the Big-Salt-Water, and how you found that long curving tooth of the giant beast washed up on the beach. What kind of spirit animal do you think it belonged to, my shaman?"

Her explanation satisfied the old man.

"Good thing I am not a healer," said Woman, smiling at Smoke Hand the whole time, "Or they would be throwing my body in the sinking grass for telling such lies."

Smoke Hand nearly smiled back at her. Flattery was winning Woman better treatment from the vile man.

There would be no session tomorrow or the next day. The shaman had a healing ceremony and vigil. He would have to stay with the young patient though two sunrises and two sunsets. If the boy lived, everyone would sing Smoke Hand's praises at Strong Man's execution the following day. If the boy died, Smoke Hand would sing the Prayer of Returning to the Sea before the dancing. That would assure family and friends that *Spirit Being* had taken the child to live with him and that no earthly magic could have saved him.

The shaman decided to send Woman and Cane Basket with the other women to collect clams in the shallow bay waters.

"Head to the flats behind the point, where the waters are calm. Pierced Nose tells me that his daughters filled their dugout full of big clams faster than he could skin an alligator. He said they could not take a step without feeling clams under their feet. The water is shallow, too, only knee-deep, so you can collect them with your hands, instead of having to use the rake. We can never have too many steamed clams when Crying Eagle's people visit. They will make the man-meat last longer."

"Now, go clean out my dugout, Woman," ordered Smoke Hand. "Make room for your biggest baskets. I want them filled up. Leave enough room for the old woman to sit. You can sit on the prow and paddle with your feet dangling in the water."

"We will fill your purging pond," promised Woman. "You will supply more clean, fresh clams for the feast than anyone else. The people will know the generosity of Smoke Hand, and they will love you even more than they already do."

"Be careful, Woman, someone is going to mistake you for that filthy man-eater's daughter," said Cane Basket, speaking Many Waters People's words.

"I hope they do," said Woman laughing. "It will make it easier to escape."

The women left to prepare Smoke Hand's dugout, leaving Storm Rider to his anxious thoughts. Bound tightly and lashed to the heavy stump, he did not see how he was going to get loose and free the others. Time was running out. Buzzard would die in three days, Speaks Twice would be crippled, and he would be blinded. There would be no escape then, no reason.

Despair stifled all hope, and he fell into a black, dreamless sleep.

Smoke Hand left quietly at daybreak. Storm Rider pretended to be asleep. He heard Cane Basket and Woman talking with him outside the hut, and then all three moved away.

"If I did not know better," thought Storm Rider, "I might think he was trying to keep from waking me."

Storm Rider was grateful for the time by himself. He had to quit accepting defeat. He could not let Buzzard die without doing something. He must think of something.

"It's no use," he cried out loud. "My bindings are too tight, my hands are so swollen I cannot make a fist. I can't even stand—my legs are dead."

The mean sentinel heard his outcry and rushed into the hut, as if expecting to find an accomplice trying to free Storm Rider. The man checked the ropes and, satisfied, started out the door, but as he started to raise the flap, he paused and, with a menacing smile, returned and jabbed the butt of his spear in Storm Rider's stomach.

Storm Rider doubled over in pain, and the sadistic spearman went back outside, grinning and humming.

"Oh, guardian spirit, show me how to get away," he pleaded, his eyes fixed on the light beaming through the crack under the door flap. "Make the

Black Faces look the other way and send them on the wrong trail when we are gone."

A dog growled outside the door. Storm Rider waited for the guard to reenter and strike him again, but his visitor was not human. A red- and black-banded mud snake crawled under the flap.

"Ay-e, guardian spirit, have you have come to help?" he asked, as the reptile slithered across the floor, stopping near his feet. It raised its head and stared at Storm Rider, as though preparing to speak.

"Storm Rider, Storm Rider," called a familiar voice.

"I hear you, but I cannot see you," said Storm Rider. "Where are you, father?"

"At your feet, my son," said the voice.

"My snake guardian is at my feet."

"No, son, it is I," said the voice. "I come to you as a snake to avoid detection."

"How did you know where to find me?"

"When my shadows were reunited in the Upper World, my spirit body was able to see what was happening to you," explained the voice. "I saw the Black Faces take you across the bay and have watched everything they have done since."

"Then you know Buzzard and Speaks Twice are with me, and there are two slave women from the swamp here," said Storm Rider.

"I know. That is why you must leave this place tonight. It is the last opportunity for all of you to get away."

"But Speaks Twice and. . . ."

"Hear me, my son. Tonight, the bindings will fall away from your hands and feet. A dugout has been prepared to take four Many Waters People home. Do not return the way you came. Follow the sign of the sacred fire that will be set before you. And most importantly, remember Bent Woman's teachings about *Golden Face Man*."

"But, father, I do not understand. Father, father, do not go. I must know more," lamented Storm Rider. "Father!"

The snake was gone.

"Was my father really talking to me through the snake," wondered Storm Rider, "or was my imagination playing tricks on me? How are my cords supposed to fall off? Where are we going to get a dugout? How can we follow the sign of the sacred fire when these devils don't even have one? How can Bent Woman's teachings about *Golden Face Man* help us escape? Father, I do not know what these things mean. Father, come back and explain."

Storm Rider went over his daydream, time and time again. He thought of nothing else all day. How was he going to get loose, free Speaks Twice and Buzzard, steal a dugout, and follow the fire sign to freedom? Distraught, he watched the golden light coming under the flap turn amber and then orange.

"Ah-e! The snake returns."

The door flap was raised, and the mean-looking guard stepped inside, Woman right behind. The guard pointed his spear with its razor sharp fish spines at her back. Anything out of the ordinary would send her inside shadow to the Upper World, then and there.

"I only have a minute," she said, smiling broadly at the guard. "He knows I bring your meal at this time."

"Be ready to leave tonight, after the guards change," she whispered. "Give the replacement time to lean against the porch post, and he will be snoring like a grumbling stomach awaiting a meal. After he goes to sleep, the three of us will slip past him and free you. Smoke Hand's dugout will be waiting at the purging pond."

"How can this be, Woman? Go without me. You cannot cut my bonds quickly enough. The guard will hear."

"Do not worry. A mud snake told me how to free you."

"A snake?"

"Ay-e."

The guard punched Woman in the back with the butt of his spear.

"Ouch."

"No more talking," he said angrily.

"Okay," Woman replied in Black Face words. "You know words untie ropes, brave warrior."

She left with a flip of her loose hair. The guard closely examined Storm Rider's knots. They were tight.

"I grow tired of her haughty remarks," mumbled the guard, as he returned to his post on the porch. "I am going to speak to Smoke Hand about her clever attitude."

As Woman whirled around to stomp out the door, the fading light fell across the red birthmark on her shoulder. It looked like a burning fire with three leaping flames—it was the mark of the sacred fire, the sign they were to follow.

18

Escape

The sadistic guard had not even reached the bottom of the shell heap before Storm Rider heard scuffing sounds as the night guard settled against his familiar backrest and his bone-tipped spear clattered on the hard clay floor. Holding his breath so he could hear better, Storm Rider heard the fat guard's guttural snort and then rhythmical snoring.

He listened intently for other sounds. Dogs were baying at the garbage dump where Buzzard was held. Small waves slapping against the shells at the landing competed with the guard's snoring. An alligator bellowed in the distance, but nothing else, except the chorus of bullfrogs, reached Storm Rider's straining ears.

Then, he sat up straight. There it was again—a faint crunching, a light step on the shells. They were here.

In the moon glow coming through the raised door flap, he saw Woman hold her finger to her lips, telling him to be quiet. Buzzard entered the door with a piece of driftwood as long as a man and about as thick as his leg. Speaks Twice followed him. Woman held the flap partly open so the moonlight fell on them.

Storm Rider looked at Buzzard quizzically. Buzzard smiled, and Speaks Twice put his hand on his friend's head.

For a moment, nobody moved. All listened to the night sounds, which seemed to be unaffected by the soft stirrings inside the temple. The guard's snoring seemed louder.

Buzzard placed the driftwood log underneath the heavy stump, Storm Rider's anchor, squatted and put his broad shoulder under the lever, then slowly stood up, his leg muscles straining.

Nothing moved! The stump would not budge. Speaks Twice grabbed Buzzard's leg and pointed to another crack under the stump. Buzzard inserted the lever, and, gathering all his strength, struggled to rise. This time, the root moved high enough for Speaks Twice to slip Storm Rider's bonds off the root that held them. Free at last! His hands were still tied, but at least, he was mobile, if only his sleeping legs would wake up.

Woman motioned them out the door. The guard would swear to Smoke Hand in the morning that he had seen nothing, heard nothing, that spirits had come in the night and freed Cloud Man and the other prisoners. How else could they have escaped while they were being so closely guarded?

The four of them slowly made their way down the back of the shell heap and though the live oaks and tall grass at the water's edge, away from the heavily guarded landing. They climbed into Smoke Hand's dugout, which Woman left tied at the purging pond, and pushed off into the silvery, moon-lit waters of the little inlet. Woman stood on the prow, push pole in hand, and maneuvered the dugout through a maze of tidal channels and flooded gator trails in the marsh grass.

Speaks Twice finally sawed through Storm Rider's ropes with a broken clamshell.

"Woman was right," Speaks Twice muttered, "It would have taken too long to remove them in the temple."

The first larger stream they entered brought a sigh of relief to Woman.

"Now paddle hard!" she said excitedly. "We need to get to Little Hill Water before daylight."

"We would make better time if we stayed in the bay," said Buzzard.

"Better time but easier to spot," replied Woman. "They can see all the way to the horizon across the bay. In the grass, we will be hidden."

"D-d-do you know where you are g-g-going?" asked Speaks Twice.

"Ay-e," said Woman. "Trust me! They will think we have gone straight across the bay because that is the shortest way to the Dead Cypress Water and the great swamp. We fool them by going through the sinking grass."

"Good, my father told me not to go back the way we arrived," said Storm Rider.

Storm Rider told the others about his father appearing to him as a snake, and the message he conveyed.

"I talked to the snake, too," said Woman.

"I do not believe in prophecy," said Buzzard, "I only believe in what I see and feel."

"It f-f-foretold our e-e-escape," said Speaks Twice.

"Ay-e, everything that Storm Rider said has come to pass so far, but we have Woman to thank for it."

"D-d-don't forget the s-s-snake. It a-a-appeared to Storm Rider and Woman."

"I have dreamed of snakes before," replied Buzzard. "That does not make me a prophet."

"Buzzard, y-y-you just don't . . . ," said Speaks Twice, interrupted by Buzzard's questions.

"Where is the sacred fire we are supposed to follow? When do we get to see *Golden Face Man?*"

"I don't know," said Storm Rider, who kept silent about Woman's birthmark.

Now was not the time to make something supernatural out of something as ordinary as Woman's birthmark. Besides, nothing was going to convince Buzzard at this moment that they were benefactors of supernatural intervention.

"When will the Black Faces know we have not taken the Dead Cypress Water?" asked Storm Rider.

"As soon as it is daylight," said Woman. "Maybe by that time we will be beyond Little Hill Island. If we make it that far, we stand a chance of getting away."

"Then, paddle harder," said Buzzard.

"H-h-how are you going to know which is L-l-little Hill Water in the dark?" asked Speaks Twice. "E-e-everything looks d-d-different at night."

"Do not worry, swamp man," said Woman. "All we have to do is taste the water and watch for the white water lilies. They shine in the moonlight."

"What do flowers have to do with finding the right water?" asked Buzzard, fearing that Woman was losing her senses in the excitement.

"The last time I came to Little Hill Island with the Black Faces, Cane Basket told me to look for the lilies. She said they grow only in freshwater, and the Little Hill Water is the second large freshwater stream that enters the bay north of Redfish Point village."

"Why not take the first stream?" asked Buzzard.

"That is the Black Face Water," said Woman. "Nobody lives on its banks but stinking Black Faces."

"W-w-we would not want to wake them this e-e-early," quipped Speaks Twice.

"What do you think they will do to Cane Basket?" asked Storm Rider.

"Maybe nothing," said Woman. "They know she is too old and crippled to have helped us get away. I think she and Smoke Hand have an understanding even though they do not like to admit it. She said if the cannibals have not discovered our absence by daybreak, she will sit outside the temple like she is waiting for Smoke Hand to let her enter. Everyone will think all is normal. Her deception should give us more time."

"I wish she had been able to come," said Storm Rider.

"She says she goes with us in our thoughts. She asks when we reach the great swamp that we think about her so she can see the land she loves through our eyes," said Woman.

"Ah-e," said Storm Rider to the nodding men.

"She journeys soon to the Upper World," said Woman. "Then, she will find peace and will have a strong, young body to enjoy it."

The first grays of morning tinted the eastern sky. The escapees found the lilies and watched the live oak–silhouetted outline of Little Hill Island slip by. If Woman was right, they now had a chance to reach the great swamp, providing the Black Faces did not discover their absence until daylight.

"I have never been past this point," said Woman, paddling in unison with the men, two on one side and two on the other. "All I know is that Little Hill Water ends at the foot of Twisting Snake ridge."

"We will have to carry the boat," said Storm Rider, watching the muscles in Woman's shoulder ripple, making her birthmark seem to leap like flames, the sacred fire preordained to lead them to freedom.

Storm Rider thought he saw Speaks Twice looking at the birthmark, but if the fisherman recognized its significance, he kept it to himself. Buzzard was not yet ready to be reminded of the prophecy.

Beyond Little Hill Island, marsh gave way to higher ground. The stream narrowed and its banks steepened. There were fewer swimming alligators and more surfacing garfish. Dense bitter pecan and swamp-oak woods claimed the banks, and for the first time in their flight, the escapees dared to hope that they might reach the great swamp.

"Awwh," exclaimed Woman disgustedly. "A mud and stick wall blocks our way."

"A b-b-beaver dam! Why now?" spat Speaks Twice.

"What are we going to do?" asked Woman.

"We must pull the dugout over the dam," said Buzzard.

As they nosed the canoe onto the dam, the paddlers noticed the pond spreading out behind the dam. Dead and dying hardwood filled its shallows, and dense stands of cattails lined the muddy banks.

"W-w-we are at the end!" said Speaks Twice. "T-t-there is no o-o-outlet."

"You mean we have nowhere to go?" asked Woman. "All this way, and we run out of water this close to the swamp!"

"Listen!" whispered Buzzard. "I think I hear paddles banging against gunwales. Black Faces are behind us."

"We must hide," exclaimed Woman.

Their last glimmer of hope was fading.

"Let me out here!" Buzzard ordered. "I will fight them while you three run to the other side of the Twisting Snake. I will die here. I will not go back and be cooked. Leave while you still can."

"Come on, Buzzard," pleaded Storm Rider. "We can all make it."

"You know I cannot run, my leg. I would just slow you down. Go. I will give you time to get to the swamp."

"Shuuh," whispered Woman, trying to gauge how much time they had before the Black Faces were upon them.

"They are near where the thick woods start," said Buzzard. "You can make it, if you hurry now."

"I-i-I've got an idea," said Speaks Twice. "H-h-hide the dugout. I k-k-know where we can hide."

"There is no place but the woods," said Woman.

"N-n-no! N-n-not the woods. They will t-t-think that is where we are h-h-hiding," exclaimed Speaks Twice.

"Ay-e!" said Storm Rider, "They will never think to look there."

"Where?" asked Woman, failing to understand Speaks Twice's and Storm Rider's exuberance.

"Buzzard, can you drag the boat out of the water along that beaver slide and hide it in the cattails?"

"Ay-e, but why?"

"We will need it after the B-b-black Faces are gone," said Speaks Twice. "Y-y-you must slide back to the pond on your b-b-belly so you will not leave tracks. They must think you are a b-b-beaver. We must all become b-b-beavers until they leave."

"Ay-e, I understand," said Buzzard.

"Will somebody please tell me what you are talking about?" asked Woman.

"W-w-we must hide in the b-b-beaver lodges. Black Faces will not k-k-know to look for us there since there are no b-b-beaver in the waving grass. The only w-w-way to enter their lodges is through a h-h-hidden under-water tunnel," explained Speaks Twice.

They hurriedly climbed out of the dugout and held onto a partially sub-merged tree while Buzzard hid the dugout in the cattails. Then, they headed for the tangled root masses on the far bank, swimming rather than wading, so they would not stir the mud on the pond bottom.

Speaks Twice dove, and before the ripples disappeared, he surfaced.

"H-h-here, this lodge is e-e-empty," he said. "Woman, hold your b-b-breath and swim into the t-t-tunnel. Y-y-you can s-s-squeeze through. Climb onto the f-f-floor inside. I will be right behind you."

"Here, Buzzard," said Storm Rider, his head emerging from the water. "Two beaver came out of the submerged roots of the leaning tree. I can see the entrance. Come on. Hurry! I think we can both squeeze through the tunnel."

"Hurry, here they come. I hear them talking," whispered Buzzard. "You go first, healer, in case I get stuck."

Four heads disappeared under the water just as two dugouts came around the turn. Shark Killer stood in the prow of the lead canoe.

"They cannot be much further ahead," he said. "The water goes no further."

The Black Faces dragged their dugouts onto the bank. Two men ran along the edge of the beaver pond searching for footprints and dugout scrapes, while other warriors spread out, searching the woods. Shark Killer and his son stood near the towering water oaks, waiting for the men to find the escapees or their trail.

"They cannot have gotten far. Strong Man is too badly hurt. They are near," said Shark Killer, peering into the open woods. "I can feel their presence."

"Where?" asked his son. "They vanish like smoke in the mist."

Gray clouds slipped across the midmorning sun, and still the Black Faces found no trace of the escapees.

"Smoke Hand warned us that the young shaman knew magic," said one of the warriors with a shrug. "Maybe he is a witch and makes them invisible."

"Does he make Smoke Hand's dugout invisible, too?" said another warrior, fearing what the old shaman would do if they returned without the prisoners or his canoe.

"They did not come this way," said a third warrior. "They must have pulled out of the water before they reached the pond."

"We must go back down the stream," said Shark Killer. "Examine every pile of shells left by the Old Ones. They are the only places where a heavy dugout could be dragged out of the water without leaving obvious scrape marks."

"Yes, and tracks would not show in the shells," said his son.

"Look for freshly overturned shells, broken reeds, and flattened grass," said Shark Killer. "They are real people, not ghosts. They leave signs of their passage. Find them. Kill the woman, and I will carry her traitorous head back to Smoke Hand. The village pole will have a new trophy."

Hurriedly, the Black Faces pushed off and descended the Little Hill Water, carefully searching both banks, not just the eastern one, in case the escapees tried to fool their pursuers by pulling their dugout out on the west bank, opposite the side toward the great swamp.

After waiting a long time, Speaks Twice slipped into the underwater tunnel and slowly surfaced among the tangled roots. Singing birds and a pair of swimming wood ducks told him that the Black Faces were gone, at least for the time being. Summoning the others from their underground lairs, they swam to the beaver dam, climbed atop it, and strained to hear any sounds that would indicate that the Black Faces were near.

Knowing their opportunity to reach Twisting Snake Water was running out, they swam hurriedly toward the hidden dugout. Pulling themselves along the beaver slide, they located the canoe, but instead of putting it back in Little Hill Water and pulling across the beaver dam, they hefted the dugout onto their shoulders and waded through the cattails to the bank. They walked briskly up the slope of Twisting Snake ridge.

Panting and exhausted, they reached the crest of the broad ridge and lowered the heavy dugout onto the ground. After catching their breath, they dragged the dugout down the inner bank of the Twisting Snake Water, energized by the thought that they were back in the land of the True People, not yet in the great swamp, not yet safe, but still close to home.

While Storm Rider, Buzzard, and Woman pushed the dugout into the dark waters of the Twisting Snake, Speaks Twice ran back up the broad bank to see if he could see their pursuers. He noticed flocks of redwing blackbirds and snakebirds winging away from the beaver pond.

"T-t-they are c-c-coming," he said, flying down the bank and wading out to the waiting dugout. "W-w-we must h-h-hurry."

Although they were now in the Many Waters People's land, their pursuers were still closer than the nearest village, and Shark Killer knew it. The Black Faces would not abandon the chase just because they crossed into the lake people's land. The danger was grave and imminent.

"W-w-we should lay a f-f-false trail on the bank to make it look like we are h-h-headed upstream," said Speaks Twice.

"We do not have much time," said Buzzard. "The false trail can only be a few steps long, something to cause momentary confusion."

Covering their footprints—but not so well as to avoid detection—the men left the muddy bank and swam out to the dugout. Woman had already turned the boat around and waited for them to climb in. One by one, the men lay across the narrow, unstable craft and swung their legs into the canoe at the same time. The four paddled madly downstream, negotiating two wide bends, before they paused to catch their breath and rest their trembling arms and backs. They listened for their pursuers.

"I do not hear them," said Woman. "But I know they come. Shark Killer will not give up just because he is in enemy territory."

"I know this part of the Twisting Snake," said Storm Rider. "Two bends farther and there is a small stream at the foot of the ridge that flows directly into the Rain Tree Water, just above the sacred tree. We can pull out there."

They reached the pullover point and were dragging the dugout down the ridge toward narrow stream when they heard voices behind them. The excited Black Faces found the spot where they pulled the dugout from the Twisting Snake. The cannibals were nearly upon them!

"We must get to the Rain Tree," Storm Rider exclaimed. *"Golden Face Man* will be there. He will protect us."

"I hope you are right," said Woman.

"Better have your knives ready in case *Golden Face Man* forgets and stays in the clouds," said Buzzard, trusting only his own defenses.

"I know what we must do," said Storm Rider. "Paddle hard."

They flew by the burial mounds and reached the Rain Tree only a meander loop ahead of the Black Faces.

"Abandon the dugout," said Storm Rider.

"What!"

"Trust my vision."

"We cannot paddle a v-v-vision, Storm Rider."

"If we stay in the dugout, they are going to catch us for sure," said Woman calmly. "I follow Storm Rider.

"W-w-we might as well try to get away on foot," said Speaks Twice. "We can s-s-split up. That way, at least one of us might get away."

Storm Rider and Woman climbed out of the dugout into the waist-deep water.

The Black Face whoop carried down the bayou sending Speaks Twice and Buzzard overboard and splashing toward the bank. Storm Rider pushed the dugout out into the current.

"Now, climb the Rain Tree!" he exclaimed. "Hurry!"

Woman and Speaks Twice scurried up the tree like nimble squirrels. Buzzard reluctantly followed them.

"Buzzard, break off a small limb and throw it down to me," whispered Storm Rider.

Storm Rider cupped his hands and threw handfuls of water onto the Rain Tree. Buzzard dropped an arm-sized limb to the ground, and Storm Rider heaved it into the dark bayou.

As if ordered by *Old Traveler* himself, the sky instantly darkened, and the wind started gusting first from the south, then the east, the north, and by the time it came out of the west, limbs were swaying and leaves filled the air like the Mighty Wind venting her fury.

"Give me your hand," said Buzzard. "I can hear their paddles splashing."

He pulled Storm Rider into the tree branches, and they climbed the tree hiding behind curtains of thick moss. They saw the three boatloads of Black Faces come around the bend, paddling furiously.

"There they are," shouted Shark Killer, as he spotted the dugout. "We have them."

The sky turned pale green, yellowed ominously, and then ice started falling fast and hard. Caught on the open bayou, the Black Faces were pelted with chunks of ice as big as hickory nuts. They covered themselves as best they could with paddles and quivers. The ice storm increased in fury, and jagged pieces as big as a man's fist rained down. Already bruised and bleeding, the Black Faces now faced mortal danger. One warrior slumped forward, blood pouring from a finger-long gash on top of his shaved head. Another dropped to his knees on the floor of the canoe, trying to cover his head with his battered, bruised arms. The men in the second canoe dove into the water and stayed submerged for as long as they could, while the warriors in the third overturned their dugout and ducked underneath.

Shark Killer stood defiantly in front of his dugout, trying to rally his men and curb their panic.

"Get to shore! Get to shore!" he cried, "Under the trees."

Nobody saw the ice ball that silenced the fearsome Black Face warrior. The sound of him falling into the water was lost in the fury of the storm. Then, as suddenly as it started, the ice storm stopped. A cold cloud rose from the ice-filled bayou, enveloping Shark Killer's empty dugout. The strange mist spread across the water and land, hiding everything under a white blanket. The escapees shivered, as the chilly mist curled through their hiding place. Despite being within arm's reach, they could not see each other, much less be seen from the ground.

The Rain Tree acted like a great cape, protecting its occupants from the falling ice. Uninjured and hidden, the climbers knew that the least sound or even a falling cypress ball would reveal their sanctuary. An eerie quiet settled around the Rain Tree. Then, they heard Black Faces talking and paddles splashing. The sounds quickly went out of hearing, and *Noon-Day-Sun* peeped through breaks in the mist.

"It is a good thing you are holding my hand, Speaks Twice, or I couldn't tell you were there," whispered Woman, squeezing Speaks Twice's hand.

"O-o-only trying to keep you from being scared," he stuttered, his face warming the chill.

"The Black Faces are gone," said Woman.

"They might be trying to trick us," whispered Buzzard. "Waiting for us to show ourselves"

"No," said Woman. "They are leaving. I heard them say Shark Killer was dead, killed by the enemy witch. Black Faces do not fight when their leader falls."

"They think Storm Rider did this, right?" asked Buzzard, a broad grin covering his face.

"Ah-e."

"Let them t-t-think that," said Speaks Twice patting Storm Rider on the back so hard he nearly fell off his perch, "M-m-maybe they will not come back to witch land."

"This man has something to say," Buzzard said. "I owe you three my life. I shall be your friend always."

"W-w-well, Buzzard, I didn't know you cared," kidded Speaks Twice, running his arm around Buzzard's neck and squeezing.

"Save the hugging for Woman, Speaks Twice," Buzzard laughed.

"Woman, now your face is turning red," said Storm Rider, grinning. "It is time to go home. I see our dugout caught in the bushes ahead."

"Our f-f-families think we are dead," said Speaks Twice. "Imagine what will h-h-happen when four ghosts show up."

Storm Rider clasped Buzzard's forearm in the warrior grip.

"Buzzard, I'm proud to call you friend. None of us would be here without your strength and inspiration."

"C-c-careful, healer," kidded Speaks Twice, "Last time you s-s-squeezed Buzzard that hard he turned into a mad bear."

"Buzzard, I would hug your neck too, except these two gossipy wrens would tell everyone I was flirting with you," said Woman. "You're my friend, too."

"D-d-doesn't anybody want to be my friend?" pouted Speaks Twice, pretending to be hurt.

"I suppose we will be your friend, too," said Storm Rider whispering something to Buzzard and Woman. "But only if you can guess what animal I'm thinking of."

"Hah, the animal guessing game! How about a s-s-snake?"

"Ah-e! You guessed right. We will be your friend," said Storm Rider.

"Ah-e! Ah-e!" said Buzzard and Woman grinning.

"Climb down and get the dugout," said Storm Rider. "I want to remain in the Rain Tree for a moment. I need to speak with my father."

The three retrieved the dugout and returned to the Rain Tree to pick up Storm Rider. The ice cloud had lifted completely.

"Be careful not to splash water on the tree," said Buzzard. "I've had enough ice for a lifetime."

"C-c-come down, Storm Rider, let's go home. M-m-my fish traps need running."

Storm Rider waved to his friends through an opening in the moss. A sunbeam warmed his face.

Stunned, the friends stared at Storm Rider's sun-lit face beaming down at them from the Rain Tree.

"Golden Face Man!" shouted Speaks Twice. "Storm Rider is *Golden Face Man! Golden Face Man* has been with us the whole time. *Wha Hay! Wha Hay!"*

"Now, I believe! I believe!" exclaimed Buzzard, holding up his arms toward the sky. "The prophecy is fulfilled."

19

Homecoming

"Sit down! You're going to capsize us," warned Buzzard.

"I'm too e-e-excited," said Speaks Twice, waving his arms and shouting. "We're home! We're home! And we're not dead!"

The dugout listed sharply, and Buzzard grabbed a handful of breechcloth, saving all of them from a wet homecoming.

Speaks Twice sat down but continued to shout and wave.

"They've seen us," said Woman. "They carry their bows."

"They don't know who we are," said Buzzard. "They do not expect the dead to reappear in a dugout."

"Ah-e," said Storm Rider, "And three of us disappeared and now we are four."

The Grand Lake warriors hid behind trees along the entire perimeter of the landing.

"I hope they don't shoot before they realize who we are," said Speaks Twice. "If they do, I won't give them any more fish."

The dugout made straight for the landing, and one by one the warriors began coming out from behind the trees. One warrior walked down to the landing, lay down his bow, and waded into the water, yelling something at the approaching canoe.

"It's Broken Tooth," said Buzzard. "He lives. He recognizes us."

"Tooth! Tooth!"

Howls erupted, and bows waved in the air. Women and children started running toward the landing, and people began lining up at the water's edge. Several men plunged into the water and swam toward the dugout, one swimmer far ahead of the others.

"Buzzard!"

Broken Tooth reached the dugout, and Buzzard grabbed him under the shoulder and pulled him halfway out of the water.

"I thought they killed you," said an elated Buzzard.

"I thought you were dead, too," blurted Broken Tooth. "I saw that Black Face hit you with his club, and you went down like a crashing tree."

"Hold on to the gunwale, Tooth. We're almost there," said Buzzard. "How did you get away?"

"When I saw you and Speaks Twice fall, I slipped over the side of the dugout, and then when I saw them surrounding Storm Rider, I pulled myself into the cattails with my good arm. I thought they had killed all of you. I lay there all night, figuring they'd soon take my head for their trophy pole, but they never really looked for me. Turkey-Buzzard-Man found me the next morning and brought me home."

Strikes Blows and a dozen warriors guided the dugout to shore, whooping and slapping the occupants on their arms and backs. They looked quizzically at Woman but knew she posed no threat or she would not have been with the lost men. Storm Rider's aunt and Blackbird hugged Storm Rider so hard, they nearly dragged him out of the dugout, and Speaks Twice stood and deliberately fell out of the canoe backwards, splashing water on everybody. His mother and father sat in the water beside him with their arms around his neck. The rest of the people crowded around, and public weeping—the most courteous form of welcome among the Many Waters People—grew so loud that it waked the sleeping curs, and cacophony of sobs, moans, barks, and howls drowned out normal conversation.

People started gravitating toward the plaza. Speaks Twice was followed by a screaming gaggle of adolescent girls and unmarried women and was obviously enjoying himself—he wore a broad grin, and Storm Rider noticed him holding his chin a little higher than usual. He saw Buzzard talking with his father, several warriors, Broken Tooth, and the rest of the Buzzard gang, and by his facial expressions and animated gestures, he knew Buzzard was telling them about their escape. Buzzard made a motion like climbing a tree and pointed to Storm Rider, and the men started nodding and whooping. Storm Rider walked beside his aunt and Blackbird, who had not released his hand since he got out of the dugout. By the time, they reached the temple steps, he had related the gist of their escape, extolling the bravery of his friends.

"Who is this Woman you owe your life to?" asked Blackbird. "She is very pretty!"

Mention of Woman rocked Storm Rider. He and the others had just gone off and left her at the landing.

"I've got to find her," said Storm Rider.

"She's right there," said Blackbird, pointing.

Storm Rider started toward her, when he saw Speaks Twice put his arm around her shoulders and walk her toward the temple steps. Woman thanked him with a warm smile. Speaks Twice's admirers looked at each other despondently and fell silent.

Many eyes followed the pair as they stopped at the bottom step. The people were cordial and even warm, but they all wondered who she was and how she came to be with the men. Woman was aware of the stares and was ill at ease. She whispered something in Speaks Twice's ear, and he removed his arm from behind her shoulder. She stared ahead, even when Speaks Twice leaned down to talk with her.

"Well!" inquired Blackbird.

"She was a Black Face slave, but she is a Many Waters person. She was taken from one of the lake villages when she was an infant."

"You say she has the mark of the sacred fire on her shoulder?" said his aunt.

"Ah-e, that is what led us to safety," said Storm Rider. "Father came to me as a mud snake and told me to follow the sacred fire. It is there on her shoulder."

"Have you told anyone she has the sacred fire mark?"

"No, but I think Speaks Twice noticed," said Storm Rider.

"I must tell Sun Woman," said aunt.

Storm Rider's aunt hurried to speak with Sun Woman, and Sun Woman excitedly followed his aunt to Woman's side. Words were exchanged, and Woman dipped her shoulder so Sun Woman could see the mark. Without another word, Sun Woman grabbed Woman and hugged her neck like she would never let go. She started sobbing, and Woman looked at Speaks Twice querulously.

"What is that all about?" asked Blackbird.

"I think I know," said Storm Rider, as he watched Sun Woman lead Woman up the temple steps to the portico, where Great Sun was preparing to address the people.

Great Sun looked at Woman's shoulder, and he too hugged her tightly. He removed his pearl-bead necklace and placed it around Woman's neck and then, hand-in-hand, Great Sun, Sun Woman, and their long-lost daughter moved to the temple apron.

The curious crowd quieted.

"People of Grand Lake village, behold! Our lost daughter has returned."

A great shout filled the plaza. The happy people rejoiced.

"There is much to celebrate," said Great Sun, raising his arms. "Our brave ones have returned to us. Our ears yearn to hear the story of their escape."

Always Frowning summoned Buzzard, Speaks Twice, and Storm Rider to the village pole. Woman looked at Great Sun. He nodded, and she hopped down the temple steps and joined her friends. Buzzard stepped forward, striking the pole three times. He told of their capture, running the gauntlet, the long days of misery waiting to be cooked, and their flight through the marsh to safety. He praised Woman's cunning and bravery and Storm Rider's prophetic leadership, which brought them home. He spoke of Speaks Twice's tenacity—how many times he would have chosen to meet death, but Speaks Twice would not let him tempt fate.

"They are my friends. I owe them my life."

The howling started, as Buzzard stepped back from the pole. One voice was heard above all others.

"Hiyee, hiyee, hiyee!" cried Strikes Blows. "Can you see that he is my son? Can you see he is a mighty warrior?"

Next, Speaks Twice struck the pole. He told of Woman's planning and guile. He spoke of Storm Rider's leadership through his vision. He spoke of Buzzard's fearlessness, strength, and inspiration. Finally, he told of his foul treatment at the hands of Painted Face Woman, and by the time he showed the rope burns around his neck, all the people were laughing and yelling.

Not once during the telling did Speaks Twice stutter.

"He is a slat off the old fish trap," shouted Laughing Otter, and the people roared again.

Speaks Twice relinquished the pole and gestured for Woman to step forward.

Woman struck the pole and timidly, hesitatingly addressed the people.

"My heart is overflowing. I am free of my captors, and I am delivered to my parents, whom I have not seen since I was a baby. Three new friends stand by my side, and one old friend lives in my heart. I am happy to be home, and I look forward to sharing words with all of you."

Finally, it was Storm Rider's time to speak. He struck the pole.

"You might think it strange that Great Sun's and Sun Woman's daughter is called Woman, but that is what the Black Faces named her. I hope she will soon be given a new name, and I suspect that two others have earned their man names. Woman is the reason we are here today. She freed us from our bonds and led us home. We owe her our lives.

"There is another woman of the great swamp who helped us escape. She remains a captive in the Black Face village, too crippled to flee with us. Her name is Cane Basket of Prairie Landing village. She asked us to think of her when we got home, so she could see the land she loves so dearly through our eyes. I ask all who hear my voice to think of Cane Basket and her plea, now—let her see her homeland once again.

"We owe another for showing us how to escape—my father. He came to me as a snake, my guardian spirit. He said to follow the sacred fire wherever it led and to climb the Rain Tree. He knew that if we followed the old traditions, we would be saved. We are here as proof of his wisdom.

"Is it coincidence that three of Many Waters People's lost sons happened to meet two of Many Waters People's lost daughters in the land of the Black Faces? No, I think not. I believe we were stolen and taken to the waving grass to bring our Sun's daughter home, and she was there to rescue us from Black Faces' cooking fires. Our paths were destined to converge. *Old Traveler* brought us together. Now, our spirits are forever joined. Hai, I have spoken."

There was a shout. Then, a few more, and quickly a great noise enveloped the plaza, as the people welcomed home a lost daughter and lost sons.

Glossary

Ah-e—Chitimacha word for yes

Alligator Entrails—basketry and pottery design consisting of slanted, running loops in a field of punctates

Alligator-Entrails-Broken—basketry and pottery design consisting of separated running loops, two per element, in a field of punctates

Always Frowning—village keeper, middle brother of Great Sun

Anoy—Avoyel tribe, or Stone-Arrow-Point People

Bear Tracks—referee at village contests

Beautiful White Water—contemporary Catahoula Lake and coulee

Beloved Men—council of elders

Bent Woman—feared high priestess and prophet of Many Waters People

Big Blackbird Eyes—basketry design consisting of circles inside running scrolls

Big Cypress Lake—contemporary Lake Fausse Point, one of a string of interconnected lakes north of Grand Lake

Big Leaf Tree—Southern Sweetbay, *Magnolia virginiana* var. *australis*; leaf tea used to treat aching joints and old-age shuffle

Big Mouth—large-mouth bass, *Micropterus salmoides*

Big Salt Water—contemporary Gulf of Mexico

Big Water—contemporary Ouachita River

Bites-Him-Hard—promiscuous woman, joking clan sister of waddling woman

Blabbers—Big Mouth Buffalo, *Ictiobus cyprinellus*

Black Drink Bush—Yaupon, *Ilex vomitoria*; tea used to treat stomach ailments and induce vomiting; said to be hallucinogenic when drunk in large quantities

Black Drink Ceremony, Dance, Feast—August celebration of renewal, involving drinking of copious quantities of the black drink, a tea steeped from the leaves of the yaupon bush

Black Dye Tree—Black Walnut tree, *Juglans nigra*; nuts used for food and nut covering to make the black dye for baskets

Black Faces—Attakapa tribe, live in the coastal marsh west of Bayou Teche and east of Sabine River; enemies of the Chitimacha

Black Face Water—contemporary Vermilion River; begins near the Upper Bayou Teche and discharges into Vermilion Bay above Redfish Point

Black Hairs—Opelousa tribe, a branch of the Attakapa, living on the upper reaches of Bayou Teche

Black Thorn Tree—Black Locust tree, *Robinia pseudoacacia*; used to make bows

Black Water Chute—contemporary Bayou L'Rompe

Bloodweed—pokeweed, *Phytolacca americana*; leaves used for food and roots for soap

Broken Plaits—Cloud Bringer's true love; also a herringbone basketry and pottery design

Broken Tooth—Buzzard's best friend

Buzzard—Storm Rider's biggest boyhood nemesis, and, later, close friend

Chestnut Eaters—Natchitoches tribe, a Caddoan group, living on the Red River

Clamshell Water—contemporary Bayou Shaffer

Cloud Bringer—old Snakebite healer, father of Storm Rider

Commoner—lower class of the two-tiered Chitimacha society

Cottonwood village—one the Many Waters People's villages, located near the junction of contemporary Lake Mongoulois and Bayou Chene in the northern Atchafalaya swamp

Cowah—Koroa tribe, dubbed the Principal People herein, a Tunican group, residing on Mississippi River tributaries above the Natchez and Taensa tribes

Crying Eagle—headman of an Attakapa village located at Palmetto Island on the Vermilion River

Dance House—House of Importance where dance regalia was stored; located on contemporary Grand Avoille Cove

Dance of the Dead—dance and feast celebrating burial of the deceased in Rain Tree mound

Dead Cypress Water—contemporary Bayou Cypremort

Dog People—one of the six Chitimacha clans; clan of Speaks Twice

Dots-Filling-In—basketry and pottery treatment consisting of punctates in-filling a broader design field

Dry Wind Moon—corresponds to month of September

Eagle Point—same as contemporary Eagle Point, a point of land projecting into Lake Dauterive

Earth Island—land of the living, the middle world of the three-tiered cosmos of Muskogean-speaking peoples; the Upper World and the Lower World (or the Wastelands) were the other levels

Eenjee—ancient Chitimacha word for father

Esteemed warriors—warriors who have killed or touched an enemy

Falling Leaves Moon—corresponds to month of October

Far-Away-Woman—a Thoucoue, or Natchez, woman, wife of Shouts-at-Night, and translator for Great Sun during Anoy visit

Father-of-Storm-Rider—name assumed by Cloud Bringer after Storm Rider received his man-name; teknonymy, a practice whereby a father changes his name to that of his son, was followed by both Chitimacha and Attakapa

Feast of Blackberry Moon—celebration of new moon in month of July

Fire Temple—temple where sacred fire is maintained, located atop earthen mound at the south end of the plaza

Fire Watcher—temple priest charged with tending to the sacred fire; in this story, he is also a Tradition Keeper responsible for passing on the history and political traditions of the Many Waters People; Great Sun's youngest brother

First People, First Ones—first people created by *Old Traveler*

Fish Island—same as contemporary Fish Island, a stream-surrounded "island," lying at the mouth of Lake Dauterive

Five-leaf vine—Virginia Creeper, *Parthenocissus quinquefolia*; roots and leaves boiled for tea to treat fever

Flat Fish—flounder, *Paralichthys lethostigma*

Flat Heads—Hasinai tribe, a Caddoan group, living on the upper Neches and Angelina rivers in East Texas

Flint Rabbit—eldest son of the Anoy chief; future chief

Ghost sickness—insanity and death caused by a deceased person's outside shadow entering a living person

Golden Face Man—Rain Spirit

Gourd head—wood ibis, *Mycteria americana*

Grand Lake—contemporary Grand Lake, location of Grand Lake village

Grand Lake village—home of Storm Rider and of Great Sun, located on the banks of contemporary Grand Lake near Charenton, Louisiana

Great Sun—head chief of Grand Lake village and of all the Chitimacha people, living in the western part of the Atchafalaya swamp

Great swamp—contemporary Atchafalaya swamp

Great Water—contemporary Mississippi River

Green head—mallard duck, *Anas platyrhynchos*

Green wing—green wing teal, *Anas crecca*

Grunter—freshwater drum fish, *Aplodinotus grunniens*

High Island—contemporary Cote Blanche salt dome, located on north shore of West Cote Blanche Bay and south of Bayou Cypremort

Howling Wolf—one of the Grand Lake villagers, whose family "owned" first rights to Blue Bank fishing grounds

Humped Beast Water—Boeuf River, lying between the Mississippi and Ouachita rivers in northeastern Louisiana and southeastern Arkansas

Inner shadow—*see* Shadows

Joining song—chant sung when inserting decorated pipe stem into pipe bowl forming the calumet

Kunti bread—bread baked from flour rendered from Greenbriar roots, *Smilax laurifolia* and *S. bona-nox*

Laughing Otter—father of Speaks Twice; well-known fisherman

Lightning-Spirit-Bird—sky spirit, sister of *Thunderer,* represented by lightning

Little Eagle Lake—contemporary Lake Fausse Pointe, one of a string of interconnected lakes north of Grand Lake

Little Hill—contemporary Petite Anse salt dome, standing in the marsh near New Iberia, Louisiana

Little Hill Water—contemporary Bayou Petite Anse; encircles Petite Anse dome and discharges into Vermilion Bay north of Bayou Cypremort

Little Long Water—contemporary Bayou L'Embarras, a tributary-distributary of the Atchafalaya River

Little Oak Water—contemporary Bayou Chene

Little owl—screech owl, *Otus asio*

Little Thoucoue—Taensa tribe

Lizard's-tail—today's Lizard's tail, *Saururus cernuus*; marsh plant used to treat wounds, sores, and teething gums

Long Black Being—supernatural monster who resembles a man but has small eyes and pointed ears and scares or harms hunters; normally detected by sharp-eared woodsmen as the step or two taken by an unseen pursuer after the hunter stops to listen for his follower

Long Water—contemporary Atchafalaya River

Lower World—the Underworld; the afterlife filled with famine, sickness, and ill-fortune; where bad Chitimacha go after death; *see* Upper World

Many Waters People—Chitimacha tribe

Mighty Wind—a hurricane

Moon of the New Leaves—month of March

Moon of Redfish Running—month of April

Mosquito Slappers—the Karankawa tribe of the south Texas coast

Muscadine moon—month of June

Noble—upper class of the two-tiered Chitimacha society, class from which village leaders come

Noon-Day-Sun—spiritual mother of humans; embodied in the sun

Oak nuts—acorns from *Quercus virginana*

Old Ones—ancient marsh dwellers, who left shell heaps marking the site of their old villages and fishing camps

Old Traveler—Great Spirit of the Chitimacha, the Creator

Outer shadow—*see* Shadows

Pale Sun—spiritual husband of *Noon-Day-Sun*, the moon

Passing on Traditions, song of—chant sung by Tradition Keeper when passing on ancient wisdom and tribal lore to a future Tradition Keeper

Peeling-bark tree—sycamore tree, *Platanus occidentalis*

People of the Rocks—Attakapa name for the Anoy, the Stone-Arrow-Point People

Persimmon People—Chitimacha tribelet living on contemporary Bayou Plaquemine, one of the eastern Chitimacha branches

Persimmon Water—contemporary Bayou Plaquemine

Pipe of the Dead—self-smoking pipe with figure of a half-defleshed, half-in-flesh body forming tobacco bowl

Plaits-Starting—notable basket maker; also a basketry and pottery design consisting of dashed lines

Pond-lily Cove—contemporary Grand Avoille Cove, a cove lying north of Grand Lake village, just below the entrance to Lake Fausse Point; well known for its extensive growth of American Lotus, *Nelumbo lutea*; rootstocks were a staple food

Prairie Landing Village—one of the Many Waters People's villages, located on contemporary Lake Dauterive, near South Eagle Point, above Charenton, Louisiana

Prayer of Returning to the Sea—chant sung by Attakapa shamans when sending a dying person's spirit back to the sea where humans were born

Pretty Island—Belle Isle salt dome, located in the marsh near the mouth of the Atchafalaya River

Rain Tree—sacred cypress tree on contemporary Bayou Portage; believed to bring rain when water is splashed on it

Rain Tree mounds—two Chitimacha burial mounds, located near the Rain Tree

Rain Tree Water—contemporary Bayou Portage

Red bellies—sunfish, *Lepomis* sp.

Red-Clay-On-His-Feet—Anoy emissary

Red Club—head war chief of Prairie Landing village

Red Earth Village—one of the Many Waters People's villages, located on contemporary Bayou Teche near St. Martinville, Louisiana

Redfish Point village—Attakapa village on contemporary Redfish Point on Vermilion Bay; village where Storm Rider, Speaks Twice, and Buzzard were incarcerated

Red seed—Mamou plant, *Erthrina herbacea*; used to treat coughing sickness

Red Sticks—Bayogoula tribe, an enemy tribe living along the contemporary Mississippi River east of the Atchafalaya swamp

Round Island—same as contemporary Round Island; stream-surrounded section of land of western shore of Lake Dauterive

Shadows—the body's two souls; upon death, the inside shadow departs for the hereafter, while the outside shadow hovers around the earthly remains frightening the living

Shark Killer—war leader of the Attakapa village at Redfish Point

Shortcut People—Houma tribe, a Muskogean group living along the Mississippi River north of Baton Rouge, Louisiana

Sinking grass—coastal marsh in the Attakapa language; called Waving Grass by the Chitimacha

Smoke Hand—vile Attakapa shaman

Snakebite healer—prestigious native doctor able to heal bites of venomous snakes; both Storm Rider and his father, Cloud Bringer, were Snakebite healers

Snake People—one of the six matrilineal Chitimacha clans; Cloud Bringer and Storm Rider belonged to this clan

Speaks Twice—Storm Rider's best friend, Laughing Otter's son, and an able fisherman

Spiny-seed plant—broad-leaf dock, *Rumex obtusifolius*; used to make yellow dye for baskets

Spirit Being—Attakapa counterpart of *Old Traveler*; Great Spirit, the Creator

Spotted Fawn—pre-pubescent name for Storm Rider's and Speaks Twice's friend; becomes Blackbird-Eyes-Shining or Blackbird after womanhood

Storm Rider—young Snakebite healer and prophet of Grand Lake village; a foundling adopted by Cloud Bringer; the book's hero

Stormy—Storm Rider's childhood name

Straight-Lines-Beginning—a basketry and pottery design consisting of short vertical lines inside an encircling panel

Strikes Blows—Buzzard's warrior father

Sunrise People—Attakapa name for themselves

Sun Woman—Great Sun's wife

Swamp bush—buttonbush, *Cephalanthus occidentalis*; used to treat eye sores

Tall grass—coastal prairie

Tattooed-All-Around—elderly spokesman for Beloved Men

Telling Traditions, song of—chant sung by Bent Woman before passing on tribal traditions

Thoucoue—Natchez tribe, living on the Mississippi River near Natchez, Mississippi; called the First Sun People herein

Thumping—method for hunting alligators by pounding stream bank with a heavy pole until a hollow sound reveals the underwater entrance to a den; the pole is then jammed into the den and when the alligator bites the pole, the reptile is pulled from the lair and killed

Thunderer—sky spirit, brother of *Lightning-Spirit-Bird;* manifested as thunder during storms

Tradition Keeper—one responsible for remembering and passing on the ancient wisdom and tribal lore

Turkey-Buzzard-Man—temple priest charged with defleshing noble corpses prior to final interment in Rain Tree burial mound

Twisting Snake Water—contemporary Bayou Teche

Two Shadows, prayer of—chant sung to reunite deceased person's two shadows in the Upper World

Underwater village—mythical submerged village founded by Chitimacha who killed a sacred white deer; located in the middle of Grand Lake; usually associated with the rare appearance of the Aurora Borealis

Upper World—the Hereafter, an afterlife of plenty, happiness, and good health; where good Chitimacha go after death; *see* Lower World, or the Wastelands

Village Keeper—official in charge of village social and political calendar of feasts, ceremonies, and arrangements; position held by Always Frowning

Wastelands—the barrens in the Hereafter; where wayward shadows go after death

Water-Runs-Red—contemporary Red River

Waving Grass—coastal marsh to the Chitimacha; called Sinking Grass by the Attakapa

Whisker Mouth—catfish, *Ictalurus* sp.; most prized was the Flathead, *Pylodictis olivaris*

White Ibis Lake—contemporary Lake LaRose; site of the mound of the Ancients, the contemporary Lake LaRose mound

White-mouth snake—cottonmouth, *Agkistrodon piscivorus*

White perch—black and white crappie, *Pomoxis annularis* and *P. nigromaculatus*

Woman—name given to the young Chitimacha slave by her Attakapa captors; stolen daughter of Great Sun and Sun Woman

Worm-Tracks-Broken—basketry and pottery design consisting of bold herringbone pattern

Yellow wood—tulip tree, or yellow poplar, *Lieriodendron tuliplera;* a tea made from leaves used to slow down heart rate

Yoron—Tunica tribe, dubbed the Trading People herein

Further Reading

Brown, Ian W.

1984 Late Prehistory in Coastal Louisiana: The Coles Creek Period. In *Perspectives on Gulf Coast Prehistory*, edited by Dave D. Davis, pp. 94–124. University of Florida Press, Gainesville.

Dyer, Joseph O.

1917 *The Lake Charles Attakapas Cannibals, Period of 1817–1820*. Privately printed, New Orleans. Copy available in Louisiana State Library, Baton Rouge.

Gatschet, Albert S.

1883 The Shetimasha Indians of St. Mary's Parish, Southern Louisiana. *Transactions of the Anthropological Society of Washington* 2:148–158.

Gatschet, Albert S., and John R. Swanton

1932 *A Dictionary of the Atakapa Language*. Bulletin 108. Bureau of American Ethnology, Washington, D.C.

Gibson, Jon L.

1978a *Archaeological Survey of the Lower Atchafalaya Region, South Central Louisiana*. Report No. 5. Center for Archaeological Studies, University of Southwestern Louisiana, Lafayette.

1978b The Land of the Chitimacha: Historical and Archaeological Data Relative to the Geographic Territory Occupied and Utilized by the Chitimacha Indians. Unpublished report submitted to the Chitimacha Tribe of Louisiana, Charenton, Louisiana.

1980 Documentary Evidence Bearing on Chitimacha Land Claims in the Bayou Plaquemine Tract, Iberville Parish, Louisiana. Unpublished report submitted to the Chitimacha Tribe of Louisiana, Charenton, Louisiana.

1982 Archaeology and Ethnology on the Edges of the Atchafalaya Basin, South Central Louisiana. Unpublished report submitted to U.S. Army Corps of Engineers, New Orleans District.

Haas, Mary R.

1939 Natchez and Chitimacha Clans and Kinship Terminology. *American Anthropologist* 41:597–610.

Hoover, Herbert T.

1975 *The Chitimacha People.* Indian Tribal Series, Phoenix, Arizona.

Neuman, Robert W., and A. Frank Servello

1976 Atchafalaya Basin Archaeological Survey. Unpublished report submitted to U.S. Army Corps of Engineers, New Orleans District.

Post, Lauren C.

1962 Some Notes on the Attakapa Indians of Southwest Louisiana. *Louisiana History* 3:221–241.

Rees, Mark A.

2007 Plaquemine Mounds of the Western Atchafalaya Basin. In *Plaquemine Archaeology,* edited by Mark A. Rees and Patrick C. Livingood, pp. 66–93. University of Alabama Press, Tuscaloosa.

Stouff, Faye, and W. Bradley Twitty

1971 *Sacred Chitimacha Indian Beliefs.* Twitty and Twitty, Pompano Beach, Florida.

Swanton, John R.

1911 *Indian Tribes of the Lower Mississippi Valley and Adjacent Coast of the Gulf of Mexico.* Bulletin 43. Bureau of American Ethnology, Washington, D.C.